FADE
TO
BLACK

BOOK ONE
THE BLACK TRILOGY

M.C. Webb

I chased the cat publishing
Knoxville, Tennessee

M.C. Webb
I chased the cat publishing
Knoxville, Tennessee
www.marenewebb.com

Publisher's Note: This is a work of fiction. Names, characters, places, and incidents are a product of the author's imagination. Locales and public names are sometimes used for atmospheric purposes. Any resemblance to actual people, living or dead, or to businesses, companies, events, institutions, or locales is completely coincidental.

Ordering Information:
Quantity sales. Special discounts are available on quantity purchases by corporations, associations, and others. For details, contact the "Special Sales Department" at the address above.

Fade to Black/M.C. Webb -- 1st ed.

"Know from whence you came. If you know whence you came, there are absolutely no limitations to where you can go." — *James Baldwin*

CHAPTER ONE

Fade to Black

Piper ~

I don't know why, but my mother, who had never shown an interest in my life before, collected me from my grandparents' home the day I saw my dad lowered into the earth. She had come and gone out of my life since I was born, but never before had I lived with her, as she did not stay long in one place. Nana said she lived "pillar to post," and my dad often referred to her as "not well," which was being kind.

I had no choice once my dad died. I went with my mother, as she now had the right to take me and my brother wherever she wanted. Kissing Nana and Papaw through our mixed tears, I was frog marched to the car where I sat in quiet wonder at how my life had changed in such a short amount of time.

It didn't take long to be introduced to silence and hunger. I was ordered to speak only when spoken to and ate when my mother remembered Nathan and I were in the home. If I complained, I was swatted with whatever was in my mother's reach.

Sometimes when she dressed for work, in a short denim skirt and snugged T-shirt, I could see the beauty my dad must have fallen for years ago. She was not a modern kind of attractive, more that she was curvy and seductive with sultry eyes and full lips. An unpolished Jayne Mansfield or Sharon Tate.

I watched admiringly and unseen as my mother would line her eyes with precision and apply mascara with counted strokes. She left for work one woman and returned another. Drunk, haggard and worn she stumbled in with makeup and clean uniform smudged and spotted by the end of her shift.

There were times, when my mother had just a little to drink, she didn't hate me as much as when sober, yet it was always obvious to me that she preferred Nathan over me for company. He never got to experience being hit with a hair brush on the side of the head or being kicked when simply in the way. My brother got whatever good our mother had. She saved all the mean for me.

Mother might have been lovely at one time, but now she drank heavily and complained about having children.

"They might give a government check, but it costs a woman her figure. Never have kids, Piper. They'll be just as ugly and dirty as you," she told me straight faced, meaning every word.

I did try to not be ugly or rotten. I kept the house tidy and the laundry clean, but nothing I ever did pleased her. My brother, Nathan, entertained himself with girls and his band.

He was far too busy to worry about a kid sister. I tried not to bother him. I knew he was working hard, writing and singing. Each passing day I would quietly grieve over the loss of my father, the absence of my grandparents, and the inevitable goodbye from Nathan.

A few days after my brother left me, our phone was disconnected. I had not seen my grandparents since the burial of my dad . My grandparents were simply shut out of my life. One of the last times our phone was used I heard my mother telling Papaw to "mind your own goddamned business!"

No matter how much I begged, my mother ignored my pleas and sank deeper into a darkness of drunkenness and self-destruction that had been hidden from me by my father. He had kept all the ugliness from me, and I had no idea this type of sickness was inside her. A shell of a woman, there was nothing to stop her from becoming what her mother had been before her.

All of my mother's family are drug addicts, and most of them spend time in prisons across the South for various offenses. They're the kind of people who bring trouble with them everywhere they go. When my dad met my mother she was on the edge of being just another statistic. I was never allowed to know her family, yet the name Akins was infamous in the South. From what little I heard from family gossip, I didn't want to know them. It was as if she never had a family. She never mentioned them. Not even once during the short visits we had at truck stop diners or a park bench we sat on, barely speaking. My dad insisted we see her. It was important we knew her. Even though she was not in our lives, she was still our mother.

We are simple people in a simple town. Average, I would call it. At least we were until my dad died in a car accident on his way home from work one night. One day, he was there. Then he wasn't. No more kisses and bear hugs. I had my last that morning. We were given a few days of crying and casket colors and Nathan shutting himself off from the world.

The nights became days, and soon it all ran together. Shortly after our once simple life had been interrupted by death, I lost my brother when he left me behind to chase down his dreams. I know he had to feel as lost without our dad as I did. I also knew he smoked pot and occasionally popped pills to deal with everything. I wasn't supposed to know this, but I had learned how to be invisible and observe things from the shadows, adapting quickly on how to silently move from room to room so not to be seen or heard.

My mother, always an impatient woman, grew colder still. Only weeks after Nathan left me, October brought us cooler weather, and my mother, a new man. Whereas my dad was the very essence of man, Daniel was childlike. He was a sometime mechanic and had taken an interest in my mother one night at the bar where she worked part time.

My mother never seemed to have money, and she stayed too drunk to do much working. Strange men began coming and going, but Daniel came around more often than the others. I often heard him and my mother in discussions that always seemed to involve money.

He stayed over one night, not long after he started coming to the house, and I found him naked, standing in front of the bathroom mirror the next morning, using my brother's razor. I stared all of two seconds and then ran back to my room, horrified, before he knew I had seen him. I didn't leave my room until I knew for certain he was out of the house.

Not long after that, my mother and I moved to Daniel's two-bedroom trailer, deep in woods I did not recognize. Lonesome took on a whole new meaning for me. I spent my days alone, eating whatever we had, straight out of the can.

Mice and spiders were my roommates. It did very little good to clean, as the trailer was rundown and old, with a threadbare carpet and plywood floors. I was not allowed to return to school, or to even speak of it.

I remained unseen, as my mother made it clear the sight of me disgusted her. Every time she saw me, she would rant about how ugly I was and how I'd never get a husband because I was so tall. No one would want me. Sometimes, I was allowed to go to Daniel's shop as long as I stayed out of sight. I was given the job of cleaning carburetors, using cut-up old T-shirts and gasoline.

Daniel was not unkind to me. In fact, he was almost my friend. My mother forbade me to speak to my grandparents, but on occasion, Daniel would let me call them, as long as I didn't say where I was or give any hints. He didn't have to make me promise. I had no clue where I was, nor the chance to tell them. Daniel stood over, ready to snatch the phone from my hand if I said the wrong thing. I assured Nana I was okay, even though I was hungry and in need of someone to care about me. Nana always cried when I spoke to her. She missed me and my brother, and by the way she sounded, losing my dad had aged her greatly in a few short months.

Normal people do not see evil coming into their lives, especially eleven-year-old children. I did as I was told, fearful that if I put a toe out of place, I'd be punished. I often went hungry—my punishment for just being in the room at the wrong time.

My mother no longer sipped her drinks throughout the day, but drank thirstily starting as soon as she woke and not stopping until she was snoring. Daniel acted as if he didn't notice. He was not a smart man, but at times I sensed deep, distant thoughts when I caught him staring at me.

He did exactly as my mother instructed, to the letter, and if he didn't, she'd slap him across the face and scream at him for hours. Daniel cowered at her raised voice and did everything he could to keep her from being upset. He would struggle with his speech as he shuddered, "I'm s-s-s-sorry. I'm so-r-r-r-ry," and run to correct whatever displeased her. I was scared for Daniel, afraid my mother would hurt him when this happened.

I guess Daniel and I got along so well because he pretty much thought like an eleven-year-old kid most of the time. Maybe even younger, although I can't say I ever saw him without some kind of beer or whiskey bottle in his hand. Other than that, he did try to make my life a little easier. He always asked about my dreams and favorite things.

I got acquainted with my new surroundings, and once counted 485 giant steps from the mailbox to the front door. It was a good mile and a half through the cornfield out back to the nearest neighbor. The trailer was black as coal if the lights were out, and our water came from a sour-smelling well. I had an old black and white TV in my room with six channels.

After we ate dinner, Daniel and I would go into my room and stretch out on a mattress on the floor to watch old movies till I fell asleep. It was nice having someone around, with my dad gone and Nathan away. I didn't know if my brother could find me if he ever tried. Daniel was the only person I had that cared about me.

When I took the chance to ask my mother about Nathan she would tell me, "Never you mind about that good-for-nothing brother of yours. He better not darken my doorstep!"

My mother was a total stranger to me. Her words were constantly slurred, her dark eyes unfocused. When she took the time to notice me, she'd only yell at me or hit me. My mother hated me. For whatever reason, my existence caused her great discomfort. I watched as she slowly turned into a monster. Her hair was seldom clean, and her heavy makeup was so smudged she looked possessed.

She terrified me. The more she was asleep, or out of the trailer, the safer I was. Her beatings were beginning to break my skin open, and bits of my scalp were going bald from her yanking out my hair.

When Christmas came that year, Daniel took me to a strange town to watch a movie for a treat. I know he wanted to avoid being seen with me in Cosby, fearing someone would recognize me. After the movie I had hot chocolate, as Daniel sipped from a flask and watched me.

When we were back in the trailer, he gave me a white box with a pretty red bow on top. I was thrilled to have a gift. I carefully untied the ribbon and lifted the lid of the box feeling my heart beat with excitement. A gold locket lay on white cotton inside.

"It's so pretty." I said gently tugging at the clasp.

"O-o-o-open it." Daniel instructed me.

There inside the little window was a picture of my dad and me, taken when I was about four. Like a monkey, I was draped over his broad back. We were both smiling. Tears began to flow freely as I touched the photo.

"Y-y-y-you can't let your mom see it. It would m-m-m-make her m-m-mad," Daniel warned me.

I nodded, still looking at my handsome dad. I missed him so much my body hurt from it.

"Now you'll alw-w-w-w-ways have your dad with y-y-y-you," he said with his stutter a little worse after he'd been drinking.

I continued to cry and hugged his neck. When I pulled away from him, tears flowing now, Daniel held my face with his rough hands and rubbed my cheeks with his thumbs. A smile stretched broad on his scruffy face.

I thought nothing of it, wrapped up in the moment of my wonderful gift. I had a split second of warning in my head, just before Daniel leaned forward and kissed me full on the mouth. He was holding my face, not allowing me to pull away. My eyes went wide, and I jumped off the couch as if he'd pinched me.

Breathing heavily, I said, "Thank you for my gift, Daniel. I need to go to bed now," and sprinted to my room.

I sank to my mattress, confused and scared. My heart pounded in my chest, and my cheeks were on fire. My mother constantly called Daniel retarded. I lay in my cold room that night wondering if this were true.

He was at least forty-five. Why would he kiss me? After my heart slowed to a normal rhythm, I began to talk myself into believing it was harmless. Just a kiss. My first, yes, but still harmless. At least that's what I tried to tell myself.

I tossed and turned most of the night, dreaming awful dreams of running in place, with my feet on fire. Thankfully, Daniel never came to my room. Around three in the morning, I heard my mother stumbling in the front door, cussing. I covered my head, trying to drown out any noises that came from her.

In the days that followed, Daniel acted like his normal self. We again watched TV together after dinner each night, laughing together at Mr. Ed and Wilber. I felt awkward with him at first, but the kiss was never repeated or mentioned, which was a relief to me.

I did notice he stared at me a lot and began to pull me closer to him while we watched TV. I was more than a little uncomfortable, but at the same time, he was my only friend.

He did not hurt me. He was just lonely too, right? My thoughts ran wild most of the time now.

I would find peace in hot showers. This was the one thing I truly enjoyed. Hot water, and the time to think and dream as I watched the water drain away my sorrows. One night as I always did, I stayed in the shower until my skin wrinkled. I turned off the water and opened the curtain to find Daniel holding my towel. I screamed and jerked the curtain so hard it ripped from its plastic hooks. I held it shut, as if I could keep him from opening it.

"D-d-d-don't be scared, Piper. I j-j-just want to look at you. That's all!" He stuttered out the words. I felt my face flush as his words sank in.

"No!" I shouted back at him. Look at me? My head was spinning. I begged him to leave. More than once. I began to shiver, both cold and scared, as he tried to get the curtain from my clutched hands. Stopping just short of force, he began to stutter again.

"I-I-I just want to look at you," he begged.

I felt heat rise to my head, and my eleven-year-old self answered, "But why?" Truly confused. I did not understand his meaning. I knew nudity was a no-no, and Nana always told me that good girls kept themselves covered. I was so embarrassed, I didn't know what to do. "Why?" I asked again. Why would anyone want to see me naked? That was just gross. I sure didn't want to see anyone naked.

He didn't answer right away, but when he did his voice came out clear. "Because you're s-s-soft and sweet. I'd never hurt you. I just want to l-l-l-look at you. That's all, I s-s-s-swear."

I thought he was crazy. What was I supposed to do? It was so gross! I could run, but he was between me and the door. Daniel could easily block my path. Oh God, what am I supposed to do?

"P-p-piper? C-c-come on n-n-n-now.

If I just do this and get it over with then I can go to bed. I felt sick at my stomach and more than a little ashamed. Then again, there was that spark of excitement that thought of someone wanting to *just* look at me, which made me feel somewhat wanted.

If looking was all, I could live with it, and Daniel was always nice to me. I trusted him. We had spent many hours together, and he had never harmed me ever. I sucked in my breath, numb with cold now.

It was the second week of January, and we had a wood furnace that barely heated one room. With great reluctance, I gathered myself, and finally I said, "Okay," through clenched teeth.

Slowly, with my eyes shut, I opened the curtain. I stood naked for at least a minute. When I did finally open my eyes, Daniel was *just* looking at me.

Pitiful and pathetic as he was, I was unafraid and unashamed. After another minute of taking me in, he came toward me. I stood stock-still as he wrapped me in my towel. I tensed when he put his arms around me, rubbing my back, up then down, up then down in long slow strokes.

"Shh, shh, shh, beautiful girl," he whispered and kissed my forehead.

He insisted I allow him to dry my hair. I just wanted to be left alone, but then again, this made me feel pretty. Cared for. Something I hadn't had in a long time. I thirsted for attention and was in the same breath afraid I was going to hell.

I gave in and allowed him to dry my hair, as long as I was covered with my towel. What was wrong with him just drying my hair? When he had finished, I felt him pick up a strand and smell it. It was creepy. He touched my hair from crown to end, then turned and left the bathroom.

I breathed deep and dressed at warp speed in my too-small pajamas. My lips were blue with cold, or maybe shock. I don't know. I went to bed feeling excited but dirty, as if soap had never touched my skin. Never had I wished for my Nana more than that night. Scared, lonely, and confused, I said a small prayer, and went to sleep watching *Who's the Boss?* on my black and white TV.

The next day I woke up to my mother vacuuming the bare rugs in the living room. A cigarette and the cord in one hand, and the handle in the other, she pushed and pulled in one spot, long enough for me to realize that it was early and she was drunk. She had probably not been to bed at all the night before.

Every few days she would go into these crazed cleaning fits. Wiping everything. Vacuuming. The woman slept in her own vomit most nights, yet when these urges hit, you had better stay out of the way, or you would pay dearly. I wiped the sleep from my eyes, and went to the bathroom to wash my face and brush my teeth.

I felt nauseated at the sight of the torn shower curtain. When I reentered my room I noticed an old movie playing. Gregory Peck. One of my favorites. The volume was turned down as usual, because I left it on day and night. I knew the film by heart and knew the words without hearing them. The movie was *Behold a Pale Horse*, one of Papaw's favorites, as well as mine.

Absently, I began to change. I had my shirt over my head with my vision blocked when the first blow landed, knocking me to the floor. I knew instantly my mother was upon me.

"Get up, you whore!" she screamed as she jerked my shirt the rest of the way off me.

"What, Mother?" I screamed back and tried to grab at the shirt to cover myself. She threw something at me, and I ducked just in time. Whatever it was it barely missed my head and smashed into the wall just behind me.

She was definitely still drunk from the night before. Her clothes were splattered with bits of this and that. Her hair was tangled, and her makeup, once so precise, was smudged under her bloodshot eyes.

She stood before me, a wild animal—mean and belligerent. Daniel came in. I didn't turn to look at him. I held my arms to cover my bare chest. Mother raised her manic eyes and looked at him. A wicked smile slowly crept across her face. Slowly, she raised her left hand. Hanging from it was my locket. She cocked her head sideways, still smiling.

"What do ya get for gifts like this, Danny boy?" she said mockingly. She took a long puff of her cigarette and looked down at me. "What did ya do for this, you filthy whore?" she asked, blowing smoke in my face.

I said nothing. For one, I didn't know what she meant, and two, I knew it would be worse if I said anything in return.

"D-d-d-deb? Let's g-g-go to bed, Honey," Daniel began.

"Shut up!" she spat at him.

I wanted Daniel to grab her and get her out of there, but he was an idiot, and at that moment, I hated him. For what, I wasn't sure, but I knew it was for something awful. Didn't Nathan always tell me to trust my gut? My gut was screaming danger from both Daniel and my mother at this moment.

My mother turned her back to me and reached into my closet, and I wanted desperately to find something to cover myself, but I didn't dare move. It was freezing, and I stood statue-still in just my panties. When she turned back to me I thought I was about to be whipped with a wire hanger, but instead she was holding the tie my dad had worn every other Sunday to church, a gift from Nathan and me the Father's Day before last.

I'd watched him countless times, tying that tie with such care and accuracy. When he had finished, he'd admire it in the mirror.

"That would put those Oxford boys to shame," he would brag with a wink.

I began to tie it for him a couple of weeks later. Every Sunday I couldn't wait to get myself ready, so I could stand on the toilet lid and tie his tie for him. When I had finished, he would look in the mirror, then at me out of the corner of his eyes.

"Not bad for a prissy little princess. Not bad at all," he would tease me, knowing I hated being called that.

Now my mother had it. She was twisting it, in and out of her hands. I reached for it, afraid she would tear it. She slapped me hard across the cheek. Laughing, she then twisted the tie around my neck, and, with strength I had no idea she possessed, she wrestled me to the mattress.

I felt the blood vessels in my eyes begin to protest at the pressure around my neck.

"Come on, Danny," she crooned in a mocking, baby voice. "Let's see what you two have been up to!"

I was fighting, literally for my life. I heard Daniel asking her to stop.

"This is what you wanted? Take it! I'm offering it to you!" she told him.

She loosened the tie enough to give me a gulp of precious air. I sucked it in, and then it was gone again. I looked to Daniel, begging him to stop her.

"Grab her," my mother demanded.

I kicked wildly. Daniel placed his hands on my ankles, and when he looked down at me on the mattress, I knew in that instant he would not help me. In that moment, I saw what he was. It had been hidden from me, maybe by my own need for a caring person in my life. I had somehow convinced myself that at least he cared what happened to me, when everyone else had left me. My dad, my brother, and my own mother.

Daniel was my friend, my father figure, a person who asked about my day, and sat with me watching TV—simple little things I so needed in my young, secluded life. Cut off from school and my grandparents, Daniel was the only person I had.

"Please!" I screamed, and my throat felt clawed on the inside. "Daniel, please don't! Mother, I'm sorry! Mother, please!"

But she was lost to me. I begged and began to shake with sobs. A fist fell hard on my mouth, and blood began to gather at the back of my throat. I had to turn my head sideways to cough it up. Words were spoken, but by whom, I didn't know. What was said made no sense to me.

Daniel released my legs, and he left my line of vision. Tears were running into my ears now, and blood ran from my lips. Mother continued to squeeze the tie around my neck, but would let up just enough to allow me to breathe before passing out.

I smelled the alcohol and cigarette smoke so strong on her, it gagged me. She bent low to my ear, and said, "This is what life is about, Piper. Best you learn that now and just accept it. You should thank me. It's not like you don't want it."

I felt the weight of Daniel climb on top of me. I fought, kicking, and scratching the best I could, but he held me down with little effort.

"Mother! Please!" I begged her. I felt my panties rip, as they were pulled off me.

I tried to fight. I pleaded, but neither listened. When Daniel entered me, the pain rendered me silent. The shock of it took what little breath I had. His breath was hot on my face. His odor, I knew, I would never forget. I jerked and twitched in misery as he pushed deeper into me.

I screamed out, and my mother's closed fist came down hard on my face. Once, twice, three times. Blood pooled to the back of my throat again. I kept my head sideways to allow it to run out freely so I wouldn't drown in it.

I coughed, but my mother pulled the tie tighter every time I did anything but lie there. Daniel reached my mother's mouth, and they began kissing above me. Frantic, I looked around my room, which was now blurry to me, as I was running out of air.

I was leaving my body. I had to, or I would surely die from this. I went still and silent. My effort left me. I wished to die.

My last memory of that day is Gregory Peck's face on my black and white TV. I was murdered. Even though my heart continued to beat, I was very much deceased. All faded to black.

CHAPTER TWO

When I woke, I lay very still, with my eyes shut tight. I listened, and then I felt. Sounds of mumbling and flesh hitting flesh came from somewhere in my room. I swallowed just enough to know my throat was both raw and swollen. Pain cut through me like a knife.

My body was stiff, and at an awkward angle, as if someone had tossed me like a pillow onto the mattress. After a moment of sensing everything I could with my eyes closed, I tried to open one eye. My lids wouldn't budge. They were stuck with gunk from crying, and probably blood as well. The hitting and mumbling got louder, and I pulled my protesting eyes wide open.

I was still naked, and at some point, my hands had been tied above me with an extension cord, usually used for a small lamp I read by at night. My feet were free. My legs were numb, and my body ached all over. The taste in my mouth was rotten with blood.

A harder sound came from the corner of my room. The only light came from the hallway, but as my eyes began to adjust, I could tell it was Daniel. His heavy feet were pacing back and forth.

The light glinted off a half-empty bottle of whiskey. He was pacing, crying, mumbling, and every other second, hitting himself in the head. I watched this, too scared to move, knowing what he was capable of.

I was freezing from the cold draft. The inner parts of my legs were sore and wet, sticky with fluids and dried blood. I remember a deer I had watched Nathan field dress, after he had killed it with a bow. I had worried the deer could still feel, even after its heart stopped beating. *This* is what it must feel like if the deer were still alive as he gutted it.

My big brother was gone, but in that instant, I wished he would burst through the door, and gut Daniel while his heart was beating. No mercy for this monster.

I jerked involuntarily, and Daniel stopped to look down at me. He sank to his knees beside me and began rubbing my head like he was petting a dog.

"Oh, thank God! I thought she'd k-k-killed you," he said in a rushed whisper, the stench of stale alcohol washing over me. I gagged at the smell and recoiled at his touch.

"You m-m-m-mustn't be afraid, Honey. I-I-I tried to be gentle. She wanted m-m-me to hurt you. She…I-I-I…" He stopped, searching for words. "I didn't want it to be this way. I planned on it b-b-being special, but now we c-c-can be with each other. I'm s-s-sorry you were hurt. That won't happen again. I won't let it." I tried to back away from him, but I was held in place by the cord. I lay perfectly still, and Daniel put his forehead against mine. I shivered, repulsed by him.

"Let me go, Daniel," I said, my voice cracking.

This man was my friend. At least, he was the only person left to me who I considered a friend, and until recently, he had shown me the attention and love I so needed after the loss of my dad.

I was eleven years old. My father was dead. My mother hated me and told me she wished I were dead. My brother, my best friend, had gone to Nashville in hopes of making it big, whatever that meant. My grandparents were forbidden to speak to me, and now I was being comforted by my rapist.

"Let me go," I whispered with all my strength. My voice was not my own. Would it ever be again?

"No," Daniel got up and shook his head. "No," he said again, and drank from his bottle.

I watched in horror as he paced and hit at his face, again speaking incoherently. I was strapped to something above my head, but I was paralyzed with fear. The realization hit me that I should be dead, yet here I was, whether I liked it or not, witnessing this crazed man's breakdown.

The pain was getting worse, and my ears thumped with my heartbeat. I decided to be submissive.

"Daniel?" I said softly.

He hit his knees again. I was so cold, I was numb, and I could no longer feel my hands.

"I need to use the bathroom."

Without saying anything, Daniel left the room. I heard the water running in the bathroom. I began to fight the heaviness that was threatening to take me under again. I pulled at the cords on my wrists as hard as I could, stopping just short of tearing my flesh. Daniel came back into the room and began to untie me. I would not speak, and I couldn't if I wanted to. My throat was nearly swollen shut now.

Daniel picked me up and carried me to the tub. I ached from head to feet. My hands tingled, and my head rushed with blood. I couldn't fight him if I tried. There wasn't an inch of me that wasn't hurting, or wasn't numb from the bitter cold.

Daniel sat me gently in the tub, and I jumped as my blue-tinged skin hit the water. I gasped from the warmth of it. My skin rose in goose pimples. Slowly, I lay back in the tub. I wanted to sink in it, and drown, be sucked down the drain, and never feel again.

I didn't care when Daniel began washing me. I sat perfectly still. No tears. Nothing. I had died in the other room at eleven years old, at the hands of someone my father had cherished, at the hands of my own mother, and this man she had allowed into our lives. I was dead and gone, but my body remained. My mind stayed still, as Daniel washed my hair and body. I shut my eyes and floated away.

When I was dry, Daniel carried me into the room he shared with my mother and put me on the bed. He began to pace again. I watched as he began to talk, and all I wanted to do was lay there on the dirty, bare mattress that smelled sour from nights of vomit from my mother's drunken binges.

"You s-s-see? We can be together n-n-n-now?" he said excited, as I began to try and focus on his words. "I-I-I mean, we can't marry till you're s-s-sixteen, but that's j-j-just a paper, right?" he smiled at me. I blinked, realizing for the first time ever that this guy was really nuts. He wasn't sweet because he was mentally challenged, but literally crazy. As he looked at me, his eyes jumped with excitement behind his thick glasses.

He raised his eyebrows, waiting for me to respond. I just looked at him and said nothing.

"You're tired," he said, as if this were just another night. "I will l-l-let you sleep. We have t-t-t-he rest of our lives. Deborah is g-g-gone, and you are mine f-f-f-forever."

At this, I willed all my strength forward and managed to croak out, "Gone?" I instantly wished I hadn't spoken, as pain seared through my throat.

"Yes. She will n-n-never hurt you again. This is not what I w-w-wanted to happen, but she gave me n-n-no choice." He began pacing again.

I had to close my eyes. I couldn't keep up with him.

"That Deborah," he said in disgust. "She w-w-wanted our agreement 'fulfilled,'" he said, in a mock, high-pitched voice. "Well, I d-did fulfill that c-c-cunt," he spat.

I didn't understand, and I wondered if he realized I was even in the room anymore.

"Ha!" he yelled, and I jumped startled. He stopped pacing and came and kneeled beside me on the floor.

"I'm sorry. I s-s-shouldn't yell. We'll have n-n-no more worries, so go to s-s-sleep and rest. We will talk m-m-more when you are better." He tucked a blanket under my chin and kissed my forehead. As he left, he snapped on my TV, which he'd moved into this room.

He left the door open, and I could hear him moving around the house. I lay in the dark, still and unthinking. My head was pounding. I tried to sleep, as my lips throbbed. My last thought was, "You wanted this. You wanted him to look at you. You wanted him to kiss you."

Knowing in my heart that I desired to be loved, but not expecting this to be the love I would get, I prayed silently for forgiveness. I prayed not to be dirty. I prayed for Nathan to come and find me and take me to Nana's. I prayed I wouldn't wake up in this nasty old trailer with a broken body, with a mother who hated me so much, and a crazy man I had thought was my friend. All of my thoughts circled back around to the idea that somehow, this had to be my fault.

I did eventually wake up. I knew immediately from the smell that I was still in Daniel's bed. I kept my eyes closed and listened to him laboring with something heavy. Then I heard the sound of plastic bags. After wrestling with whatever he was doing, Daniel dragged the bags outside, and the backdoor shut behind him. When I could no longer hear his footsteps on the porch, I opened my still protesting eyes.

I realized that while I had been sleeping, Daniel had used some kind of cable to tie my wrist to the brass headboard. It was dark outside, and the only light I had was from the silent TV.

I scooted to the window above me and peeked underneath the filthy blue blanket that covered it. I could see by the dim porch light that Daniel was pushing an empty wheelbarrow with one hand and with the other he balanced a shovel over his shoulder. I quickly put the blanket back in place, scared he would see me. I could hear him on the porch, dragging something again.

After a minute of silence, I pulled the blanket aside slightly again. My teeth chattered as the draft from the window swept over me. Daniel had something in the wheelbarrow now and was headed into the cornfield. He disappeared between the thick, frozen stalks, and I think I took my first breath in several minutes.

I was sore, but my head was clearer. I began tugging at the plastic cable, which tied my left wrist to the bed. I don't know how long I worked on it, but it didn't budge. I had no idea if my mother was in the trailer or not, so I tried to be as quiet as I could. I listened hard for any sound, outside or in. My stomach growled, and my mouth was dry.

After a long time of tugging and pulling I was exhausted. Finally, I gave up, and lay back in the bed. The smell made me nauseated. I tucked the blanket around my feet the best I could with one hand. I was cold to the bone. My stomach ached with hunger. For a long time I lay, watching the TV lights flicker across the ceiling.

I dozed off, lying in the filthy bed. When I woke up again, I tried to focus on the TV, but the images came in fragmented pieces without making sense. I remember a shampoo commercial, where the woman was smiling, her teeth brilliantly white, and tossing her hair back and forth, pleased with its beauty. I wanted so badly to know what that was like. Being clean again. Being pretty. Being happy.

My head pounded, and I bled between my legs. The lip that my tooth had bitten through throbbed painfully. I drifted in and out of sleep for a while. It was near sunrise when I saw a flicker of light in the cornfield through the one-inch gap between the blanket and window. The smoke from a lit cigarette announced Daniel's approach from out of the frozen stalks. He was pushing the wheelbarrow, stopping every few feet to take a drink from a bottle, and a puff of his cigarette. I froze, watching his progress. When he reached the steps, I arranged myself as best as I could to look like the dead.

I waited, listening to his entrance and the sound of him discarding his winter coat and boots. When he came to bed I didn't move, trying to breathe evenly, to make it seem as if I were asleep. Daniel put his cold, rough, whiskered face against my cheek. The smell of cheap whiskey burned my nose. I stayed still as he kissed my face and laid back to sleep. His heavy breathing became soft snores almost instantly. I lay looking at him in the light of the TV, wondering if my mother had gone. Her clothes and makeup were still scattered around the room. When she returned, what would happen? I could not survive another beating, and I would rather die than be raped again.

I watched an Alfred Hitchcock movie until the sun was bright. On the edge of sleep once more, sore and hungry, a thought hit me hard. It might have been the movie, but I knew for certain my mother was not coming back. The realization was there, and it was undeniable.

It was her in the trash bag. It was her in the wheelbarrow. She wasn't coming back, because she was freshly buried in the cornfield. I knew this without question as I stared at Daniel's hands and the dark stains on them. It wasn't just dirt, and at that moment, I didn't know how I felt about it. I wouldn't cry and couldn't if I wanted to. Somewhere in my little-girl mind, I felt that I had asked for all of this.

I had wanted attention and had loved when Daniel gave it to me. I was starved for a friend. For love. I'd wished my mother gone. Maybe I'd even wished her dead. Now, I had gotten that wish, and I was paying for my evil ways.

CHAPTER THREE

In the days that followed, I healed. Daniel never mentioned my mother, except to say she had quit her job and told everyone she was heading to Nashville, to live closer to Nathan. and it was believable. This was in fact her plan, he said, but Nathan knew nothing of where we were, and more importantly, no one I wasn't with my mother, so no one would be looking for me. This cleared me from ever returning to school.

Daniel repeatedly told me no one wanted me. Not my brother, my mother, or Nana and Papaw. He reinforced this when I tried to run from the house one day, after he allowed me to take a shower without him present. He caught me, and whipped me with the old leather belt he wore daily. Huge, bloody welts appeared on my legs and back. After that was over, he cried and said I made him hurt me, and why would I want to leave him? He was the only one that loved me and wanted me.

By my birthday in February, I was in a dog collar with a chain that slid through its locked ring around my neck. This, as Daniel explained, would allow me access to the bathroom and the bedroom while he was away at work, without his having to tie me up each time.

I was no better than a dog on a leash, or maybe even worse. My life was isolated from the outside world. Daniel hung plywood over the windows so I could not see out, or more importantly, so no one could see in. No one ever came by, and the mailbox was far enough away from the hillside that no postman would make the trip up the hill.

Daniel said this was for my protection, so that when he was at work, no one would be able to break in the house. I knew this was a lie. The trailer was a dump, in the middle of nowhere with one road in, and one road out. I did not know which side of town we were on, but I watched the sun through a two-inch space the plywood did not cover at the bottom of the bedroom window. The sun rose on the right and I knew somewhere Nana was watching it with me. My mind was saying nobody would want me now, I was so dirty, but my heart kept saying, every sunrise, Nana and Papaw were waiting on me. I hoped somehow Nathan was too. I missed my brother so bad, it physically hurt me to think of him.

Life went on without me every day. I got to eat as long as I did whatever Daniel wanted. When he was on top of me, I would become the people on TV. It was the only way I could escape where I was, and what was happening to my dead body. I became numb to it all. I did everything Daniel wanted, so I could eat mostly, and he would allow me to read while he was at work.

I quickly became pale and thin. Within a couple of months my ribs began to show through the old T-shirts I was permitted to wear. I would sit with my knees pulled up inside the shirt, trying to keep warm. I had a thin blanket, but no socks. It was a frigid hell, that much I was sure.

I read of Jonah in a small Bible that was stiff from never being opened. What he described, I understood. I took comfort in his escape from the whale, or rather the deliverance God provided him. I did not believe I would be delivered from my own hell. As Daniel repeatedly told me, no one would want me anyway. They were not even looking for me.

We had a huge ice storm in March that year. Daniel and I stayed in bed for a week. It was so cold in the trailer, I would breathe just to watch my breath for entertainment, when I was not watching the black and white TV. After the storm finally passed, the woods finished shedding the weight of ice and snow from its branches and brush. They looked bare in the distance. Under the bed, I had found a scope from a hunting rifle Daniel had changed out for a new one, and with it, I watched the birds and deer when he was gone. The scope became my secret treasure.

I craved being outside, and seeing the birds and deer gave me a little bit of freedom in my dark world. Every morning, as soon as I heard the heavy steps out the door and Daniel's truck start down the drive, I went to my crack at the bottom of the window, and I would watch as the sun rose high in the blazing blue sky.

It was the end of March. I was sick at my stomach and felt weak all over. When Daniel did allow me food, it was very little. He told me he despised fat women, and I was perfect the way I was. I was skin and bones. The night before I had four saltine crackers and a cup of cold chicken broth out of the can. I drank the broth down, grateful for every drop.

This morning I was light-headed and felt like I needed to sleep a little longer. After ten minutes of lying still I had to guide myself, careful not to choke on the chain I was attached to, into the bathroom to throw up. I drank water from the sink and lay on the floor heaving and sweating.

I prayed that God would let me die a real death on this floor. I asked that if Jesus came and took me, I would not be buried next to my mother because that was way too close to the devil for me. I prayed my Nana and Papaw were okay. I prayed Nathan made it big, with a song everybody would know the words to one day.

I woke up, almost disappointed, two hours later. After washing my face, I began to feel much better. Placing my hand on my chain I went back to the bedroom, turning the TV up as I came in. *I Love Lucy* was one of my favorite shows and one of the only things I watched with the volume on. I loved listening to Ricky's Cuban accent and tried to mimic it, pronouncing the words just like him. After it went off, I turned the TV back down and got my scope to watch the woods again.

Today was beautiful and clear. Sunny and bright, the woods were alive with activity. I watched birds bring their babies worms. Spring was near. I was so caught up in the birds' daily feeding, I almost missed the barn in the distance. Once I spotted it, I began to cry real tears for the first time in weeks. My shirt was soaked before I realized what I was doing. I thought maybe it was a mirage, like they showed on Bugs Bunny, so I watched and waited for it to disappear. The sun was to my left now, shining off the glass window on the top of a huge blue barn.

Never had I seen a more beautiful thing than this. I knew it well. It was the barn of the Logue family. It had been the source of great humor in the county for many years. My papaw would say, "Looky yonder, at that ugly blue barn." Then he would chuckle and shake his head. "There ain't no missing that thing, no sir," he would say with a smile. I liked it, because everyone else would paint their barns red, but being blue was different in a place where everything seemed the same.

I was afraid if I looked away now it would be lost in the woods. It was not until I heard the truck pull in that I stopped looking for signs of anyone in the woods. I hoped with all my heart that I was not imagining this unbelievable sight. Had the ice storm not come, I would have never seen through the trees. I said a prayer, and with all my heart I thanked God for the storm.

I had no way of knowing exactly how far that barn was, but knowing its general direction I knew I could find it just by watching the sky. The sun would be my guide, just as my dad, Nathan, and my papaw always taught me, when I would go hunting with them in the woods for days. I knew the patterns of the sun and the moon and the seasons by heart.

I knew without even thinking that if I could reach that barn, I could continue over the hills and be only a small ways away from Nana and Papaw. The only problem with that was, what if what Daniel told me was true. Was I not wanted, or loved any longer? The very thought brought tears to my eyes again, and then with the sound of heavy boots on the porch, I remembered I was dirty and unworthy of a family anyway. I was now Daniel's pet, attached to a dog leash. That's who and what I was. No better.

CHAPTER FOUR

Every day, as soon as Daniel left the house, I would look for that blue barn. It didn't take long to lose sight of it through the woods, after the trees put out their leaves. I continued to be sick off and on. I stayed hungry, but I seemed to gain a little weight over the next couple of months, nothing too noticeable.

I found myself obsessing about how to get free, and to that blue barn. I had very little energy and tired easily when I worked on the rings that held me captive. I knew if I did get away, Daniel would kill me. He assured me of this many times. I also knew I was dying slowly anyway, and it would be worth the chance, just to see home again.

Home was the place I knew better than anything else, in the dark or in the bright light of day—my grandparents' home, old as it was, and big enough to get lost in. I thought hour by hour of Nana's cooking, and the feel of Papaw's calloused hands touching my face. His crazy songs my dad told me to never sing in public, and especially Sunday dinner after church. I remembered Nana's old dusters she would wear on off days. I loved to get lost in them in the closet when I played.

I thought of the smell of wood polish and the sound of breaking runner beans. All that mattered in the world was getting to that blue barn. I was consumed by it, but I was trapped in the collar that refused to let me go as much as Daniel did.

In late May, I noticed a difference in Daniel and the way he would look at me. My brown eyes stayed bloodshot, and circles formed beneath them. My skin became even paler, and my once reddish-blonde hair hung limp and dull. I was withering like a tree that had been pruned too much and refused to grow any longer.

Something about the way I looked did not please Daniel. He was rougher with me and seemed disgusted with my weight gain. It was not until he asked me if I were pregnant that I even thought of the possibility. I had started my period just after my eleventh birthday. I had missed it, but I had no idea about babies. When he asked one night, looking at my swollen belly, if it were so, I immediately said no, being ignorant and naive. The next day, Daniel brought home a book about girls and their bodies, along with a pregnancy test.

I was pregnant, at twelve years old. I did not know or understand what was happening to me.

Daniel would not allow any talk about it, and he was cruel most of the time now. When he drank heavily, he would slap me and whip me with his belt. His drinking became heavier, as my stomach became bigger.

Judging by what the book for girls Daniel gave me, I was at least five months along when, in a drunken rage, Daniel whipped me so hard from head to feet, my flesh separated and peeled away from the wounds. If I whined or complained, Daniel would pour pure alcohol on my open sores. It burned me to the point that my mouth watered from the agony. I could not scream, or I would pay for that as well.

Daniel beat me until he was exhausted from it. When he finally stopped, he laid back on the bed and began smoking, ordering me to lay down beside him. Holding my breath so not to whimper from pain, I did as he said. I closed my eyes and got my breathing even again. My side hurt, and I wondered if Daniel's intention all along was to beat the baby out of me.

I began to really look at him for the first time in months. He was dozing slightly now, his mouth slightly parted completely relaxed. I was convinced he was not human, but evil in the flesh.

A lit cigarette dangled from his fingers, hovering over the ashtray. It was the first week of August and miserably hot. I had on my dirty T-shirt, and panties, which clung to my skin from sweat. The cotton rubbed at my injuries, causing them to burn. My body was not taking to the baby well. I was in my own little hell, sick and swollen.

I checked again. Daniel had passed out in his clothes, and barely sticking out of his pants I saw, with sheer delight, his keys, a set I knew contained the key to the locked dog collar around my neck. In an instant I saw in my mind, me running to the barn I knew to be on the hill. By the light of the TV, I began to slowly work the keys from his pocket. I was sweating profusely, and the cigarette in his hand was nearly burned to the filter.

I moved as fast and as quietly as I could, fearing he would wake from the sound of the loud thumping of my heart. When the collar was unlocked, I peeled it away taking pieces of my skin with it. With the thing finally off of me, I sat in stunned disbelief at what I had just done.

I stared down at the collar in my hands. I do not know how or why, but I made the decision in that instant and placed it around Daniel's neck. Sliding it through the small space between his neck and his pillow, I held my breath, and moved like I was playing the board game, Operation.

When the lock clicked down in place, Daniel's eyes snapped open. He was on top of me choking me before I could blink. His fist flew at me, hitting my face, my stomach, and my sides. I fought him for my life. Blood gathered in my teeth and, and ran from the corners of my mouth.

You will not die here, I thought. Although I knew I had prayed for it, I knew now I wanted to live.

I sucked in air that was chalky and ashy. Clutching the keys in my closed fist, I began to hit back connecting with his left eye with the point of a key. Only giving me a moment of pause as he grabbed at his eye, I began trying to slide out from under the weight of his body.

As soon as I could I scrambled to my feet and ran. My head swam as I made it to the door, reaching for the knob when Daniel screamed a horrible scream. It froze me midway in turning the knob. I took a chance and looked behind me.

The bedroom was ablaze. Smoke poured from it, and flames were climbing the walls. The plywood sparked like it was soaked in gasoline. Horrified, I turned to go and help him out of the room. I nearly fell from the dizziness that hit me. I knew if I went back in that room I was a dead girl either way. He would kill me, or I would die from the fire.

I backed up to the door and turned the knob. I watched the fire in the open doorway just long enough to make sure Daniel was not coming out of the room to get me. I dropped the keys still clutched in my hand and ran through the backyard, into the woods. Bits of the ground tore at my feet, but I ignored the pain. I was halfway to the cover of the woods when I heard Daniel screaming for me to help him, screaming for me not to leave him there to die.

When I reached the trees, I turned back and watched the fire spread through the trailer. No more screaming could be heard. I stayed in the same spot, watching it burn, until I heard the county fire department coming up the drive. I ran heaving and bleeding for at least an hour through the woods to that blue barn.

I did not want to see the firemen. Daniel had told me that if anyone ever found me, I would be locked up in a girls' home. All I wanted was to go home, if I still had one. I stopped long enough to study the sky making sure I stayed on the right path that would lead me to where I knew the Logue family lived.

I hurt everywhere. My swollen stomach felt foreign as I moved. I had spent a long time indoors, shut away from the woods I loved so much.

The noises through the trees didn't scare me. I tried to run, in case hogs were around. I knew the beasts could be vicious and would easily eat a human. I kept a steady pace, willing myself to go on.

Just before dawn I hit the dirt road that led to the Logues' driveway. It was muddy, and I stumbled through the mud with my bare feet, trying to hang on to what little strength I had. The barn was not far now.

Just a little further, I thought over and over.

I tripped and fell in a puddle, and for the life of me I could not get up. I was soaked and exhausted, hungry and weak. I lay watching the sky, saying my prayers, praying that Nana would bury me with my daddy when they found my body. I lay for so long, my fingers shriveled from the damp.

Flies and mosquitoes bit at me, but I could not swat them away. When the sun came up and began to dance on the trees, I watched paralyzed, knowing the birds would be around me soon, biting at me, thinking me road kill. I couldn't blame them. It was their nature after all.

The heat and the smell of me drew them my way. I lay, letting the bugs feed on me, knowing this was the process of dead bodies. I accepted I was dead, so why stop them? My eyes were swollen shut now. I drifted away.

I was at the point of giving in and allowing the pain to take me deeper, when I heard someone shouting and the opening and closing of a truck door. Strong arms picked me up. I was carried to the bed of the truck, and I thought Daniel had found me. He had gotten out of the trailer, and I would be going back now, where I would die, and be buried in a cornfield, never seeing home again.

CHAPTER FIVE

I heard my papaw's snores. I smelled bleached white sheets. It was a heavenly sound and scent. I believed I was dreaming. I lay perfectly still, waiting for the putrid smell of Daniel's filthy mattress to hit me. After a long moment of feeling my foreign surroundings, I began to realize I wasn't dreaming at all.

When I opened my eyes, I saw Nana sleeping in a makeshift bed beside mine. I lay staring at her. It was dark outside, and the light from the bathroom fell on Nana's weathered face. She looked like no other woman I'd ever seen. She was beautiful. Even being in her sixties, she shone with light. Tonight she wore no makeup. I thought this funny and completely out of character. She would not leave the house without her face perfectly lined and colored. I had the sudden urge to laugh. Her neat blonde hair was fanned out around her face, making her appear even more angelic.

I looked to see Papaw asleep in a chair at the foot of my bed. His head hung to the side, resting on the chair back. I wanted to give him my pillow, afraid he would wake with a sore neck. I tried to sit up a little, but my body was so stiff I couldn't move. I felt oddly heavy, and my head foggy.

I must have made a sound, because I saw Nana jump. I turned my head to look at her. She looked at me blurry-eyed and smiled. Then she was at my side placing cool hands on my cheeks,

"Thank you, oh Lord. Thank you," she breathed then kissed my forehead.

I wept as she held me. She didn't sound or act like she didn't want me. She was holding me as if I were not dirty.

I felt her body shake from sobs as Nana's arm circled and rocked me. I was safe. I was home. Wherever Nana was, I was home.

After what seemed like forever, I heard, through her chest, Nana call to Papaw.

"Nathaniel? Nathaniel!" she said twice, and he was there crying with us a second later. The smell of his cologne made me cry harder. It was my favorite smell in the world. I felt wet spots in my hair from their tears and the pressure from their kisses.

We had our private reunion for a while. I felt heavy with drugs. Absently, I knew there was no more bump in my belly. I'm not sure if I was sad, or relieved, but I felt that somehow evil was no longer in me. I would have recovery. Lots of recovering. I had not yet realized the damage that had been done to me.

From the moment he stood waiting for me to exit the shower, Daniel had injected me with poison, a poison still swimming in my blood and my mind. It began working its way through me, possessing all parts of me. It would rob me of many things if I allowed it, but how do you say this to a twelve-year-old kid? How do you undo what has been done? How do you mend the aftermath of evil?

CHAPTER SIX

I was released from the hospital a week later. I was on super-strong antibiotics. Nana wanted me to heal in her "birthing room," where she practiced her midwifery.

I loved this room and the hugeness of it. Tucked away were the instruments and items Nana used to deliver her babies, but it was a simple, pale yellow color, with all the comforts you could ask for. Nothing about it looked clinical.

The room was surgically clean but was fit for royalty. Papaw had it built for Nana years before, so she would be able to stay at home and work. This would also have allowed her to keep an eye on the many children they once planned to have, but sadly never did.

My dad was the only surviving child among three miscarriages and a stillborn baby girl. Nana could still barely speak of the babies she lost. I always thought she blamed herself for not being able to have more kids. We had cousins that visited from time to time, but for the most part it was just Nana and Papaw.

Now, just two weeks after being discharged from the hospital I was settling in the birthing room, I could move around in the big bed and oversized chairs comfortably. I slept a lot and when I was awake I stood the streams of sunlight that filled the room, letting it drown me head to foot.

I missed this, never knowing what a glorious thing sunshine was before I was forced to live in the dark. I watched the sun rise the fall day after day in silence.

The birthing room became more than a place of other's births, it became a sanctuary where I could feel safe if only for a little each day. I could rock in the padded rocker, or soak in the birthing tub that was at least three times the size of a normal tub.

I enjoyed the tub most of all and soaked in it often, placing my toes over the pulsing jets, breathing the warm mist that floated in the air while I soaked and felt almost normal.

I sat, as always, in uninterrupted silence. Nana said silence healed the mind, and she allowed me to take my time talking. My mind wandered over the bump that was now gone from my middle. I touched the puffy line under my belly button with my index finger, feeling the rigid thin jagged flesh where I know I was opened up and emptied of the baby.

Nana sat on a stool, always within my reach to wash my back or hair for me. I looked into her eyes after touching my scar and watched as an expression of the deepest pain entered her face. Her eyes crinkled slightly as if witnessing me thinking of surgeon's hands inside me had somehow injured her. She got down on her knees beside me, as I soaked in warm milky water of "healing" salts.

The water was running, and steam rose from the spout. Nana's light blonde hair looked oddly withered like a sunflower faded in the dark. She seemed to search for what to say. Reaching for my hand, she drew it to her chest not at all concerned with its wetness.

"Love?" she whispered to me. "It's gone. They couldn't save it," she said sadly or maybe Nana was relieved?

I felt nothing, as she told me what I knew already, I just watched her lips move as she spoke softly. I was aware of a movement inside my stomach like bubbles then it was gone. Silent. Dead.

I hadn't spoken yet. I heard the doctors tell Papaw and Nana I was in shock, and my mind would need to recover as well as my body.

"It's the scars unseen we need to be concerned with," he had told them grimly.

I sat wondering if I may be mentally damaged and that's why Nana was speaking low and with caution. Maybe if I looked closely in the mirror I wouldn't see me, but a disfigured person that would need a scarf to hide my face when I went out in public like the Muslim women in papaws stories.

When my skin began to wrinkle, I stood and allowed Nana to wrap me in an oversized towel and brush and dry my hair, like I was smaller than I was. Truth is, I was much smaller than I was aware of at the time.

My once shiny strawberry blonde hair hung limp and lifeless like fragile little twigs. My collarbone and ribs looked grotesque, sticking out like a horror movie. My brown eyes looked dull even after days of sleep still set too deep in their sockets.

After my hair was brushed and dried I slipped into one of Nana's soft knit gowns. I had my own nightgowns at the house, but I preferred Nana's things that smelled like her, as if I could wrap myself in clean things, and the aroma could drown my thoughts.

I believed, as I slid in between the sheets, that maybe I had died and this was heaven. The cool clean bed covers, the goose-down pillows, the clean gown. But the reality of it was, I wasn't at all cleaned. I was soiled to the bone. Daniel made sure of that. No matter what I put on, or how long I stayed in the tub, I was still nasty on the inside.

Nana stayed with me every night, as I tossed and turned. She sat silently in the oversized chair in the corner of the room, where I'd seen new mothers nurse their babies. She was waiting on me to talk. I knew that.

I wasn't ready for her to know how deep the poison had gone. I was now being weaned off of medications I'd been given. Sleep was hard for me without a pill now, but Nana felt it was time I tried on my own.

I drifted to sleep, or what I considered sleep, but was more like moments of suspension then a crash back to the here and now. I may have slept an hour each night, and every time I looked over at the chair, there she would be, a solid reminder that I was loved. I was too broken at that moment to feel it, but I knew in my head it was so.

The days came, and each one was the same as the one before. I stayed in bed, trying to recover. My wounds were deeper than the bruises or cuts. I had my meals in bed, and I remained silent. I watched the sun rise and set. I watched Nana as she spoke to me. I was afraid if I slept long, or began to speak, all of it would disappear, and I would wake in the trailer.

Nathan came and sat quietly with me. Much of the time, he just stared out the window, watching the sun with me. Nana continued to sit with me, and Papaw came in to tell me my favorite stories. Up and down his eyebrows rose and fell as he did this. It made me physically ache for my dad. Little by little, each day I felt my heart close up around the broken shards within it.

Sleep was my enemy. I would wake suddenly, thinking Daniel was on top of me. Nana would come sit on the bed with me until I calmed down, but finally, after several nights of this, she remained in her chair, watching me by the soft glow of light coming from the bathroom.

I looked for her when I woke enough to miss her. I found her shadow in the corner. I knew she could see me better than I could her, mostly because she wanted it that way.

"Nana?" I said in a hoarse voice, for the first time.

"I'm here, love," she said, but didn't come to me.

She would not push me to speak, but in her way of thinking, she had given me enough silence. Now it was time

I purged myself of the things making me sick. Like a stomach virus.

I stayed perfectly still and thought of what I wanted to say to her. Of how I would tell her. I watched the moonlight dance across the ceiling for a long time.

"Nana," I said finally

"I'm here," she said, still not coming to me.

"It died?" I asked in a whisper.

Knowing I meant the baby, she said, "Yes, honey. It had died. That sometimes happens."

I could not explain why this was on my mind. I had never thought of being a mother. I don't even think I had realized what that was at twelve, but I knew that there had been a living creature inside of me because I had felt it move. Now I knew it wasn't there, and I needed confirmation that it was not alive but dead, like my father.

Nana sat silent. I could hear she was holding her breath, ready to hear what I had to tell her. It was easier not to see her loving face and see the anguish as I flinched in pain or cried for no reason.

I told her the things that had happened and where I had been for so long, pausing only to wet my lips occasionally. Nana never interrupted. She allowed me to tell my story without asking questions. When I finished I lay numb and silent for a while.

When finally it was out of me, my mind was clearer. I turned a little in Nana's direction. Even though I knew she loved me I did wonder if she could still love me after knowing everything.

"Will you tell me what has happened since the funeral?" I asked.

She sniffed and began clearing her throat.

"After your father's funeral, Deborah asked us to give you and your brother some time before we made a visit. The insurance money paid for the funeral, and when she began to ask for money she felt entitled to. Your papaw tried to reason with her which only made her angry. She just wanted money and had we considered what she was capable of we would have sold everything to pay her. But had we given her anything we feared we would never see you. We tried to talk her into letting you and Nathan stay with us. I think this made her even angrier. She insisted that we not come and always had an excuse for you not to visit. I wanted to respect her, but I also wanted you with me. In the end, I thought it would keep the peace between us if I did as she asked. We decided to give her a little time."

Nana coughed, and then continued.

"After weeks passed with still no word, Nathan came here, and told us your mother was drinking heavily. He said he was headed to Nashville and would be in touch. He asked us to check on you. We did, but by then the apartment was empty, and a notice was on the door. We looked everywhere. We could not find you, Piper. There was no trace of you or your mother anywhere. When we asked around, a lady told us you all had moved to Nashville with family. Nathaniel and I immediately began searching for you there. We heard nothing. The police wouldn't help. She was your mother."

Nana made a face at this.

"She had the right to move, and to take you with her. We hired a private investigator, who reported different men Deborah was seen with, but none knew anything. He then searched the place your mother is from, thinking she might have gone back there, but turned up empty. We searched Nashville for you as well. We never gave up. Nathan checked in, and said he thought you would turn up."

Nana breathed deep, trying to compose herself.

"Matthew Logue found you on the holler road that morning," she began again before I could ask. "He brought you to the hospital and called us immediately. You were in bad shape. An infection had formed, and that's why you had surgery. There was little hope, but you got stronger as your body and mind slept. You know the rest of it. You have had many people wanting to visit. When you are well you should see them, but now I think you should rest."

I knew Nana well enough to know she wanted to think in silence. I felt better after talking with her. We had skated over some things we needed to talk about more, but there would be time for that. For now I was content and as happy as I could be, knowing I really was loved and wanted.

I allowed sleep to come again, just before dawn. Daniel's voice carried me away saying, "They'll never love you, and you know it."

I had nightmares on and off all morning until Nana finally gave me something to help me sleep. Maybe this was the first time I understood relief could be found in a pill.

CHAPTER SEVEN

Time came and went as I spent my days reading or watching TV. I sat on the back porch for hours at a time watching the leaves change from to vibrant orange and yellow until the last of the foliage died with the autumn. Winter came mighty and quick. By Christmas, Cosby had three inches of snow.

Nathan, Nana, Papaw and I spent a quiet New Year together around the fire in the great room. I had reached the point of wanting to talk much or see anyone. I felt if neighbors or church people came by they would see I was filthy. I shied away from any visitors.

It was January before I was strong enough to remain awake an entire day though I wanted to sleep, but Nana insisted I stay up to get my body on "a normal schedule" again.

Time carried me on, never pausing to allow me to catch up. Matthew Logue and his brother Josh came to see me. I was easy to tire, so Nana allowed me to stay propped in the bed as they came to visit.

Truthfully, Nana knew being surrounded by an oversized comforter, as I sat upright, gave me a small feeling of security while I had visitors. At first it was just the pastor that I agreed to see. He did not push me to talk and did not reach for my hand. I think he sensed my discomfort and kindly sat with me and prayed small prayers of strength and healing.

Next came the little old church ladies that smelled of sweet bath powers and had a blue tinge to their perfectly combed white hair. I loved when church ladies came because each one always had something sweet for me to eat, but it was the boys, in particular Matthew I tried to hold off the longest. I was terrified and waited anxiously the day they were permitted to come in my room.

The Logue family lived "up the holler" as Papaw would say, "the holler" being the hollow road. The Logue family lived about two miles from our home and I had known the boys all my life. I played with Josh countless evenings in the woods that hugged our properties together.

The Logues and my family, the Mitchells, were two of the oldest families in Cosby. Although my family had a vast amount of land, we only kept two to four horses at a time, to the Logues' twenty. We rented our land to hunters, who stayed in our tiny cabins, scattered here and there in our woods. They were perfect for those who wanted to "rough it," without using tents.

Everything was carefully marked, and tree stands stayed in place months at a time. The cabins consisted of four bare walls, a tin roof, and dirt floors. There was a hollowed out area with a stone chimney for fires in most of them. This was income, but not Papaw's passion, which was veterinary medicine.

My papaw, Nathaniel John Mitchell, was the county veterinarian. He also taught hunters the proper way to kill and field dress the animals they hunted on our land. We had lots of deer, elk, wild hogs, and turkeys to name a few of the hunted.

We had hundreds of acres of land that shared a border with the Great Smoky Mountains of Tennessee. Cosby was often overlooked on maps, because it lay in the shadows of the mountains.

There was a season for everything, and strangers rented parts of our land to hunt nearly all year round. On days I had free time, I helped clean the small shop Papaw used for his "patients." The Cherokee Reservation was just past the office.

When Papaw rented his property to others, he wanted them to kill either to eat, or to feed others. No waste. That was his rule, or no game—literally. From those who hunted and got their kills but chose not to keep the meat, Papaw would take the carcasses, clean them, and deep-freeze the meat to give to families who needed it. Our family always had fish, duck, turkey, pork, or venison year round. It's a way of life around here.

Papaw treated all the wildlife, farm, and domestic animals in our county. Mondays and Tuesdays, he would wake early and make house calls then stay at the office to treat those with appointments. His small office was by the main highway in town, a few miles away at the mouth of the holler road.

Wednesdays were surgery days. Then Thursdays and half of Friday were for either teaching hunters how to field dress their kill, or prepare the meat for families in need. He stayed on-call through the weekend, but in his downtime, he walked or drove an ATV to check the land for illegal traps and unauthorized hunting.

Papaw loved what he did. He considered it a calling to help those that did not have a voice of their own. When I asked once, confused at the huge, dead twenty-point buck he was sending to a taxidermist for a hunter who frequently rented from us, "Why then do you allow people to kill the animals on our land?"

These were the animals that pranced in our backyard and could often be seen through the thick, almost smoky, morning mist—the "smoky" of the mountains. He grew serious, thinking. Collecting his words, wanting me to truly understand, he explained. "Hunting controls a population of animals that would otherwise starve to death, and this way, they can be used for nourishment and warmth."

I guess I understood that reasoning. I never asked again. I just accepted that his judgment was correct, and from what I could see, he knew everything anyway. He was the most intelligent man I ever knew. From world conflicts to the Bible, front to back, he had the answers for me whenever I was ready to ask them.

I listened to Papaw talk many times with Josh and Matthew from the birthing room as they inquired about my health. I pictured Matthew, the oldest o the two at fifteen, as a Greek demigod-like creature like Hercules or Purseus. The feeling of his strong arms as they scooped my lifeless body from the mud causes butterflies inside my ribs.

Only a frigid January afternoon I listened from my propped up position in my bed as Papaw greeted the boys, their parents, Mrs. and Mr. Logue had sent flowers earlier in the week. They had told Nana to give me their love and said they would wait to visit until I was up for company. They were a nice family, headed by the grandpa Logue, who was a semi-retired dairy farmer.

The Logues had a farm, complete with cows and chickens, but most important to me was that big blue barn. The boys had always been my friends. I was closer to Josh, who was my age. Josh was my coconspirator in many pranks through the years. He was free-spirited and wild. He had a mischievous and fun personality, with big broad shoulders and a tangled mess of brown hair.

Josh had often brought me home by way of piggy back, injured because he'd talked me into jumping wide ditches or climbing a tree that I had "no business climbing", as Nana would say, scolding us. I thought Josh made it his life's ambition to be the polar opposite of his older brother, Matthew.

Matthew was two years older than Josh. Handsome and smart, kind and well spoken, Matthew was going to be a doctor and "travel the globe, helping people in third world countries," as he told me this day, as we sat talking in the birthing room.

I knew this story well, because Josh never missed an opportunity to tease him about it. Josh wanted to play football, and after that it didn't matter. Matthew watched me when Josh and I spoke to each other. He stood behind his younger brother, politely and quietly waiting until we were out of things to say his green eyes seemed to x-ray me, but oddly this did not make me uncomfortable.

Nana stuck her head in the door, her favorite apron tied around her waist. She looked like a perfect picture of a fifties housewife in a Norman Rockwell painting.

"Josh, love," she said sweetly. "Would you help me a second? I need a jar open and am in a desperate situation."

Josh clumsily left us to rescue Nana. The situation was most likely a pie that needed filling, but I had a sneaky suspicion she wanted Matthew and me to have some privacy.

Matthew pulled a chair close to my bedside. I felt heat flood my cheeks and I was deeply thankful to have the comforter to hide my shaking hands in.

"Are you feeling better today?" Matthew asked me seriously.

I nodded, looking down at my lap. I was embarrassed that he found me the way I was, in a filthy T-shirt and the bump in my belly. I must have smelled awful too. I was thankful to Matthew, but I knew with horror that he must know just how dirty I really was, then and now, no matter how much I bathed, or how hot the water got. I could never get clean.

We sat talking about this and that. We talked of what books I'd read recently. I had not been allowed many books those months I lived on a dog leash, and I went cold inside remembering the awful book Daniel had given me about girls and sex.

See? The dirt was always with me, no matter the innocent nature of the conversation. I wondered if I'd ever have a thought again that would not be tainted with a memory of Daniel.

Matthew and I spoke about *Treasure Island* and *Oliver Twist*, but the conversation died away quickly. I was so nervous, but couldn't say why. He pierced me with his dark blue eyes. Those intense, all-too-knowing eyes, as if he could see right through me. The same eyes I knew had seen me in the worst state I had been in in my life.

I nervously told him, "Thank you," before he said good night and was preparing to go. He looked surprised and turned his head, looking at me sideways.

"What for?" he asked incredulously.

This embarrassed me further. I thought it was obvious. I looked away, knowing I was blushing.

"For stopping," I said in a small voice, "and helping me."

I took a chance to glance at his face, and he looked sad for a moment.

"I was meant to head out that morning, Piper. Never intended to, but my grandpa was out of coffee, and I wanted to grab some before he woke up, you know, to save him the trip?" He shrugged. "I was up finishing a paper for English, so I thought I might as well go and save him the hassle of driving, since it's getting harder for him. He loves his morning coffee."

Matthew looked down and then back up to me, and said, "Thank God you're all right, Piper. Everyone's just been worried sick, and never stopped looking for you. Some thought you moved away, and wasn't coming back. My mom was especially worried about Mrs. Mitchell."

I didn't say it, but I felt it. I felt I did move away, and I was never coming back. I was still gone, and all that was left of me was the shell of the girl I'd once been. Before my daddy died. Before my mother, along with Daniel, murdered me. Something in my face must have shown what I was thinking.

Matthew took my hand in his and squeezed it. I didn't protest, but I just sat there, as he held my hand.

"You're going to be all right, Piper. You just have to look beyond all this. It'll be sunny again someday for you. I promise."

I quietly wiped my eyes. I was thankful to have a friend that knew my secret and didn't run from me. I was dirty still, but for a moment, I was Piper Mitchell and could climb the trees with the best of the boys and could swim like a fish in the river on the back of our property. I was the Piper that put frogs in different places in the house, just to hear my Nana scream for Papaw to save her. Nathan and I would hide and watch her dance around frantic and terrified of the "wretched things!"

Just for a moment I smiled, exhausted, at Matthew. Then I slipped silently inside the dark places within my heart once more. I wanted to believe this handsome boy. What was beyond and unforeseen for me? Something I had not thought about in a long time.

CHAPTER EIGHT

Even after months of recovering I struggled to find a consistent mood. I functioned in a kind of sleep walk, going about the day doing the things normal people did.

I brush my teeth and hair. I bathed and wore clean clothes, but I lived inside my head without rest. Nana took me to speak with a doctor after finding my in the same position staring at a spot on the wall for more than an hour straight. When she asked me what was I thinking about, I could not recall. That was an hour lost and it was happening more and more frequently.

After seeing a doctor I was prescribed medication. It helped some, but it made me feel funny all the time. My head would swim, and I wanted sleep all day. The medicine seemed to worsen my zombie-like state of mind. Nana had me stop taking the pills after just a couple of months, and instead opted for old remedies she learned from her grandmother back in Germany.

Day and night, she would make me sip herb teas made of things I couldn't pronounce. They did soothe me, or maybe it was the kindness and love I was shown. I'd been denied the needs of a child, like loving arms to hold me. I instead had arms was inescapable.

I would wake many nights with this distinctive smell in my room, only to realize it was the memory of things I'd never be able to wash from my mind. Nana and Papaw did try to love all this out of me, but despite all their efforts, I walked life daily with a dark cloud following me.

I came to accept that no matter the laughter, no matter the happy times, I shook with fear at the smells I couldn't forget and the skin-crawling dreams of Daniel climbing on top of me. I learned to live with the heaviness in my heart and found that there really were ghosts, or rather dead people that walk the earth, for I was dead in spite of my heartbeat.

I played a good role and tried to be normal. Nana never fell for my act. Papaw accepted me broken, the way I was. To him, that was far better than not having me at all.

As time slid by, the days got a little easier. Routine was my friend. Matthew and Josh were always around which awakened resentment in me, especially with Matthew. I hated that I'd never have a boyfriend or a first kiss with someone as good as Matthew. I'd never take joy in school dances or anticipate my wedding night. Soon, I became bitter at the thoughts.

Nathan came home every other week. I loved my brother and could tell the months that had gone by had changed him greatly as well. One day, while riding Betsy, one of Papaw's more gentle palominos, I found him by the river smoking a joint. His brown hair was long now, like a rock star. He inhaled and patted the rock beside him, indicating I should sit with him.

I sat with my brother watching him smoke. The smell was like that of a skunk, but it was not at all unpleasant. On the contrary it made my mouth water.

"What's that like?" I asked him nodding at the joint.

He inhaled deeply, looking at me from the corner of his eyes.

"It keeps me calm. Never ever tell Nana you saw me smoking this." Nathan said sounding a little ashamed.

"You're still afraid of her?" I said with a giggle.

By now Nathan was a grown man that was twice the size of our grandmother.

"Hell yeah. She'd skin me alive."

I laughed at the thought.

"I'm serious. Don't tell her nothing Piper."

"I won't," I promised then remembered his reason. "Why do you need to be kept calm?"

I was genuinely curious. He sat for moment in thought, as we watched the water flow by hypnotically. Nathan picked up a rock and tossed it.

"I have a hard time living with what's happened to you. It's all my fault, Piper. If I'd stayed, this would've never happened."

He dropped his head and took a drag from the joint. I shook my head in protest.

"Nathan, if you'd stayed, you would probably be in that cornfield with her." I shivered inside as I said this.

Nana had told Nathan most of my story, of course. He said nothing to me about it, but I knew we would have to talk one day.

No one knew where she was but us. Actually, no one knew anything that one of us hadn't disclosed. Since Daniel and my mother were dead, Nana wanted me spared from all that would come with being known as "that girl," for the rest of my life. I was thankful for this.

We did not hide it, or never speak of it. It was all just better "left to God," as she would put it. We agreed to leave my mother wherever she was in that cornfield. I didn't want to talk about her. I couldn't stand the thought of her, not while the image of my daddy's tie in her hands was so very fresh to me.

Sitting and watching the river now, Nathan didn't say anything. There was a comfortable but heavy silence with us. Finally I broke the silence.

"Can I try that?"

Nathan looked at my face as if he heard something but was unsure what exactly.

"Not just no, but hell no," Nathan said shaking his head.

"and why not?"

"Just cause. It's not good for you," he said sternly then tossed the joint in the water.

"There," he said, proud of himself. "I'd better not hear of you doing stuff like that either. I mean it, Piper," he warned me seriously, which was kind of ruined by the grin that crept over his lips.

I elbowed him in the ribs.

"You're no fun, Nathan," I pouted, but felt good he was looking after me, even if it was fairly hypocritical.

He walked with me, as I guided Betsy to the stable, and then he walked me back to the house with a big arm holding me close to him. For a few minutes the hole that was in my chest was almost filled.

I was homeschooled for a little over a year to keep me on track for high school. It took some adjusting to social gatherings a little at a time. By the following Christmas I was in school and doing pretty good.

I rode with Matthew and Josh every morning and afternoon, as Matthew was allowed to drive. I think this helped Nana's fear, as she never wanted me alone, left to only my dark thoughts. Josh and I were in most of the same classes together, and I had to help him with homework because most of his time was taken up by weight-training for football. Even off-season, his schedule revolved around football training.

Matthew and I would wait in the truck until Josh was finished in the afternoons. Josh normally took only an hour after school, so Matthew and I would talk and do homework, or read as the windows fogged up. I would draw on the windows, and more than once I caught Matthew watching me, with sadness in his eyes. I didn't feel bad when I saw it in his eyes, like I did with others. After all, he was my hero.

He had pulled me out of thick mud and had gently lain me in the truck bed. That was something I would never forget. In my mind, Matthew could damn well feel however he wanted, because he'd earned that with me. I enjoyed being with him and hearing about other places in the world he wanted to visit someday. He was so open-minded and God-fearing, two qualities that sometimes clashed in our small country town, but for Matthew it only added to his appeal.

Matthew was allowed to drive to and from school, church, and the store. He was more responsible than most adults. He came over and studied the Bible with Papaw at least once a week. Matthew was the ideal son, friend, brother, and with a pang of the deepest regret, I knew he would be an ideal husband for some pretty and clean girl as well.

He got along great with everyone. Over a year had passed now, and I would be fourteen in February. I was not blind to the fact he was gorgeous, and my darkness would fade slightly when he was around. Not that any boy would ever have me, I was convinced. I was dirty and spoiled, and Matthew would marry a girl as clean as he was. The thought of it sent ice through me. I hated Daniel for ruining me. I secretly wished I could kill him all over again.

I rode home sad at this thought, the last day before Christmas break. We three rode silently, bouncing our way down the holler road, heading home. I leapt from the truck when Josh let me out, as I always rode in the middle of the bench seat. With a low "Thank you, and see you later," I walked as quickly as I could to my front door.

I guess they said goodbye, but I wasn't sure, I was too emotional at this point and needed to get away before I started crying. Josh and Matthew both knew I was weird, so I never bothered to explain my sudden shifts in moods.

I wore my pain and darkness like a coat on the coldest of winter days. I wanted to shut myself in my room and lock myself away, so I couldn't contaminate anyone. As Daniel had said, nobody would ever want me. It was a sad fact, and I might as well get used to it fast.

When I walked in the front door, I was brought up short by someone screaming. I dropped my bag, and ran through the kitchen, following the sounds. I had long since moved to my dad's old room upstairs, on the second of the three floors. Judging by the noise, the birthing room was back in business.

I stopped outside the door to listen like I always did when someone was about to enter the world, and take his or her first breath. I always waited anxiously for that tiny cry. Nana surprised me when she called from the other side of the closed door.

"Piper? Love? Is that you?" she called sweetly.

I didn't want to be heard. I figured I would have to leave and give the mother privacy, but then again, it sounded like Nana might need something. I decided to answer.

"Yes, Nana?"

I heard low talking and then the door opened, causing me to jump about three feet.

"Come in and give me a hand, will you?" Nana said, and I stood shocked. I'd never been allowed in the room before, not while a baby was coming. I'd heard dozens through the door, but never been inside, not for a birth.

Nana sat down on a rolling stool, and I stood in the doorway, unable to understand what I was seeing. A woman lay with her feet in the air on the hospital bed that normally was folded in half, tucked away in the corner of the room. The bottom of the bed had been removed and stirrups held her legs apart and in place. The woman was breathing heavily, her chest rising and falling rapidly.

Nana said in a soothing voice, "Come now, dear, you're nearly there, Just a bit longer, and he'll be here. Piper?" she said, not looking at me "Come in, and shut the door, please."

I moved woodenly, not knowing if I wanted to be there or not. Once the door was shut, Nana motioned for me to stand next to her. The woman on the bed tossed her head back, heaving. I suddenly realized she was not a woman at all, but a girl, not much older than I was.

"That's a good girl," Nana said, patting her leg.

"Piper, this is Lana. Lana, this is my granddaughter, Piper." Nana said properly, as if we'd just ran into each other at church. I looked up into the girl's face, which was covered in sweat now. Lana cocked her head sideways and grinned at me

"Hey," she said.

"Hey," I replied awkwardly.

I watched her face turn red and screw up in pain. Her breath began to pick up. Despite the circumstances, Lana was completely at ease. Nana got up and pushed me to sit down in her stool. I shook my head, horrified,

"What? I can't, Nana. I don't know—"

Nana shushed me and handed me gloves.

"Hush now, you need to be ready. Just listen as I talk. There's really nothing to it."

Lana screamed, and I froze, seeing something round bulging from her lower half, which was now in my direct line of vision.

I wanted to run from the room, but I was also transfixed by what was happening. I was mortified, but I could not look away. I put on my gloves hurriedly. Nana placed my hand where the baby was crowning.

"Just like baby horses, no?" Nana asked, her beautiful German accent more pronounced.

I wanted to say it was nothing like the horses I'd helped Papaw deliver. Nothing.

"Feel the pressure build with each contraction? That's when you push through the pain."

I didn't want to feel, and yet I wanted nothing more in the world. I placed my hand on the stretching tissue, and watched in amazement at the life within coming forth.

Lana began to scream, causing me to start shaking all over.

"It's going to rip me in two!" she said through gritted teeth.

Judging by what I was seeing, I didn't think she was too far off with her assessment. The tiny head progressed a little further out, then retreated.

"Doing good, Lana! Next time, I want the biggest push you can give me, okay? Come on now," Nana coached.

She guided my hands to be ready and began whispering in my ear.

"Here it comes, Piper. Be ready now."

Tears were filling my eyes, making me blink rapidly. Lana screamed, and bore down, straining with the labor of it. Her knuckles were chalk white from the death grip she had on the bars on either side of the bed.

"Here we go! Piper, keep his head up! He's coming," Nana said sweetly.

She sounded far away from me, although I felt her directly beside me. I was fully wrapped in this moment. The baby's head was out now. I was in shock, but adrenaline was rushing through my body.

I placed my gloved hand under its head, and Nana continued to coach Lana. I tuned everything out. I couldn't say it was an out of body experience, but I think it was close.

A minute later the baby was out, wailing and balling his fists at me. I held him, slippery with goo, not caring about anything else in the world. I felt hot tears slide down my cheeks. Daniel had not killed everything in me after all.

Nana was beaming with pride, and my heart fluttered wildly with excitement inside my chest. I could feel an overwhelming joy and peace looking in this creature's eyes. A living, breathing thing was here, and I helped get it here. I looked, with my eyes full of tears, for Nana's face. She was telling Lana something, and then she looked at me.

"Good girl," she said winking, and gave me one of her angelic smiles.

I blinked the tears away and watched as Nana cut the cord. She began to tell me what to do. I placed the baby in a blanket rubbed the protective white paste off his face. I suctioned his nose and mouth—just like baby horses, I thought.

After the baby was as clean as I was going to get him, I started toward the mother, but Lana began shaking her head.

"No, he's not mine," she said, without an ounce of humor.

I felt my face pinch with confusion. I held the little boy in my arms and watched as Nana sewed Lana up. Nana would turn her head to the side to tell me something, explaining why this and that was necessary. She was coaching me. I didn't think I'd ever shown interest in the work of a midwife, but she was coaching me nonetheless.

Lana, as Nana later explained as we left her to rest a while, had gotten pregnant by a married man. The baby was going to live with the man and his wife, raising him as their own. Lana didn't seem to have any concerns about this decision.

Later that evening I checked on her, she openly admitted as much to me.

"I mean, honestly? He's going to be much better off with his family than with me," she said sleepily. "And besides," she added, smiling at me. "I'm going to be an actress. I wouldn't be able to give him the attention he deserves."

I just listened, knowing the first rule of delivering babies is you never, ever judge the mothers. Not their age or color or reasons. Lana and I talked and got to know each other a little as I cleaned around the room, killing time, and enjoying the company, even as odd as it was.

Lana was a high school dropout, who worked at a diner on the edge of our little town. She was saving up her tips and longing for the day she got away from her "drunken whore of a mother" and "super-sized" granny and their tiny trailer in the Westland trailer park. She was going to be a famous actress when she finally got away.

I wished I had some kind of dream, but for now all I knew was Daniel, and my mother had made sure I would never be able to do anything without their presence in my head. They were with me always, along with the awful words they'd said, and the things they'd done.

By now it was late, and Nana had taken the baby somewhere. Lana had signed a bunch of papers that a lawyer for the family brought over. It was practical, but it still made me sad. I went to bed excited that I delivered a baby for the first time but sad that it was gone and that I would not know what he would grow to be. The little pieces of my heart still hurt at the thought of never being loved, and never being clean enough to have a family of my own.

CHAPTER NINE

Christmas was a huge deal at the Mitchell home, this year especially, now I was well enough to enjoy it. We cooked and baked for church folks and neighbors. Nana and I took food to the less fortunate families that otherwise would not have anything. I loved every minute of it.

When we visited the Logue family with baked pies and homemade fudge, I sat and watched *Mickey Mouse Christmas* with Josh. Matthew, I assumed, had grown tired of me by now and didn't feel the need to see me. I sat rigid and upset that he hadn't at least come to say hello to me.

I could hear Mrs. Logue and Nana gossiping in the kitchen. Leaving Josh to Mickey, I began to wander around the living room, looking at the decorations. The pictures of a happy family sat all over the room, scattered in different places, including pictures of the elder Mrs. Logue who had died a few years ago. After she died, Mr. Logue refused to leave, so the family moved here from Florida to take care of him.

Something caught my eye and I looked out the window. There, setting on the hill was my blue barn, the image that started my dreams of escape from Daniel and the personal hell I was forced to live in. A light was on in its loft. I instantly turned and left the house, telling Nana I'd be back in a few minutes. I shut the door, not waiting for a reply.

I climbed the hill to the barn. I loved that thing—blue and ugly, but a symbol of home to me. I opened the doors and looked inside. Nothing. Just the dusty inside of a barn. I climbed the steps to the loft and found Matthew propped up on his elbows reading.

"Oh, hey," he said, with that crooked grin that made me blush. Laying the book down beside him, he sat up

"I'm sorry," I stammered, and I began to back away.

"No, stay," he said, getting to his feet now. "I was trying get some things caught up." He nodded toward the papers and books. "I have to stay ahead if I'm going to get into Duke." He grinned again.

He was so handsome. He had wavy dark brown hair clipped close to the scalp, and green eyes. He was clean and lovely. He stood a whole head taller than me, and I was pretty tall for a girl. The boys at school made sure to tell me all the time.

I got lost for a minute in those deep green eyes. I realized he was saying something and tried to tune back in.

"Piper?" he said, and I blinked back to earth.

He was clean, and I was dirty. I would never be a part of his clean happy family, no matter how much I wanted it. The smiling, happy people in the pictures I saw moments ago would never include me.

I swallowed my hurt at the thought and said stupidly, "Right."

Matthew looked at me, and frowned. "You okay?" he asked.

Getting control of myself, I said, "Yes, I just wanted to see the barn. I saw the light and wanted to see it."

I looked around me, sadness starting to bubble up my throat, tears threatening to surface.

"You wanted to see the barn? Why?" he asked, confused.

I remembered he didn't know my story. He knew I was dirty and unlovable because he found me, but he didn't realize why I would want to see the blue barn. Matthew didn't know it was a symbol of hope in a hopeless trailer that had held a little girl prisoner for months. I paused, and thought this was an innocent enough question to answer.

"This is where," I stopped, and swallowed my emotions and then finished quietly, "I was running to."

Understanding dawned on him, and his face went soft.

"Anyway," I said, feeling uncomfortable. "I better get back before Nana misses me." I turned to go.

"Wait. Hold on just a sec." I stopped on the top step and turned to see him rummage around in his bag, emerging with something in his hand.

"Three different girls tried to corner me at school, but I dodged them all," he said sheepishly. "I brought this home, hoping to get a chance to use it."

He opened his hand to show me a small strand of mistletoe. I looked at it, not understanding.

"Okay," I said, not catching on.

I was dirty. Not at all kissable, but this clean and beautiful guy placed the mistletoe over my head and said, "May I?" in a nervous whisper.

I was dumbfounded. He wanted to kiss me? Heat rose to my face and I felt suddenly light headed. I just nodded numbly, not knowing I was even moving my head. I wanted nothing more in the world than to taste those pink lips of his.

Matthew stepped down on the step with me, and leaned into me, kissing me so softly. At first it was just him touching my lips with his. I was terrified, and almost shaking with nerves. My cheeks burned, and my head rushed.

Something must have shifted with him because he began to kiss me deeper. Forgetting the mistletoe, he wrapped his arms around my middle. My mouth parted, and our tongues touched. Feeling him press into my body, I jumped back as if he'd burned me.

Breathing heavy now, I shook all over. Daniel's face was there for just a second. He had succeeded in ruining this wonderful moment for me.

Matthew reached to get my hand, concern on his beautiful face. I began to cry, confused.

"Piper?"

Something in his voice was gentle, but commanding. I looked up to his face.

"It's me, Piper. Just me," he pulled me to him, to hug me.

He smelled like cedar and musk. I loved him, but I was dirty. I wanted to kiss him, but I was diseased in my mind. I would never be free from the stranglehold of my mother. My body and the scars I had would always be a reminder I was not worthy. But damn it, for just a moment I wished to be just that.

CHAPTER TEN

Not long after the kiss, I found by accident the relief that came from cutting. I absently picked at a scab. I picked at it with so much focus and control. I was relieved when the blood began to flow freely.

This was something I controlled completely, and it released my mind from bonds I didn't know were there. I began to cut myself daily. I had so many emotions and no control over them. I hurt so bad in my mind, the physical pain relieved me of it and felt good.

When the first shard of broken glass released blood from my upper arm, I immediately felt better. Not in a soothing way, but in a gratifying way. I could control this. I could cut, and not draw blood, or I could cut, and make myself bleed as much as I thought I needed to. I was dirty and diseased, and therefore I needed to bleed from the sickness.

Escape came to me in bloody droplets. The more I cut, the less I cried. It somehow turned everything off. I now had marks on the outside to match the ones on the inside. I was tempted to cut too deep, but stopped just shy of it. I knew what I was doing was twisted, but I was twisted, so it also made perfect sense to me.

Matthew didn't try to kiss me again, though we spent hours talking in person and on the phone. It was months before anything physical took place between us, other than hugging. He just got me. He understood without me saying that I wasn't ready.

Most girls my age bragged about the things they would do with boys. It made me feel out of place, but I had just not got to the point of not hearing Daniel's nasty words in my ear.

I turned fifteen and finished my freshman year of high school with honors. Nana was beside herself with pride. I wasn't sure, but at times sad thoughts showed in her seraphic face, and I secretly wondered if she was just happy I was semi-normal.

I did have my darkness. That was always there with me. It haunted me most nights. I would wake with dry heaves, thinking of the taste of Daniel, or the smell that rose from his rancid flesh after days of boozing. I hid this as best I could, not wanting to add to the worry I was causing Nana and Papaw already. I went day to day with a smile on my face and a heavy heart.

The summer came fast and furious. Lana began to hang out at my house more and more that year. She would come to eat and watch TV. I knew, as did everyone in the county, that Lana lived with her grandmother and her mom. Her mom, Nicole, was what Nana called a "lot lizard." Nana said she was the kind of woman who hung out at truck stops and did things with truckers for money to buy drugs and beer.

Nana would check on Lana's grandmother, old Mrs. Morris from time to time but would never take me with her. She said she was scared to death I'd catch a disease. I thought—but didn't say—I already had a disease, though it left no physical signs. In my mind, I couldn't catch anything worse than what I already had.

On days that Nana visited the expectant mothers, she had me stay home or work in the office with Papaw. On a midsummer's morning I walked to office to help my favorite Veterinarian and found him sweeping.

"Hi, Papaw," I said as I walked in.

"Well, hello, my Piper," he said brightly.

I was taller than he was now, and I bent my head to kiss his rough cheek. Just as my dad could never seem to keep a smooth face, neither could his dad. Papaw had five o'clock shadow by eleven in the morning. His hair had been chalk white since before I was born.

"What ya up to today, kiddo?" he asked.

He returned to his sweeping, as I got a coke from the fridge.

"Nothing. Nana's visiting Mrs. Morris. Need me to do anything?" I asked, hopping up on the counter.

Before he could answer, a man came in, followed by a younger version of himself. Taking his hat off, the older man nodded in my direction.

I hopped off the counter and went to stand behind it. Strangers made me immediately wary. I felt I was always anticipating someone tying me up at any moment.

"Mr. Mitchell. It's been a long time," the man said, in an accent I couldn't place.

He stuck out a big hand to shake in welcome. He was a dark man, maybe Spanish or Italian. He had jet-black hair, and big, broad shoulders. His eyes were so dark they looked black. I was struck by his resemblance to Brutus from Popeye.

"Maurice Duchete! How ya been?" Papaw said, pumping the man's hand in return. "What's it been? Ten years?"

The man smiled, creasing his brows together. "Yes, sir. I guess it has," said Maurice.

The younger version of Maurice was standing in the big man's shadow. He eyed me slyly, and I felt heat rise to my face. I looked at him and then quickly looked away, aware I was blushing.

"This is my boy, Jean-Paul," Maurice said proudly.

Jean-Paul shook Papaw's hand politely. "How do you do, sir?"

Just as politely, Papaw said, "Nice to meet you, son."

Maurice then inquired about my dad. My heart clenched at this question. Papaw only brought up my dad when he was in certain moods, and this was not one of those moods now. He was unreadable, but I know the toll my dad's death had taken on him—his only child, dead and buried in our family cemetery, up in the hills.

Papaw had a sad smile for the man. "Nate passed not long ago." He paused. "Car wreck," he finished, in explanation.

The man, Maurice, looked sad.

"Nathaniel, I'm very sorry for your loss," he said sincerely.

If we had a dollar for every time I'd heard that said, we'd never have to work again. But I believed this man was sincere. Maurice turned his gaze to me, and Papaw followed it. For a moment, I thought he had forgotten I was there.

"Oh, yes!" he said proudly. "This beautiful young lady is my granddaughter. This was Nate's greatest gift to me during his too-short life."

I felt proud for a second. Papaw loved me. Me? But I'm dirty and diseased, I reminded myself. Now I had the nasty cuts to prove it. Unseen by the world, I made sure I kept the fresh cuts open, to remind me that bleeding meant being alive, because the other feelings would certainly kill me.

The men talked about reservations and tree stands for the coming hunting season. I was bored with the conversation, so I said my nice-to-meet-yous and good-byes. The younger man, Jean-Paul, never took his eyes from me. I figured he could see I was dirty. I left before his dad noticed it too.

On my walk back home, a car pulled up beside me. It was a miserably hot August day, and school would be starting back up in no time. Lana rolled the window down and smiled her best Hollywood smile.

"Hop in," she said, with her wicked grin.

"Where we going?"

"Who cares? Get you country ass in the car before I melt." She waved long fingers back and forth to fan herself.

I ran to the other side, and we set off to I-didn't-care-where.

We ended up at the river, a spot we would swim and rope jump into deep water. Handing me a swimsuit, Lana got out of the car. Unashamed, she immediately began to undress. Her body was perfect, and there were no ugly scars or cut-marks. She was not dirty as I was.

I got out of the car feeling ashamed.

"I'll just swim in this."

I had on a shirt with three-quarter sleeves, and jean shorts I had cut off myself. My cuts were on the insides of my upper arms, and a few on my stomach.

"Oh, no, you won't! You need some sun. You're as pale as a vampire, missy." Lana reached for the button on my jeans.

Nothing was weird or uncomfortable to Lana. She would often curl up against me like a cat, when we sat on the couch to watch TV. Although I had problems with physical contact, I was trying to overcome them. I had no choice with Lana, and I felt oddly safe with her. Nothing Lana did ever made me uncomfortable.

Except for now. I jerked away from her. She was my best friend, and we had been spending a lot of time together since the baby was born, but I had never shared anything with her that I was ashamed of. Nothing about my mother, nothing about Daniel.

I thought about it daily. I'd had a mother who could have given me to Nana, who continuously told me I was loved and wanted. No, my mother sold me. For what I don't know, but it destroyed who I was supposed to be.

"Stop!" I said, mad now, as Lana kept trying to get my clothes from me.

After noticing I was not playing, she stopped. Taking off the oversized sunglasses she sported, like the movie star she was going to be, she searched my face. I refused to meet her eyes.

"What is it, Piper?" Concern etched her gorgeous dark eyes. "Tell me," she demanded.

I opened the car door. "Just take me home."

Lana put her arm out, blocking me from getting in. "Livia Piper, I will hog-tie you until you tell me what is wrong!" I could hear in her voice that she meant it.

I began to cry for no reason. I was not hurt, but ashamed. I would give anything to be like Lana, and let Matthew kiss me without freaking out. I was a mess. I had cuts all over me, because I was a freak.

I'd never get the smell of stale tobacco and Daniel's sweat out of my nose. I would never get clean, no matter how hard I scrubbed my skin. I couldn't bleach the images out of my mind, out of my heart.

Lana hugged me and rubbed my back. After I got control of myself a little, she pulled away from me and got something from under the front seat of her grandma's beat-up old K-car. Without speaking, she led me to the cliff, where we sat Indian-style. I watched quietly as she placed something in paper and rolled it tight, licking it with her tongue and then putting the whole thing in her mouth to wet it.

Pulling it from her lips, she grinned at me. "This will make you feel much better, and then we're going to talk."

I didn't protest. I watched as she lit up the joint. It made my mouth water, in spite of the smell of skunk. Then I smoked my first joint with Lana. There was no denying it, I felt much better. The weightless sensation carried me away almost instantly. My mind unraveled and my shoulders relaxed for the first time in a long.

We talked and talked. I told her little bits, and finally broke down and told her about my cutting myself. I felt freer with each word that left my lips. She looked at me, wanting to see what I had done to myself. I took my shirt off, and showed her the mutilation of my arms. She never judged. Never seemed disgusted. She bent her head and kissed my self-inflicted wounds.

Lana's jet-black hair shone like glass in the sunlight. I was floating on a cloud. I allowed Lana to kiss me and to hold me. I understood we were both kindred spirits, broken in many different ways yet all were relatable. Lana explained to me how she believed we did what we needed to survive. If cutting made me feel better, then she understood.

"My gran feeds herself all day and all night. The only time she's not eating is when she's sleeping. She does this instead of this," she said, indicating the joint between her two perfectly manicured fingers. "For some unknown reason she believes hers isn't a sin, but mine is. We both do what we do," she said with a shrug.

I'd never thought of things that way, but she was absolutely right. We talked about heavy things, then funny things. Being high was the first time I had unraveled my inner wrappings, and allowed myself to be in the present. I laughed till my jaws hurt.

We skinny-dipped and lay on the rocks, unashamed by our nakedness. We finally dressed, and began making our way back as the sun set. I giggled all the way home. I hung my head out of the window, letting my long, wild hair fly through the wind.

I was still smiling stupidly when she dropped me off at home. Nana was waiting on me at the door hands firmly placed on her hips. She chewed me up and down. Then, when Lana had enough time to get home, she called her and chewed her out as well. I knew she was just nervous. She worried all the time. I wished there was something I could do to take the worry from her.

As I went to the kitchen to get dinner, I wondered if I could get Nana to smoke some weed with me. Then she wouldn't worry so much. I laughed out loud at my thought, and Nana shot me a disgusted look.

Nana thought we'd been drinking.

"All the girls to run around with, and you run with that one," Nana was saying to me.

I think the irritation at me was gone, and now she was going to coach me. Forever coaching me. I acted as normal as possible, but later over dinner, I told her we swam and giggled by ourselves. No drinking, which wasn't a lie.

"Nothing bad," I said, and honestly believed it.

After I'd gone to bed, I heard Papaw saying, "Gracie, you got to let the girl live a little. We both know she's lucky to be alive."

Nana never brought it up again, but she sternly told me the next day I was to always leave a note to say where I was going and who I was with, and that I shouldn't go drinking. Then she proceeded to cover my sunburned nose with aloe from the plants she grew in her window boxes.

She swore the herbs she grew cured everything. Oh, how I wished that were true. I'd bathe in them, if they would cure me.

The funny thing was, the more I was with Lana, the safer I felt. Mostly, I felt safer with myself. I was getting comfortable with Matthew now, and as we waited for Josh to finish football practice the following October, I let him hold me and kiss me. I was now a sophomore, and Matthew was a senior, making plans for college. I was so excited for him, but when he talked to me about Duke, I wept inside.

I didn't want him to leave me. I wanted him to stay with me forever. I never said this out loud, but it's how I felt. We were unofficially attached to each other. He walked me to classes, picked me up, and drove me home each day.

We went to the movies on weekends with Lana and Josh, who shamelessly made out, to the point that Matthew and I would not sit with them any longer. The more I prayed time would go slower, the faster it went. It was December before we knew it.

CHAPTER ELEVEN

Rifle season was about to begin. I saw Maurice and his son, Jean-Paul, several times. I saw them when they came from the south to camp for the week in one of the hunting cabins. Jean-Paul would stare holes through me. I didn't know what to make of him. I was guessing he was around twenty years old. His skin was not as dark as his father's, but his eyes were the same shade of near black.

He was a very attractive man, and from the little he said, he seemed very intelligent. He was kind to me, a gentleman from another place and time. When father and son would join us for dinner, he would bow slightly when I entered the room, or stood until Nana and I had taken our seats at the table.

I began to be suspicious of the increasing visits, after I overheard Maurice and Papaw talking one night on the porch, their cigar smoke so thick you could cut it.

"Forgive my curious nature, Nathaniel, but your granddaughter? How old is she?"

Papaw chuckled

"Too young, Maurice."

They sipped brandy and rocked in their rocking chairs.

"Sixteen? Seventeen?" Maurice asked.

Papaw chuckled again.

"Piper is not yet sixteen and she might as well be twelve."

A heavy silence took my Papaw, and I knew he was thinking of me being twelve. I would do anything to relieve him of the burden of that knowledge.

"I only ask, because my Jean-Paul seems mighty taken with her."

Papaw snorted.

"No offense to you or Jean-Paul, but I'm hoping Piper stays with me till my dying day. She is more joy than anything I've ever known."

I placed a hand over my mouth to silence my cry. He was the joy in my life, and I, a dirty, spoiled girl, didn't deserve the love he and Nana gave me so freely.

A poke to my ribs made me jump.

"What are you doing?" Nathan whispered.

He was dressed in his too-short pajamas, and his brown hair messy, the worse for wear. I put my finger to my lips, grabbed his arm, and led him out of the room.

"Nosy," he teased me, when we got to the living room.

I stuck my tongue out at him.

"Takes one to know one."

We crawled under the Christmas tree, and lay looking up into the lit branches. That had been something we did with my dad. He would have us lie on our backs, and tell us Santa stories. I missed him every day.

Nathan and I lay in silence, watching the lights, lost in their dance. My brother's visits were further apart than they used to be. Nathan had been looking tired and worn out. I worried about him constantly. The late nights and partying were catching up to him.

My big brother would be twenty-two in two weeks, but had already begun to show signs of aging. I knew he drank heavy at times. Though I was aware of the signs, he didn't share with me the extent of his drug use. I smoked weed with Lana, but that was our secret. Nathan would probably throw a fit if he knew, so I chose not to share this with him.

The grandfather clock ticked hypnotically.

"Piper?" Nathan said, breaking the trance.

He said my name in a voice laced with sadness.

"Hmmm?" I said, still dazed by the lights.

Nathan hesitated, and I begin to dread whatever he was cooking up.

"You ever think of her? Think of her out in a cornfield alone?"

I had to think about what he was saying before I replied. The truth was, Nathan had never known just how cruel our mother could be. She saved the worst for me. Nathan had the Mitchell name, but it was a little known fact that he would never know his real father.

The mother we shared was cruel to me even before my father died. I know that now. I didn't see it before, but she found pleasure in my discomfort. She was jealous of me.

I was neglected and starved for the affection I never got from her, but Nathan never knew this, because he received her love, in the warped and twisted way she could love.

"No," I finally said flatly. "I try not to ever think of her."

I felt him shift, probably trying to find the right words to say.

"She held me down while a man raped me, Nathan. She hated me from the day I was born. No. She's exactly where she should be, and I'm lucky to not be with her." I said this in my dead voice, because admitting these things was channeling the dead girl inside me.

Nathan took a deep breath and didn't say anything else. He held my hand a while, then went back to bed.

It was hard to imagine such evil in our lives, but it had been there all along. My dad married my mom even though he knew she was pregnant by someone else. He thought she just hadn't been loved enough, and he could show her what love really was. He could fix what was broken in her.

He couldn't though, and I think at times my mother knew that if she didn't act right, he would cut her off, and she'd be just another trashy Akins girl. Daddy gave Nathan his name simply because no matter what, Nathan was his son, and Nana and Papaw accepted this with open hearts and minds. Nathan has never been treated any different.

Over the Christmas break from school, Jean-Paul came around often. Nana teased me about him, but as nice and beautiful as he was, I was deeply in love with Matthew. Nathan left right after his birthday, gone again to chase his dream of being a musician, playing in what Nana called "honky-tonks." She said this word like it tasted bad.

My sixteenth birthday was coming up fast. Nana wanted to celebrate with a sweet sixteen party, decorating the house in, of course, Valentine pink and red. I thought I would die of embarrassment, but stayed quiet. Nobody could throw a party like Nana. The food alone drew people from all over.

"I am going to say that monetary gifts will go towards your college education, or whatever you choose," she said about the invitations. I knew deep down, she wanted me to be a midwife.

"Whatever you think, Nana," I said with my back to her.

I now smoked pot nightly, sometimes more than that. I kept my eyes averted, for fear Nana would catch on.

When I smoked, I had way fewer nightmares, so Lana kept me in stock. My allowance kept her in stock. We were two peas in a pod. My bedroom window was directly over the porch roof, so I would sit out there and smoke Lana's finest weed. I didn't cut myself as often when I was high. I stayed calm, and had worked my way up to kissing Matthew for more than a few seconds.

We worked our way up to make-out sessions that left me breathing heavy, and Matthew red in the face. Now waiting on Josh after school consisted of petting and long kissing sessions. Our body heat kept the truck windows fogged up. If Nana or Papaw knew of either the weed or Matthew, they never brought it up.

I think Nana was happy while I was happy, and learned to only intervene if I showed signs of trouble. My grades were good. I was delivering babies and helped with the land and the shop. I even visited shut-ins with Nana. I also made house calls with Papaw when I could. I worked hard and practiced good manners. That was really all that was expected of me.

I got sixteen pink roses from Nathan. Nana placed them in the center of the "Grand room," as she called it. The Grand room was huge, and was big enough so guests could have room to dance to the grand piano. Half the room was now home to a huge U-shaped sofa, centered in front of the giant fireplace, which was big enough to stand up in. It really was the perfect gathering place.

"Now all the party guests can see what a wonderful brother you have," Nana told me, as she fiddled with the roses.

"They already do, Nana, or most of the girls do," I said sheepishly.

Nana wrinkled her nose, but said nothing. She was well aware of how popular Nathan was with females.

The guests arrived, and before long the party began. My school friends danced and laughed. The adults hung out by the food and gossiped. I opened presents and squealed, almost like a normal girl.

I always knew in my heart, I was dirty and diseased. Daniel was in my head, telling me that these people didn't love me. I was unwanted and unloved. Thank goodness Lana took me to the bathroom with her, after watching the stress enter my face. There was no fooling Lana. She knew me very well by now.

"Chill out, would you?" She paused to sniff powder up her nose. "This is your party. Quit freaking out."

I wanted to try this powder, but she wouldn't let me. She said weed was one thing. This was "a whole other monster." She fished in her huge bag, and pulled out a bottle of prescription pills.

"Take this. It will calm your nerves."

I did so without asking questions.

When I came out five minutes later, I noticed the crowd had swelled. Jean-Paul was leaning against the kitchen counter, talking quietly with Nana.

I put my arm through Papaw's and whispered, "What is he doing here?"

He turned to look at Jean-Paul, then back at me.

"What?" he asked innocently "It's your party, and he likes you. What's the big deal? Matthew is not the jealous type. He won't be bothered by your male friends, surely."

After I thought about it, I couldn't argue. He and his dad were here for this week, and it would be rude not to invite them.

Jean-Paul seemed to watch me everywhere I went. When I would meet his eyes, he would lift his glass to me or bow his head. He was handsome, but there was a mystery in his eyes. Something about him made me cold inside.

Papaw had told me he was Cajun. "They're different folks for sure. Louisiana people always are. I think it's all that French nonsense."

I smiled at Jean-Paul when he looked my way, and I left it alone. Around eight, Papaw took me outside in a hot-pink blindfold to give me my gift. It wasn't a car, which I was secretly hoping for but knew we really couldn't afford. Nathan took my dad's old Camaro, so I was left driving Nana's Oldsmobile. I drove Papaw's truck better, but he always needed it. I didn't mind.

Someone took my blindfold off, and by the whiff of cologne I guessed it was Jean-Paul. He did smell wonderful. There, by the front steps, was a brand new, navy-and-yellow Yamaha four-wheeler. A broad grin stretched my face.

We used these to get from here to there on the property, but I had wanted one that could drive me through mud. Papaw's was pokey, to say the least.

"If you can ride Tootsie, you can handle this, I think," Papaw said, beaming at me.

I squealed in genuine delight this time, and clapped my hands like a small child.

Papaw handed me a key.

"Be careful. It's a monster," he warned me,

I leaped down the steps and instantly looked for Matthew. I finally had one I could keep up with him on. I searched the crowd, and found his face.

"Come on!" I yelled excited.

Matthew grin and came my way as our friends watched him walk my way. His long strides closed the distance between us in seconds and I couldn't help but swell with pride when he placed his hands around my waist in front of everyone.

We set off to the woods. I knew I shouldn't go far without my helmet, but I wanted to at least try it out. A few hundred yards out, I felt funny. I slowed down, put it in neutral, and got off. My head was spinning. I had all forgotten all about the pill I took in the bathroom with Lana.

"You okay?" Matthew asked concern in his voice.

I put my head between my legs and took deep breaths. The cold was bitter and tore at my chest. The ground beneath me felt soft and I swayed slightly.

When my head eventually stopped spinning, I stood up, feeling light-headed and more than a little drunk.

"I'm okay, just all the excitement I guess." I told him.

"Come on," he said, tugging at me after I convinced him I was good.

"Let's go to the barn, okay?" I said in his ear. He nodded and shifted gears.

I put my arms around his waist, and my face into his back to block some of the cold. He drove straight into the barn, and shut the doors. He held me, knowing me enough to know something was off with my behavior.

I simply couldn't tell him I had taken something Lana gave me. I could not bear the thought of him thinking badly of me. He was perfect. My hero.

It suddenly dawned on me that in a few months' time he would be gone from me to an unknown place. Duke University. It might as well be Africa.

Taking his hand, I led him up to the loft. I had feelings I had never had before. I felt numb but alive with excitement. When we reached the top, I turned to kiss him. He kissed me back, and then pulled away.

"Wait," he said, chuckling at my eagerness.

"No," I said, pulling back into him. If I didn't do this now, I never would.

Matthew pulled away from me again leaving me to blink rapidly.

"Wait." he said in a stern mock voice, holding up a finger,

I stuck out my lower lip, and crossed my arms, waiting. He reached out to take my right hand, and on my ring finger, he placed a band encircled with small black diamonds. My head was buzzing, and my body tingled all over. I didn't know what to say.

"Happy birthday," he whispered, and I heard the nerves in his voice.

"Oh," I said, my senses delayed.

Matthew cleared his throat looking shy. His green eyes blazed at me causing my heart to speed up. He was so handsome I could look at him all day.

"It's a promise ring," he announced like that cleared up all my questions.

"It's beautiful," I said.

He bent his head to me, looking me in the eyes. "It's a promise ring," he said again, but more seriously. "I will promise myself to you, and you to me. If you agree? We will survive the separation of college and med school, and if you will let me, in a few years I want to put a bigger ring on this finger," he said, touching the ring finger on my left hand.

Understanding struck me dumb. I was loopy from the drug and not at all sure I'd understood. I searched his face for confirmation of his words.

I was a castaway child. I was dirty and unwanted. Yet here was an angel, sent to me to not only rescue me from death, but to rescue me from myself. I cried. I couldn't help it.

I always thought this thing between us was only temporary, and that Matthew would marry some sweet southern belle. I didn't know if it was the drugs, or the love I felt, or fear, or appreciation, but I wept—to his amusement.

"You agree?" he asked, hope evident in his voice. How could he doubt my longing to be with him always?

"Of course, of course, of course, of course. Yes!" I swore.

Excitement shone in his handsome face.

"Look, Piper," and he gestured wildly in the air at things unseen. "The future, Piper. It's wide open. *We* write our lives. *We* do. Not the ones who have done us wrong, but us. Together we can do anything. We will travel and help people in need. Maybe you will deliver babies, while I tend to expectant mothers." He smiled.

I began kissing him. His mouth. His neck. All over. My body caught fire at his words. I began tugging at his clothes, pulling at his jacket. I think I shocked him a bit, because he didn't seem to know what to do with me.

"Piper?" he said, chuckling with my lips on his. I didn't answer. I was afraid to stop.

"Piper?" he said, in deep heavy voice in my ear. "Are you sure this is what you want?"

I answered by putting my cold hands up his shirt.

"Oh, yes, Matthew. More than anything," I breathed in his ear.

I felt his body turn forceful and hungry then. Finally resistance caved, and we began to undress one another hurriedly. I was not at all ashamed or embarrassed. I wanted to be his wife, lover, and friend forever. What would stop me now, but silly notions?

I knew I was supposed to wait until marriage, but I had thought about this for many hours, and decided it was just a man-made law, and man has screwed up everything anyway, so what if spiritually, Matthew and I were married already? I, at sixteen, already felt like a wife, and I was ready to act like one.

We lay kissing, naked on the blankets Matthew sat on to study. He kissed my neck and breasts. I quivered from cold and excitement. My breath caught, and I began panting with excitement. He was skilled with his hands. A doctor's hands.

He touched me softly, yet obviously starved. I reached for him wildly, driven by mad desire to have him inside of me. I was high on more than drugs.

We made love the way teenagers do. Clumsy and fun. Loving every inch of each other. Playing and laughing. We were young lovers with a plan. We had the whole world by a string, and our futures were very bright ahead of us.

We lay breathless, intertwined in each other, the aftershocks of lovemaking leaving us now. For a while at least, I forgot I was dirty. I forgot no one could ever love me. And for once, Daniel never came to mind.

Matthew took me home, and I went to bed, still buzzing from the pill, the promise, and the sex. It was a great sweet sixteen. I had a ring, and I had a plan.

When I woke at three in the morning, sweating and scared, I should have listened to the warning bells ringing in my head. I woke feeling Daniel on top of me again. I hated him all over. I hated my mother all over again.

I wanted to be with Matthew, but I would have to get used to being without him for the years he would be away, only able to see him in summer and holidays.

I lay in my bed, listening to the soft snores coming from Papaw down the hall. I gave up going back to sleep. I was restless, and my heart was troubled. I couldn't shake the feeling something was wrong.

I opened my window slowly, and stepped out to the roof. I had my favorite homemade quilt wrapped tight around my body. I lay back and lit my half-smoked joint. I inhaled deeply and felt my body begin to relax. Was I feeling guilty?

In the most important way, I had lost my virginity. No, I did not wait until we were married by law, and I was only sixteen. I stared into the clear sky above and inhaled deeply on my joint allowing me mind to roam.

Why does the world try to stuff everything into a box? People are forever saying this or that about the way life is. My great-grandmother was married with two kids by my age, and just because people or certain religions decided something wasn't right, didn't mean that it wasn't. I didn't want to feel guilty.

I loved my God, and Jesus was my savior. It just worked my nerves to think you could slap a label on something and call it "wrong."

Buzzing, I tried to relax these thoughts out of my head. I knew Nana would think it was wrong for me to smoke weed, but I'd rather smoke weed than pop some antidepressant meds the doctors tried to feed me. No. I would not feel guilty.

I closed my eyes, and took in the night sounds. This was when I had the most peace—alone on a rooftop, stoned. The quiet sounds rocked me gently. I put the burned-out joint in a cup of sand I kept out here for these occasions. I turned to go back inside, when something in the woods caught my eye.

By the moonlight I saw a glint of glass. It was tiny, but my keen awareness picked it up. I froze in terror. I stared at the flicker in the distance. And as I stared, trying to make out a shape, it was gone. I stayed perfectly still, watching the woods.

Hunters were not allowed this close to the house. Territories were marked very clearly, and the ones out tonight knew the boundaries well. A terrible thought hit me like a ton of bricks. Daniel was in the woods, watching me. He didn't die in the fire. He was there now, plotting my death or my capture.

That was absurd. Nana said they recovered a man from the fire, burned to a crisp, a dog collar attached to his neck. No trace of my existence was found. Nana never made me tell the police.

My medical records were sealed and my refusal to speak at the time only confirmed the suspicion that I'd had an accident. Nana thought it best to spare me the attention. Justice had been served. We knew the truth, and no one else needed to know.

So who was this? It was definitely the scope of a rifle. I'd recognize that anywhere, and at any distance. I watched closely but never saw it, or anything else, again. Buzzing now from the weed, I made my way back inside, hoping I could sleep, and dream of when I would be with Matthew always, and have little kids running all over the place. But as I lay down, thoughts of dread filled me. Unexplained fear kept me wide-eyed till dawn.

Who was in the woods so close to the house? Why did I, after a wonderful night, feel like something bad was about to happen?

CHAPTER TWELVE

Winter did not let up that year until the end of March, and it was bitter cold and icy till the end. Spring lasted less than two months. In east Tennessee, temperatures are either cold or hot. We have short falls, and short springs. Summers are brutally hot, and winters are freezing cold.

By May, Matthew was set to start at Duke University in the fall. We spent as much time as we could together. We would spend evenings in the blue barn, and the days we were not in school, we stayed on our four-wheelers, discovering new parts of our woods.

It was a Saturday the end of May, and temperatures were already in the eighties—hot and sticky. Matthew would walk the stage to receive his high school diploma later that night and I could feel the clock ticking down. I wanted to attach myself to him and refuse to let him go.

We decided to take our four-wheelers to the cliffs and spend time together. Our precious time together would soon be restricted to a few weekends a year.

We made love on the cliffs in the sun. We then ate sandwiches and pickles, drank Cokes and shared a piece of Nana's chocolate pie. We sat quietly, watching the sky change above us, until finally it was time to pack up and head out.

I had a new dress for the ceremony ready and I needed time to fix my hair. I wanted to be extra pretty next to my handsome boyfriend. I couldn't wait to see Matthew in his cap and gown.

On our way down the mountainside on our four-wheelers, Matthew, always the gentleman, wanted me to go before him so he could watch me.

We could not go side-by-side because the path was too narrow, and had a sharp, elbow turn. He took my helmet from my hands, and placed it on my head. Snapping it in place, he kissed my nose through my open visor.

"Be safe," he said, and I began my descent.

I felt like a pro now with my Yamaha. It was powerful and drove smoothly across rock or ditches. After five minutes of careful navigation, I was at the bottom.

There were so many trees that I could not see Matthew as he made his way down. He would give me time to reach the bottom and then begin his descent. I waited. I waited so long that I started trying to see back up the hill. No Matthew. After ten minutes, I killed my motor so I could listen for him. My heart clenched, and a strange nagging in my brain told me there was something wrong.

I took my helmet off. I couldn't drive back up the narrow path for fear I would run into him, and create the problem of either me going down backward, or him going up backward, both dangerous things to do on such a narrow path with deep ditches on the left side.

I sat, squinting through the woods for any movement. None came. I began to panic. My reactions were not great. Lana had introduced me to Xanax a few weeks back, and I had a two-a-day habit now. Those, along with the weed, kept me pretty loose.

I began the steep climb up. I hadn't walked far when I saw the green of Matthew's four-wheeler through the trees, but I didn't hear the motor. I climbed some more, wanting to hear something, but still I heard nothing. I got to a point where the hill was so steep that I had to pull at branches to help me climb. My fear was rising.

"Matthew?" I said.

No answer.

"Matthew!" I said louder.

No answer.

I willed my legs to climb harder. Almost there.

Sweat poured into my eyes, and terror poured into my heart. Something was wrong—very wrong. Finally, I rounded a bend, and I saw the ATV on its side, the front wheels still spinning. I couldn't breathe.

"Matthew!" I screamed "Oh, God! Matthew!" No sight of him.

I looked under the four-wheeler. Not there. I looked further up the path, thinking maybe he'd fallen off up there and the ATV had rolled down on its own.

I began to scream and scream. Frantically, I looked here and there, and then I spotted him. He was lying face down in a ditch, about fifty feet up the hill. I dug my feet into the mud, trying to get to him, screaming his name all the while.

When I reached him, I turned him over, and wiped blood and dirt off his face. There was a gash on his forehead, deep and long, from his hairline to his eyebrow. His blood was thick, and starting to dry on his face. I shook him.

"Matthew," I whispered again and again sobbing.

No response. In my state of panic I could not recall how to take a pulse. I begged him to answer me. If I were honest, I knew he was dead, but my mind would not allow me to think such things. Impossible things like a world without Matthew Logue. I kissed his lips then placed his head softly down on the grass. Numbly I, ran back to my four-wheeler, and raced off toward Matthew's house.

I had no way of lifting him. I had to get help. The doctors could fix him. They could fix me, so they could fix him. I pulled into the Logues' driveway, and raced toward the house. Matthew's dad was carrying grocery bags in from the car. Such a normal thing to be doing and I wanted to laughed at the absurdity of it. When George Logue saw me heading toward him, he paused and waited. I skidded to a stop right in front of him.

"It's Matthew," is all I got out.

His eyes swept my top and blood covered hands. George dropped the bags he was holding, and ran to the garage to get Josh's four-wheeler. We drove back to Matthew, and all the while, I kept chanting in my head, "Please, God. Please, God. Please, God."

We got to the bottom of the hill, and I told him we would need to climb one at a time. He motioned for me to get on the back of his ATV, and I raced to get there. We made it to Matthew's overturned four-wheeler. Climbing past it, I tapped his dad's shoulder to let him know this was the spot. He pulled in between two trees so the ATV would stay put on the hillside.

George Logue was a big man, but he moved to get to his son with the speed and lightness of a much smaller person. Sliding down into the ditch, he assessed the situation. He tried to get Matthew to breathe, but nothing changed. Matthew was motionless. Still. Quiet. Dead.

George scooped Matthew up and got him onto the ATV. He strapped his son's body to his, then turned an ashen colored face to me.

"You'll be all right getting back to your ride?" he asked.

I nodded, and watched him go, helpless. I stood still. I hadn't realized I was crying until I noticed my shirt was nearly soaked through. I stood for a long time, looking around the ground, for what I don't know. I was so numb and foggy. It wasn't until I got to my own ATV that I figured out what it was I had been looking for.

Matthew had a head injury. That was a fact. Another fact was he always, always, always wore his helmet. I couldn't find his helmet. That's what I was looking for.

I retrieved my helmet from the ground and placed it on my head. I was cold in spite of the heat. I drove home, not thinking. I don't remember what I told Nana when I got there, but we were at the hospital ten minutes later. Mrs. Logue was rocking back and forth. Her hands clutched her face.

She was wailing, "Not my boy. Not my boy."

The doctors pronounced Matthew dead. His parents signed a form to allow the hospital to donate any of Matthew's organs that they could. I watched this from the outside of my body, only taking in bits and pieces.

Josh stood, arms crossed, staring at the floor, not moving. He was not crying. He showed no emotion. In that moment, I thought we must feel as dead as Matthew was. I walked to Josh, and we held each other in silence until it was time to go. Nothing more to do.

Somewhere a graduation celebration was starting without its honoree. Nana and Papaw took me home. When I entered my room, my dress for that night's graduation was hanging on my wall mirror, still in its light plastic bag, taunting me.

I had been so proud of my grown-up dress. I had imagined Matthew would think me pretty, and I thought of the ease of slipping out of it later, as we celebrated alone. I tore it down and threw it aside. I couldn't bear to look at it.

I went to my stash of pills and took a handful. I no longer cared. I wanted to die in that moment. My hero was dead, and with a jolt of horror, I realized my husband was dead.

I would never be Piper Logue, like I had scribbled on my folders and every blank piece of paper. I would never walk down the aisle in Nana's dress, with Matthew waiting for me at the end.

It was a stupid dream, and I had been a fool to buy into it. I had no promise. I had no plan. I allowed sleep to come. I didn't wake up for hours. Nana came in and kissed my forehead, but I had no memory of hearing her—just the whisper of the kiss, and the smell of her bath salts.

It was four in the morning when I opened my eyes. Something had awakened me, but I laid still, trying to figure out what I'd heard. A knock on my window made me sit straight up, wide-awake now. Looking, I saw Josh through the glass.

I got up and went to open it for him. He motioned for me to come out. I got my stash of weed and then climbed onto the porch roof, where I had spent so many nights recently, dreaming of my wedding day. In my heart, I had known it had to be too good to be true. People like Matthew were too good for dirty girls like me. Daniel was right. I never would be happy.

I sat next to Josh without speaking as he rolled tight the joint. The sky was starting to change color. Josh lit the joint inhaling deeply then handed it to me. We smoked it in silence, trying to numb ourselves, until we couldn't feel the pain and absence of his brother, and my lover.

After a few minutes of us passing the joint back and forth, Josh finally broke the silence.

"We have to pick a casket tomorrow," he said mechanically.

I just nodded and took another hit. More silence. It wasn't an uncomfortable silence. If Matthew was my husband, Josh was definitely my best friend. Lana was my best friend too, but I only got to see her when she wasn't working at the drug store now, on her days off.

Josh I saw every day. At school, we ate lunch together. At home, we roamed together while Matthew studied or helped tutor younger students for extra money, money he loved spending on me. The money was unimportant, but the care he took of me was priceless.

That would never happen again, and the thought took me under, to a dark place. I began to weep, my body shaking. Josh wrapped me in his arms, and I noticed he too was shaking with sobs of his own. We clung to each other as the sun rose. I glared at it. I had been hoping it would stay down, so I could forever walk the dark night alone.

Time would not stand still. I would have to go through with the funeral. The burial would cover two people. I was dead when Matthew found me years ago, and he breathed new life into me. When he died, I died again right along with him, returning to the dead girl I knew I was.

Josh and I said good-bye to each other when the sky grew bright, and he returned to his home, to his broken family. I remained on the roof and watched as my papaw started his day, walking to the barn with a bucket of oats for the horses.

He spotted me, and if he thought it was odd for me to be sitting on the roof, he didn't say anything. He yelled up and asked if I wanted to come with him.

Give me five minutes." I said.

I hurried back inside and dressed at breakneck speed. I couldn't stand the thought of staying in my room, with the dress I bought just for Matthew. I threw on clean clothes and stopped to look down at the blood on my clothes scattered on the floor. I held it to my face. The loss of Matthew was agony. And it had just begun.

CHAPTER THIRTEEN

We buried Matthew close to his grandmother in a churchyard a few miles away. He was dressed in a dark blue suit. There were dozens of people there to show their respect. People cried and talked about how wonderful Matthew was and how handsome. I didn't shed a tear. The Logues had me, Nana, and Papaw sit with the family. Mrs. Logue hugged me and told me to be strong, that Matthew was in heaven now.

I didn't want to be strong. I wanted to be mad as hell and demand heaven release him, send him back to me, where he would stay until we were both old and grey and could die at the right time, together. But I didn't share this with Mrs. Logue. She wept in a sweet, broken way.

The men's faces were stony, but the slump in the shoulders of the older Mr. Logue told me he was having a hard time keeping it together. Josh held my hand through the service and again at the burial. I concentrated on the tendons in his big hand as a distraction of what was taking place around me.

The high school honored Matthew for his work in science and the goals he set. Most of all they honored him for his contagious, optimistic attitude and the kindness he showed others. I had been loved by the perfect man. I knew that.

Funny how I saw Matthew while alive as mine, as my lover and husband. I never gave much thought to how he was just as kind to everyone else in his life.

The preacher said Matthew was in heaven, and he would be performing work for our Lord now. I hoped that was true. If there ever was an angel, Matthew Logue was it.

Nathan came home and stayed a few days. He, Josh, and Matthew had always been buddies, and he admired Matthew a great deal.

Nathan had recently signed with a Hollywood studio to do music for a soundtrack. I was happy for him, but in a distant and disconnected way. I was too busy grieving the death of my hopes and dreams to care much. Lana stayed with me the first couple of nights. Nana left us alone, to talk and be girls. I lay on the bed stoned most of the time. I drank too.

Lana informed me, while she opened a bottle of Johnnie Walker, "There is a reason country singers drink their sorrows away. It's what we are supposed to do." Then she filled my glass.

This was a vast contradiction to what Nana believed.

"Alcohol never did anything good, except create unwanted babies and make whores out of their mothers," she would say.

I didn't care. In my mind, the more I was absent from the present, the better off I would be.

Lana knew a lot about a lot of things. Like vodka doesn't smell on your breath, and what pills went well with what drinks. She never would leave much at a time with me. Lana knew all too well the cutting could easily go deeper if I wished it to. The right combination would set that course of action. She was well aware of this.

I walked through summer like a zombie. I would be somewhere and could not remember how I got there. I slept some days all day.

Josh and I spent our junior year quietly. I would watch him practice now, not wanting to wait in Matthew's truck alone. Most of that year was a complete blur to me.

Jean-Paul began to hunt year-round. He tried a few times to talk to me, but I was busy being drunk, and grieving. He was pleasant enough, but he was not Matthew. I was polite and to the point.

The following summer as Josh and I hung out at the riverbank tossing rocks and talking, he decided to drop a bombshell on me.

"We're moving, Piper," he said without preamble.

My head snapped up to see if he was serious.

"Why?"

This is where Matthew is. This is where I am. I was going to be abandoned again? Why did time not stop as I wished it to? I was dirty and no one wanted to be with me, I reminded myself.

"Mom can't handle it here anymore. Dad is at his breaking point, and Grandpa is agreeing to go with us to Florida now. I'll start my senior year there, and I am being scouted by UF for a full scholarship."

He paused a minute to let me take all this in. Josh watched my face cautiously as if expecting me to faint.

I said nothing. What could I say? No, please don't leave me? Don't you know life is over? We just need to sit here and wait to die?

I kept my eyes down, so he couldn't read me.

"When?" I asked the water.

"Mom's there now, getting the house in order. Dad hired an agent to sell the farm. We will be leaving by August, so I can get enrolled in school and have a couple of weeks to get settled."

He said all this in a rush, as if it would hurt me less if I got it faster. That was three weeks away. My heart ached. I couldn't say anything.

I'd lost Matthew, and now I was losing Josh. Lana talked of being an actress, so she'd be next. Of course, I'd be alone. Just as Daniel always said I would.

Josh sat down, and put an arm around me. Matthew was taller, but Josh was bigger. At six-one, he weighed in at an impressive two-twenty-five. Big and beefy, but quick on his feet, the way linebackers are supposed to be, as he had proudly told me.

I laid my head against his shoulder. He sighed and kissed the top of my head.

"You know, in the old days," the sheepish grin pronounced in his voice now, "the brother would take the place of the one who had died. I could easily love you, Piper. I do in the ways that count. You could come with me. We could go to college together. My family loves you already. It'd be easy."

I snorted a laugh and elbowed him in the ribs.

"Yeah, right. We'd kill each other," I said, but then I caught myself envisioning the idea of being with Josh.

It would be an easy life, but Josh was not in love with me. I was more of a kid sister, someone he loved to tease and hang out with.

"I do love you, Josh. Like a fat kid loves cake," I smiled up at him sadly, meaning it.

Josh smiled back at me, just as sadly.

"You got to go on, Piper," his voice cracked with emotion.

His words stung me, and I looked down to stop the tears from showing. He put his hand under my chin and lifted my face to look at me.

"I'm serious. My brother believed in life. He planned to save lives, and make the world a better place to LIVE. You dishonor his memory by staying in mourning."

His words hurt. I knew he was saying the truth. I cried on him, and when all my sobs were gone, I promised him I would move on, and I would live my life. I promised I would visit him in Florida, and he promised to visit me here.

We were family and nothing, not even death, would change that. I wanted to crawl in a hole and die, but Josh saying I dishonored Matthew's memory had prodded me to not give in to that feeling.

I said my good-byes to him on August first. Lana kissed him deeply, and I blushed from the heat coming off them. I hugged all the Logues, and waved them good-bye until they were out of sight. We all walked heavyhearted back to the house.

Lana spent the night. She wouldn't tell me, but I had a suspicion the power was off at her house again. Nana checked on her grandmother often, and I could hear her mumbling when she hung up the phone about just how worthless Nicole Morris was.

"Trashiest thing breathing, I tell you," she'd exclaim, shaking her head.

Nicole would apparently regularly steal her mother's social security checks and blow the money on her booze. She had several children by different men. None but Lana lived with her, and Lana only stayed for her grandmother.

Even though I promised Josh I would move on, I couldn't find a place to start. I started my senior year alone and sad. I stayed doped up. I was a pro at it now.

I took up to four Xanax a day, smoking weed on my way to and from school. Papaw got me a small Toyota truck. It was clean and comfortable, but most importantly, he said under his breath, it was "safe," like this was a dirty word.

Papaw was not as outwardly affectionate as Nana, but I felt the love he had for me. I was helping Nana with babies all the time now, and even delivering them on my own as she supervised and coached me through it. I helped Papaw in the shop, but could not stay in the room if he had to put an animal to sleep.

I would go out in the field with him to teach hunters how to field dress and preserve their kill. This didn't bother me so much since the animals were dead already. I did what I had to do to keep breathing.

The weather was mild my senior year. I helped Papaw a lot, and this meant spending time riding horses to the hunting cabins. Four-wheelers only got you so far through the trees, so we rode horses through dense patches of woods. Some hunters preferred horses, so they could have the experience of a "real hunting trip."

We had mostly standing reservations, with hunters that knew the land well. Some brought their families to Cherokee and then rode over to hunt. We had an abundance of wildlife.

I myself did not enjoying hunting anymore. I had gone with my brother and Josh a few times, but it's so boring, waiting for a deer to show up, and even when one did, it wasn't always the right kind of deer. It had to be a certain age or if not the right time of year it had to be a buck. Too many rules for me.

It was different from walking the woods with my dad as a kid. We would hike, or take the horses out and spend the day, or sleep in sleeping bags at night. Dad didn't care for hunting much. He once told me, "Your papaw does enough for both of us." I would smile at the differences between father and his son. Dad's general nature was much like Nana's, free spirited and kind, with at times too much understanding. She was cultured in so many ways. Papaw was what Hollywood would perceive as a "hillbilly," but an educated one at least.

Papaw met my Nana during the war. He lied about his age and spent three years in Germany. He spotted Nana walking with her father one day.

"She fell deeply in love with me that very moment! Couldn't keep her hands off me!" he would tell me with a wink.

Nana told it differently. "Your papaw followed me around like a lost puppy for a month! I tried to teach him German." Then she would throw her hands up and say, "Stubborn man, your papaw. Never as much as a word he would speak. More because he didn't want to, than not being able to learn it."

Nana had strawberry-blonde hair, and blue eyes. Papaw's hair had once been mousey brown, but he had been white-headed for years now. His eyes were still deep brown, same as mine. The same as my dad's. I got Nana's hair though. I guess I got my build from my mother. I was curvy and tall. I had a pale complexion, as Lana always told me.

"You need to sunbathe," she complained to me regularly.

I would stick my nose up, and ignore her. Almost everyone was pale next to her dark skin. Lana never knew her father, but she thought he might be part black.

The day before Thanksgiving, I drove home slowly, smoking a joint. I was taking pills and smoking pot all of the time now. Lana could easily get what she wanted. She would use her beauty shamelessly, and her boss, the pharmacist, would say or do anything to get her attention.

Lana was warm and loving, but sex was never an emotional thing with her. She enjoyed being with men, yet never wanted to tie herself to any of them. It would be just another day on the job to blow her boss in the bathroom, and in turn he would look the other way as she took what inventory she wanted, a little at a time. It gave new meaning to "tit for tat" for me.

Nana and Papaw were not stupid. I was pretty sure they knew about me smoking pot, but they remained mostly ignorant about the pills. I think they were so thankful to have me in one piece after Daniel that I could do no wrong.

I parked in the drive, and headed up the back steps, prepared to start cooking, as it was my night to do so. I didn't expect company, but we had it. Lana sat in a kitchen chair, peeling potatoes, long legs spread wide around a bucket. She looked up at me with pleading eyes, probably wondering how she got into this mess. I looked into the living room, and saw Maurice and Jean-Paul talking with Papaw. I ducked back into the kitchen.

"Hey," I said.

Nana turned from the sink and smiled that big smile of hers.

"Hello, love. Good day at school?" she asked.

"It was okay. I'm glad I'm off." I joined in peeling potatoes.

Lana's long nails were normally in perfect condition, but they were filthy now, as she struggled with the knife. I took the knife and peeled my first in seconds. She stuck her tongue out at me.

I sat peeling potatoes, watching the men in the living room. They seemed to be in deep conversation.

"You should go say hello," Nana told me, looking to see where I was.

"Why?" I asked her.

"Because they are your guests for Thanksgiving, and you're a good Christian girl. Maurice has had a death in the family recently, and you should make them feel welcome. It's rude not to," she said, nudging my shoulder.

I wiped my hands on her duster, ignoring Nana's protests, then walked to the living room and stood at the door as the men talked. They were talking about things needed. I could follow the conversation but was relieved of the effort when Jean-Paul stood up and walked to me.

I supposed we were friends, maybe acquaintances. I'd known him for a while, but this time his greeting was not a simple hello. This time he came directly to me, and in sight of Lana, Nana, Papaw, and Maurice, reached out his arms and hugged me.

I surprised myself by automatically returning the hug. I smelled his scent, which was woodsy and smoky. He was handsome and strong. In spite of my misery, I was momentarily happy at his attention.

"Are you well?" he asked, pulling away from me, looking at my face searchingly.

I stuttered for a second and heard Lana snort. I felt my face turn crimson.

"I wanted to say hello to you and your dad." I looked up into his face and wished I hadn't. Boy, was he pretty. I had the sudden urge to touch his face, to see if it were real.

He had skin the color of light mocha, hair shiny and black, eyes just as dark. He smiled at me as if he knew my thoughts.

I smiled back thinking my face would crack.

"Would you like something to drink?"

I tore my gaze away. What was the matter with me?

"Papaw? Mr. Duchete?" Papaw held up his glass of tea, and Mr. Duchete said, "Please, call me Maurice, and no, nothing for me. Thank you." I glanced at Jean-Paul.

"No, thanks," he said, with his eyes on mine.

I turned and went back to the kitchen feeling flushed. Lana had a wicked grin firmly on her face.

"Shut up," I said and continued to mutilate my potatoes.

Nathan arrived home that night. He was skinny, and his face was drawn. Nana fussed about his eating, and Papaw played guitar with him.

It was almost a normal time for us. Jean-Paul and Maurice were out of place in their very nice, and I'm sure very expensive, dress shirts and slacks. The rest of us were casual in jeans and T-shirts, except for Nana who always dressed for dinner. Her dress was never fancy, but like the lady she was, it was feminine and soft.

We listened to the guitar playing, and idly chatted until the end of the evening. We talked about who would sleep where, and exchanged good-nights. Lana would sleep in my room, as she always did when she stayed over. Maurice and

Jean-Paul would take a guest room each, and Nathan wanted to sleep on the couch in the grand room.

He could have taken the pull-out bed in Papaw's office, but opted for the couch instead. Nana made him put sheets on top of the cushions before he could lie down. She was a tiny thing beside Nathan, but he didn't dare argue with her. He looked as meek and mild as a child when he spoke to her.

Obediently, he placed clean white sheets over the cushions, as Nana instructed him on precisely how it should be done. I hugged them both good-night, feeling happy and peaceful for the first time in ages. At the top of the stairs, I turned to see Jean-Paul heading to the hall bathroom, his toothbrush in hand.

I smiled at him feeling self-conscious.

"I'm sorry for the recent death in your family," I said truly meaning it.

Maurice had gone into his room already, and Lana kept walking toward mine not waiting on me. The door shut behind her.

"Yes, thank you. A beloved cousin. She was into drugs for a while and could not be saved."

I went icy inside. I wondered what drugs. Nothing I did, surely. I just took pills and smoked weed.

I turned to go to my room, flustered by his stare.

"Piper?" he called to me, when I reached my room.

I stopped; hand on the doorknob looking back at him.

"Yes?" I said.

"May I take you to dinner while I'm in town?" he asked simply.

I took a breath and thought of Matthew. I missed him every minute of every day. Then I thought of what Josh told me.

"Yes. That would be nice."

He shot me his playboy smile and walked to the bathroom. Once inside my room, Lana pumped me for information. Nana came by, and poked her head through the door.

"You girls don't stay up late now. We will have to get to cooking very early, okay?"

I hugged her and kissed her cheek.

"Yes, Nana. Good night."

Lana blew her a kiss causing Nana face to light with beauty with her smile.

"Good night, Mrs. Mitchell, and thanks for having me."

As soon as Nana had enough time to walk to her room I turned the lock on the knob. Lana and I snuck to the roof and lit a joint.

"He's gorgeous," she said. "But the age difference doesn't bother you?"

I looked at her confused. I would be eighteen in a few months.

"He couldn't be more than twenty?" I asked her.

Lana laughed. "He's twenty-six," she said.

I gaped at her.

"Twenty-six? Are you sure? And how do you know?" I eyed her suspiciously.

She shrugged.

"Can't remember, but I think I heard him talking to your papaw. What difference does it make anyway? That's not much when you're a grown-up."

I was going to be a grown-up. Had I ever been a child? I took a drag off the joint. A voice came from my window behind us.

"What the hell are you two doing?"

I jumped and Lana squealed.

"Shh!" Nathan said, climbing out to join us.

I slapped his arm. "You nearly gave me heart failure! How'd you get in? My door was locked."

Nathan took the joint from me and inhaled it deeply.

"Please. No lock can keep me out," he said, not letting a whiff of smoke out as he spoke.

I shifted slightly uncomfortable. I'd never smoked pot with Nathan. It was an odd feeling and I half expected him to chastise me.

We talked a good while, as the night sky got inky black. Nathan told us how he had been busy with another soundtrack for a Hollywood studio, working from Nashville. Told us of the celebrities he had seen.

"You know me and Piper have a cousin who acts, Molly Rowland?" he asked Lana sounded a bit prideful.

"No way," Lana said, excited. "Why have I never seen her here? Or why haven't we visited her?"

Lana turned her dark eyes on me as if I'd kept this secret from her on purpose and we could have been in Hollywood all these years.

I shrugged. We were not close with Molly. She was a Hollywood star and we were the cousins in the country. Her father, Roger, was a major Hollywood agent to the stars and is the reason Nathan got the first chance at recording for movies.

"What about Ryan Knox? I know him, you know." Nathan bragged further. "He's a weird cat, but his best friend, Sheldon, is a kick-ass performer. Nothing he can't play or sing. Very talented. I'm going to travel with him a bit."

Lana sat still, not talking. She acted different with Nathan. Almost ladylike. I had a sneaking suspicion she liked my brother more than she would ever admit.

Nathan poked her thigh.

"You wanna go for a walk?" he asked her sheepishly.

As if someone flipped on a switch, she beamed. "I sure do."

I rolled my eyes and lay back on the roof, pulling my quilt from Nathan. They climbed through the window, and a few minutes later I heard them laughing in the woods. They had been each other's bed-buddy every time Nathan came home. I tried to ignore them, but I was also jealous.

I went in, popped a couple of pills, and lay down. I thought of where Jean-Paul would take me. I had a dull hope that maybe I would enjoy the company of a man again.

Daniel's voice in my head was saying, "You ain't nothing to nobody. I'm the only one that can stand you. You're trash to them. They don't want you. They can never love you. You're diseased!"

I put my hands over my ears to try and shut this out. I drifted away to sleep only to wake up feeling Daniel on top of me. I jerked with fright,

"Shh! It's just me," Lana said, climbing in beside me.

She wrapped her cold hands around mine, and I could smell sweet tobacco on her hair, the cigarettes Nathan smoked. Lana looked at me in the soft lit room. Her dark hair gleamed blue in the light of the small nightlight I always left on. I tried to adjust my eyes.

"You okay?" she asked.

"I hope I will be someday," I told her.

I shivered from the cold coming off her body.

"Piper?"

"Hmm?" I said sleepily.

Lana didn't say anything at first, and I was nearly asleep again when she spoke

"Will I ever be okay?"

I wrapped my arms around her body, hugging her to me.

"If there was ever anyone who will be okay, I believe it will be you," I told her.

She buried her face in my chest. It felt wet with tears. I never pushed Lana to talk about things. She talked when she needed to. I knew most things about her.

I knew she had no idea who her father was. She had a horrible mother who was gone most nights, not knowing or caring about her daughter. She had a morbidly obese grandmother, who lived like a pig and reminded Lana daily that she was just like her mother.

Lana was using pot and pills for the same reasons I did. She had to escape her mind to get relief. We slept holding each other that night, my wildflower best friend, feeling loved by me, if only for a night every now and then. In the morning, she would return to herself—mischief-loving, loud, and funny.

When the sun was bright the next day, I looked for signs of the sorrow she felt the night before. I saw none. I was struck by the notion that we were as alike as we were polar opposites. We both had brown eyes, but she was dark, and I was pale. She was living life at full speed, when I was content with just moving. I loved her. She was imperfect, yet perfect in every way.

We ate our turkey dinner happily and chattily. Nathan turned on the game, and the men retired to the grand room. I wanted to join them, but of course the women cleaned. We had friends over for coffee and desserts later. It was a great Thanksgiving.

Jean-Paul did not bring up our date, but sought me out to chat on this or that every so often. He stood almost seductively close to me as he talked. My head was a little fuzzy when I was around him, but I had to admit, I thought I could like it.

While I was in the kitchen with Nana washing dishes, I asked her opinion of Jean-Paul.

"He's an onion that one," she said and nodded.

I laughed, "An onion?"

Nana smiled, "He has many layers. He is rough around the edges, but in some ways spoiled. He needs a woman in his life. He seems kind enough, I suppose. Why do you ask this, love?"

I sat down at the table, glancing around to make sure we were alone.

"He asked me to go out on a date," I said in a low voice.

Nana was silent for a long moment. She dried a dish and then came to sit with me. I said nothing, as I knew she was thinking.

Pouring tea into her cup, she knitted her brows.

"You like him?"

"I think I would. He's awful kind." I told her.

She pinched her lips together and shrugged. "It's a date. Go out. Find out if you like him or not."

I nodded again.

"He's twenty-six," I said flatly.

"Does this bother you?" she asked.

I looked at her. I had thought she would disapprove of this, not be so matter-of-fact.

"No, I don't guess so," I said.

Nana shrugged again.

"There are worse things. As long as he is what you want, age don't matter none." She held up a finger to make a point, "Within reason. If he was thirty, I'm not sure that would be good for you, Piper, but go. Get to know him. Go out. Have fun." She touched my cheek.

I thought maybe she just wanted me out of the house—to live, as Josh had said. I hugged her and left the kitchen to find   Lana.

CHAPTER FOURTEEN

The date Jean-Paul took me on was dinner and a movie. The time I spent being held prisoner by Daniel, I watched old black-and-white movies. Those were my only joys as I lived each day in hell with him. I could escape just for little while inside of one of the characters.

I loved movies, and I still found myself staring blankly at the screen if one of Lucy's movies was playing or if Papaw had on a western. I could sit for hours forgetting to eat if a marathon ran all day.

Jean-Paul was delightful and refreshing. He was kind, and well-spoken. He told me stories about growing up in Louisiana. He explained that the rich, warm color of his skin came from his Cajun descent.

"If you marry me, and we have children, I hope they have your skin tone. I don't like mine very much," he told me seriously.

I didn't know what to say to that. This struck me as a bold conversation for a first date. Not that I knew the proper talk of first dates, but I was sure it didn't involve marriage and kids. He noticed.

"Does that make you uncomfortable? Me speaking of marriage and children?" he asked with mild curiosity.

I swallowed.

"I just never think about it anymore. After the accident, I kind of forgot about a husband and children. My life was so planned out before."

I couldn't bring myself to say, "After Matthew died," but Jean-Paul understood.

"Well, maybe you will begin to think about it again. Maybe you can entertain the idea of me?"

He eyed me hopefully.

Wow. I was shocked. I just stayed silent. He held my hand during the movie. I was comfortable, whether that was because of the Valium I'd taken, or because I genuinely liked him, I wasn't sure. I did feel the crusted edges of my heart soften just a little. I wanted to hope that maybe I could love him. I could try. I wanted to live, but to move on would mean forgetting what Daniel said about me. It would mean letting go of Matthew, and I wasn't sure I could do that yet. Matthew was such a bright light that he drowned a lot of the dark in me. The chance of anyone ever being that again had to be next to none.

After that first date, Jean-Paul and I began to see each other when he was in town, and we spoke on the phone a few times a week. It's was strange talking with a man that was not Matthew.

I found myself looking ahead. Future was a foreign word to me, but I was trying. By my eighteenth birthday, I had a ring.

Once the solitary diamond was presented to me I felt wooden and spoke mechanically as if my body worked, but no heart was beating inside it. I said yes. I'm not completely sure why I said yes except I couldn't find a reason to say no.

Nana and Papaw sat down and spoke to Jean-Paul of his intentions and where we would live and on and on. Jean-Paul told me he wanted to live here, in Cosby, with me, and raise our children here. He was still in the beginning stages of building his company.

Right now, it was just him and a semi, hauling meat and produce from the South. Jean-Paul had said to me many times that his goal was to have a fleet of trucks. He would commute back and forth for work every few days and be gone for a week or two at a time.

"We would live here if Piper wishes. I am happy at the thought" He told them.

This pleased my Nana and Papaw. The last thing they wanted was to see me move away. I had no desire to leave home myself. Then Jean-Paul said the words that got them completely on board with our marriage.

"While I'm building my business as an independent driver and owner, may we live here in your home, while we save to build a house?"

With glee, Nana and Papaw agreed. The house was huge, and I think they dreaded being alone in it. Nathan was a little less happy about it, but agreed that if it made me happy, then he would support me. Jean-Paul and I set a date for June.

"A June bride. Just graduated, and then married. I'm so happy for you, love," Nana told me at least once a day.

"It's a good thing I got my career lined up then, I guess, huh?" I said, smiling.

Nana and I would be midwives together. I was handling full-term deliveries and was learning more and more. I loved it. Nana told me it was in my blood. This made her swell with pride each time she said it.

It was all so practical, so normal. These things did not come to me easily. The life I had planned did not turn out the way I wished so this was a good enough plan B.

I was counting down the days till my wedding. I cared for Jean-Paul, but the truth was, I had settled for never being in love again. I would be satisfied like the brides of old who married not knowing their husbands. Maybe eventually I would get to a place where I was deeply in love with him. Right now I settled for being in love with the idea of love.

He could take care of me. We would be husband and wife, not expecting too much from one another. We would grow together. Jean-Paul loved that I was a midwife and supported my working although when I spoke of working calling it a "hobby." My work was special and important. Jean-Paul at times belittled and found it humorous.

He liked that I worked mostly at home, occasionally helping a woman who delivered in the hospital, and that wasn't often and was only a short drive away. Nothing like a "real" job of 9 to 5.

I gathered from little comments Jean-Paul made that he was relatively old fashioned and expected me to be as well. Taking care of the home, having babies. Like a true fifties housewife.

"Your being a midwife is excellent, but know I do want a clean house and things a man needs when I am home," he would tell me.

I never could tell for certain if he were merely teasing me or warning me. He lit up at the idea of me cooking for him and being home when he got there. Jean-Paul had told me his mother and father had married and divorced young. He had lived with his mother until he was fourteen, at which time he wanted to stay with his dad. She had moved to South America a few years ago, and he only saw her on occasion.

"I maintain contact, but I work a lot and she has a life of her own," he would say, adding dryly, "She knows how to reach me if she needs anything." And that would slam shut the door on the discussion.

We were going to have a garden wedding, outside at sunset. In April, I had my dress. Both dresses actually—one for my graduation, the other to say my vows in.

I spent evenings talking with Nana. By this time I did not pay attention to my drug use. I began to pop pills when my body needed them. My body began to rely on them more than my mind.

I should have been concerned with this, but I wasn't. I bought whatever was on hand. I didn't know their names, only their color and what was for sleep or daytime. I was up to at least ten pills a day.

I had money from the allowance I was given every month plus babies I helped with. Add to that Lana's discounted drugs and I was in good shape. I cared nothing for shopping and spending, so I saved whatever I didn't use for gas and school for the latest baggies of whatever my best friend could get a hold of.

I knew I would never be rich being a midwife, but again, money had very little value to me. We did not shop a lot. We stored most of our own food. Nana taught me how to cook every night, whether I wanted to learn or not.

I sat on a counter as Nana coached me, forever coaching me—how to knead dough, how to press pastas, how to tie up a turkey. Every day had a lesson.

I began to worry for Nana. She was in her late-sixties now, and her rich peach-colored skin had turned grey over the last few months. She was often short of breath. I was useless. I tried to get her to a doctor. I begged, but she blamed it on all the excitement.

"I'm only tired, love. Now go do your homework, please," she would insist.

One particular day, she was trying to help me as I delivered Teresa Humphrey's twins. The dad was ridiculous and no help at all.

All of a sudden, Nana was saying, "That's a good girl. Come on now," and then broke off, as if she forgot what she was going to say. She stumbled to a chair, looking like her vision had vanished.

"Nana!" I screamed, but she waved at me to continue with Teresa and her frantic husband. I finished and got them comfortable for the night, and then I demanded Nana go to the doctor. I would not take no for an answer this time. After much arguing, we arrived at the ER. Nana looked terrible. I was terrified. I took three Percocet to help me stay calm, but the fear stayed in knots in my gut.

Hours later, the doctor delivered the news in a dry, unhopeful voice. Nana had a mass on her colon that had attached itself to the wall of her uterus. It was in her lungs, liver, and spreading quickly to her brain. Her body was consumed by it.

I stood still, as the doctor looked at me sorrowfully. I wondered if he had treated me years ago? He continued to tell me about the treatment, and then the dreaded news that there were likely only six weeks at the most before it killed her completely. I blinked rapidly, as if we could disappear from this room and be normal and happy.

This was not happening. They had made some kind of mistake. Please, God, let this be a mistake, I prayed. But we stood in the room, with its funny smells and too-bright lights.

When the doctor finished saying whatever he was saying, I sat rigid and cold. I couldn't speak. I couldn't hear. All of my senses were shut down except the callused hand of my grandfathers in mine.

We both were shown to Nanas room. I forced my eyes in focus and my ears to hear. When they wanted to admit her, Nana nearly fought them.

"Please, do what they want." I begged.

Nana turned her clear blue eyes on me and I went still inside at the sternness in them.

"You will not allow me to spend whatever time I have left on this earth in this foul place. Take me home, love. I want to be in my own bed, watch the sunrise from my own pillow."

Her eyes left mine and settled on a place behind me. It was Papaw she pleaded with, and I knew, as always, he would do anything to give her what she wanted.

She was prescribed powerful medicines, and sent home to die. Nothing could be done. A nurse would come to check on her, but that was it. Only death would cure her.

Papaw and I carried Nana to her bed. I called Nathan and explained the best I could. He promised to be home by lunchtime the next day. I made her favorite tea and biscuits, but she didn't eat.

I slept in her room, on a pallet on the floor. I never once heard Papaw's snores. I knew he would not sleep. He would watch her through the night, and then doze in his favorite chair in the grand room.

In the morning, I woke to find Nana sitting up, looking down at me sweetly. Her graying hair framed her face, and the fine lines around her eyes showed up in the sunlight. She smiled at me.

"Go wash up, love. We need to talk," she told me seriously.

I took a Valium and brushed my teeth. I called Jean-Paul, but didn't get an answer. I glanced at my calendar. He would be here in a couple of days. He must be on the road now. I fixed toast and honey, poured coffee, and climbed the steps to Nana's room.

I found her dozing, with her head on the pillow, softly snoring. I set the tray down, and walked to the window. I loved this place. The mountains were all around us.

At any given time you could spot a deer or bear in the distance. Papaw placed electrical fencing in areas that kept most wildlife, primarily the black bears, away from the house.

It was late April, and the trees were filling out with their light green leaves. They would be tropical green in a few weeks, when the humidity was upon us. I could see a fox with its young in the distance. The woods were alive today. I turned to see Nana watching me.

"Hey," I said smiling.

She looked so pale and weak. The grey tinge of her skin unsettled me. I went to the tray on the bed, and held out some coffee to her.

"Want some?" I asked.

She raised a hand to take it. How had I not noticed how thin her arms were? Because I wasn't paying attention. I was busy with my own misery.

Guilt bubbled in my throat. I hated and resented my drug use for the first time. I got my own cup, and sat cross-legged on the bed in front of her. We sipped coffee for a moment, and then Nana gave me a serious look.

"Piper, I need to speak, and you need to listen. Okay, love?"

I nodded, knowing I wasn't going to like whatever she was about to say. Nana breathed deeply.

"I've known for a few weeks I was sick. I knew I was going to die from this."

I started to speak, and she shot up a hand and closed her eyes. I fell silent and waited for her to continue.

"This is life, Piper. No use fighting it. You get what you get. You have to obey God, be good to your family, and then it's over. I thought my life was over when your daddy died. I do not like to speak of pain in front of you because you have so much of your own."

I shifted uncomfortably. I thought I had her fooled by now. Of course I didn't.

She looked out the window and continued.

"I'm not sad, love. I've had a beautiful life. Your daddy passing nearly killed me. Then when we couldn't find you," she paused, remembering that time. "When we couldn't find you, it hurt beyond any words I can give you, but even more than hurt, I was consumed with fear, and fear is about the strongest emotion a person can have."

She looked back at me with watery eyes now.

"Don't be afraid, Piper. You were a blessing to us from the moment you were born. You're a blessing now. When the good Lord calls me home, I don't want you to stop living again, the way you did when Matthew went. That boy's in heaven, and the fact is, I'm going to see him and your daddy sooner rather than later."

I was crying now, not standing the thought of it.

"Piper, there's something else I need to tell you, honey. I should have told you already, but I hated to make you feel worse than you already do."

Nana paused and reached for two Kleenex on her bedside table then placed one in my hand and blotted her eyes with the other.

"When you were found, when you were in the hospital, the doctors told me you would probably never be able to have children. Carrying a baby that young messes up your insides."

She looked at me sadly.

"Your body withstood much damage. Matthew knew. He was with us when the doctors told us. In fact, that boy rarely left the hospital."

She shook her head and let me take all this in.

Matthew knew. Another reason to love him. He would have married me, knowing we couldn't have children. One more reason to hate Daniel. As if I needed another.

"Okay," is all I said.

She was dying. I wasn't about to add to her pain by telling her I knew I was diseased, to the point of being a freak. Daniel told me already. No, I just listened. Nana talked and talked, until her voice was nearly hoarse.

I wasn't to feel bad she told me or question God. I was to remain faithful that all would be well and God does all things perfectly. We sat together and talked the day away.

Her wish was for me to find peace in my heart. She admitted she knew I didn't love Jean-Paul the way a woman loves her husband, but he could take care of me and our home, if that's what I wanted.

She said she wanted to be buried in the pale pink dress at the back of her closet. It was a dress she wore when she danced with Papaw, while still in Germany. She would write her family in her hometown and tell them good-bye.

Then there was nothing more to do but wait. I cried myself to sleep that night. I heard Nathan come into my room. He stood for a while as I pretended to sleep. I couldn't talk to him. I was emotionally drained.

Lana came over and got in my bed early the next morning. I doubted she'd even been home. We shared a joint after breakfast and spent time with Nana, playing cards and listening to her stories. When Jean-Paul arrived that weekend I was nearly shocked by how coldly he greeted me.

"I called. No one answered," he told me flatly

"Nana isn't well, I have barely left her room." I began to say, but was caught off guard by his hand squeezing my arm.

"You are supposed to answer when I call," he said through clenched jaw.

"Jean-Paul, you're hurting me."

I tried pulling away only to be gripped tighter. A tense moment of warning hung in the air, and I searched his face to see if he were actually serious.

The phone rang, and like someone had flipped a switch behind his eyes, Jean-Paul loosened his hold on me. For a moment I had the impression he would have slapped me had he not been interrupted. Slowly he patted my arm and smiled.

"I only worry is all. I'm sorry. I don't know my own strength sometimes."

He assured me he was truly sorry and didn't realize he had squeezed so hard. He urged me to explain what had happened during his absence. I let the incident go as the attention needed to stay on Nana. Jean-Paul sat and talked with Nana for hours. He called for me to join them for a minute, telling me that we should be married right away.

I had completely forgotten my wedding plans. My graduation. Life was on hold. All that mattered was Nana. I agreed not at all certain what I was agreeing to.

We, or Jean-Paul rather, decided we'd get married the following Sunday after church. I wanted Nana to be with me on my wedding day. I wanted to give her peace as she was leaving me. I told myself it was the right thing to do.

Nathan grudgingly agreed. He had sores all over his arms. He tried to keep them covered, but I saw them when he was shirtless in front of the mirror. When I asked what they were, he said he had had an allergic reaction to a cleaner.

I left it at that, but something was definitely up with him. Truth is, none of us paid attention to much of anything but Nana. She was all that mattered, as we were all that mattered to her.

Jean-Paul and I were married that Sunday. We had a small, simple ceremony. Lana was my bridesmaid, and Maurice was the best man. Papaw walked me down to the pastor on the porch of our home. Nathan hovered in the doorway in a sour mood. We said our vows in front of our little family. When all was done, I helped Nana back to bed. I wanted her to rest and preserve her strength.

On my way down the steps, standing in the front doorway, looking as if he were out of place was Josh. Happiness flooded me nearly knocking me to my knees.

"Josh!" I screamed and leaped into his open arms.

I knew I missed him, but I had no idea how much till that moment. He squeezed me tight, and buried his face in my hair. Of all the chaos and upside down way life was leading me, this moment in these huge arms was my normal. Josh was the only thing that made perfect sense to me.

"God, Piper, you're gorgeous!" he said holding me at arm's length, and I beamed, drunk on his sweet smell.

"I've missed you so much, Josh. Please tell me you're staying for a while."

He smiled at me, looking for an instant like his older brother, making my heart ache.

"For a while, yes. Spring practice starts up soon, but for now, I'm yours," he said, and I hugged him again.

Foolishly, I began to cry on his shoulders. Josh felt my body wilt and hugged me tighter.

"Hey, what's wrong? I thought you'd be happy to see me." he said in my ear.

"Oh my God, Josh. I am so happy you're here." I sobbed now shaking.

Josh held me until I finally calmed. Pulling away he kissed my forward and raised a rough hand to wipe my cheek.

"Feel better?" he teased.

"A little." I smiled and wiped my eyes.

When finally I was cleaned up I led Josh to the living room, where a few guests remained. I detected a note of ice when Jean-Paul greeted Josh. It was strange to me, because I was so used to his kindness.

Jean-Paul never once showed indifference, but I saw a glimpse of it this day. Josh must've ignored it, certainly wasn't bothered by it. We got caught up on his parents and grandpa. He and Nathan talked about projects that were coming up. Josh would attend the University of Florida.

"It'll be nice to play in the South Eastern Conference," he said with pride.

I looked out of one of the huge windows in our grand room. My heart longed for Matthew. We would be married now, or close to it. He could have studied Nana's cancer and come up with a cure. The world lost a wise and unique man when Matthew left us.

What was wrong with me? I'd just married a man, and here I was still grieving another. Josh touched my cheek with the back of his hand. I looked at him, tears in my eyes now. We carried the same sorrow. I wore it like a coat most days, and now Nana was leaving me too.

I had to admit I felt better now Josh was here. I learned some of their family property was being sold. Old Mr.

Logue refused to sell to anyone who had any plans other than farming the land.

"He's stubborn, but I can't blame him," Josh told me.

After Nana woke from napping, Josh sat with her a while. I stayed in the hallway and listened as they talked about me.

"She's tough as nails, Josh, but her heart is as soft as cotton," Nana was saying.

Josh chuckled.

"Yes ma'am. Piper is special for sure," Josh said, and I had to grin at the sarcasm in his voice.

"You'll check on her from time to time? Make sure she's happy and safe?" Nana asked seriously.

"I promise, Mrs. Mitchell. I will," Josh told her, as if taking a vow.

I rolled my eyes at this, but it didn't bother me. It was only natural Nana wanted some reassurance of my safety.

"I have a funny feeling, Josh," Nana started.

Then she had to stop and catch her breath. It tore at my heart to hear her struggle, and I had to fight the urge to go in the room.

"I can't put my finger on it, but I have a strange feeling about Jean-Paul. Like he's got demons he has to fight or something," Nana told Josh in a low voice. "You mustn't think me a crazy person. I just want you to be aware of it."

Josh then spoke in a low voice, and I had to strain to hear it.

"I've never spoke of this, ma'am, but he's a bit odd to me. Piper ever mentioned anything unusual?"

Now I was feeling paranoid. What were they seeing in Jean-Paul that I wasn't? I absently touched my arm knowing the answer.

"Oh, Lana has been giving Piper medicine to help her not feel so worried all the time. Piper will eventually have to start feeling again. She's such a good girl. If she thinks him anything other than a gentleman, I don't know about it," Nana said.

Before I could hear how Josh would respond to that, Papaw called for me from the kitchen. I tiptoed away from the doorway.

Truth was, I was unnerved by Nana knowing I was taking pills, and the funny feeling, almost of confirmation, about how Jean-Paul was perceived by both Nana and Josh.

I had to store that away to think about later because Papaw had nearly set the kitchen on fire using the microwave. He was trying new things, at least new to him, and for now, he was proving that you really can't teach an old dog new tricks. I sighed and patiently began to explain why a metal cup can't be placed in a microwave.

CHAPTER FIFTEEN

Before we said good-bye, Josh handed me a piece of paper.

"This is yours," he told me smiling.

Excited, I opened and read. I read and reread.

"What's this mean, Josh?"

I understood what it said, but I didn't understand why I was reading it.

"It's yours, Piper. My parents wanted you to have it. It joins your land anyway, so no big deal."

He shrugged and pretended not to notice my tears.

I hugged him, crying hard on his shoulder.

"Hey, now, you're going to ruin the threads," he teased me.

"Thank you. Please tell your parent and Mr. Logue thank you. It's too much really."

He kissed my forehead, and I watched him go, wishing with all my heart he would stay. As soon as the door had shut behind him, I ran up the stairs to Nana's room to show her what I had.

I knocked softly and opened the door not waiting on a reply.

"Guess what," I said, waving the paper around.

"You got a puppy," she said with a giggle.

"No. The Logues gave me the blue barn!" I said, as if I'd just won the lottery.

Nana's face went soft.

"Oh, Piper. That is so nice of them." She put on her glasses and read the property note. The barn and the land between it and our land was mine. She looked up with tears in her eyes.

"They always wanted you to find your way home. Then and now," she said, smiling.

This pronouncement made me sad.

"I'm not lost now, Nana. I'm where I'm supposed to be. I'm married and I'm home with you and Papaw. I'm happy, so, please, don't worry anymore," I tried to convince her.

By the way she eyed me, I could tell she was still unconvinced.

"Are you? I want to believe you married for love, but I know you too good to believe that. Tell me, love." She placed a cold hand on mine, and said, "Tell me, what's going through your head right now."

I folded my property note and set it aside. I lay down beside my Nana and told her the truth, or most of it.

"I tried to look ahead and prepare for what's real. If I had to keep up the land by myself, I couldn't. I want to make for certain that you and Papaw are okay. Financially taken care of."

I couldn't admit that I didn't love Jean-Paul, at least not out loud, because I had said vows that made that a sin.

"Matthew is all I ever planned on. He was my one true love, and he's gone. Never coming back. I guess I thought Jean-Paul is the best I'll ever get, and he has the means to take care of our land, so we won't ever have to lose it."

I felt better now that I had confessed this to her. Nana turned slightly and asked me to look at her. Our lives were so consumed with her cancer, her medications, and nurse visits that it wasn't until Josh visited that I realized Nana felt we did not include her in our lives anymore, and this was the very reason why she had wanted to keep her sickness from us.

Me telling her what she already knew reinforced her place in my life, the way it should be. Nana coughed and sipped her water before she responded.

"Piper, do you believe in love?"

I nodded

"I used to, but I've already had my one true love."

Nana signed sadly.

"I loved a boy once, before Nathaniel. I know what you mean, but I'm where I am supposed to be. Not because I was told to be. This world," and she gestured broadly to the ceiling, "will try and put you in a box. This is that way, and that is this way, and so on and so on. Piper, you do what you want and nothing else. If you do the things that the world expects of you, there will be no evolving into the woman God put you here to be."

Nana paused to catch her breath. I wanted desperately to give her relief from the smothering effects of her cancer. It was robbing her of life. I was helpless, useless, as I watched the days take her slowly from us all. She waved away my offer of water.

"Do you understand what I'm telling you?" she asked in earnest.

I nodded. "I think so," I said, but Nana shook her head.

"My family disowned me when I divorced my first husband."

I frowned.

"What?" I asked, shocked.

Nana nodded.

"I married the man my family wanted me to. I did love him, or thought I did. It lasted maybe six months, and I got out of there. Turned out he liked boys better than me, and my family, especially my mother, thought I should keep my mouth shut and live with it." Nana shrugged. "I was with my father the day I met your papaw, trying to earn a place in the family again. I was trying to be a good daughter. That fact is, if I'd stayed with my first husband I'd never have left Germany, and I'd never know these hills, or you, love." Nana smiled causing the creases around her mouth to deepen.

"You've never told me this. Why?"

Nana's eyebrows rose.

"Because it's neither here nor there. It was non-essential information, at least until now. I fear you have married young because you felt it was the 'right' thing to do. I'm not saying I know your heart, love, I'm only saying, don't ever pass up an opportunity to live, and I mean LIVE. Love, you haven't been living lately. Those pills have you so numb, I'm not sure you know how you feel." She said this gently, without judgment.

I looked down at my hands, ashamed.

"I'm sorry, Nana," was all I could say.

"Promise me, Piper, that you will live? You will laugh and cry. You will dance and sing in the rain? You're here for a reason."

She placed her finger on the old bedspread, and I took her meaning. "Here" meant breathing, lucky to be alive.

I nodded, but said nothing.

"You will stop numbing yourself with pills?" she asked, and I promised meaning it.

I felt guilty the last few weeks whenever I took something. That was a feeling I'd never associated with my "medicine" as Lana called it.

"What should I do, Nana? I'm married. Are you saying I shouldn't stay that way?" I asked, confused now.

"No, love, I'm saying you need to do what you feel. It may be you love Jean-Paul, but I don't think you have allowed yourself to know what you feel." She brushed a hair from my eye. "You don't deliver babies because I wanted you to, do you?"

I shook my head, "No. I do it because I love it."

Nana smiled. "Just as long as it's what YOU want, love, and the same goes for your marriage. Just take the time to feel, Piper. That's all I'm asking."

I hugged her, noting how small she felt.

"I will, Nana. I promise."

Papaw came in then. I wasn't sure if he had heard the conversation or not, but he gave me a meaningful look.

"I'll let you rest now, Nana," I told her, and went to check on the kitchen.

Nana was cheerful and sprite. I would listen, as she and Papaw talked at night. Just rumbles through the closed door, but I knew them enough to know they were enjoying their time together. They were old friends, as well as lovers. They'd had over forty years together. They buried their only child, and raised their grandchildren as their own.

I knew Jean-Paul and I would never be this way. I accepted it. We just didn't have what you would call a loving relationship. It was very formal. I would take the time to get to know my feelings about him. I owed it to him. I had taken the plunge, so now it was sink or swim.

We agreed to put off our honeymoon until a more fitting time. This included the sex. We would wait until we had time to spend with each other which was fine with me.

I was taking care of Nana now, while running a house and delivering babies. I had enough credits to graduate, and I opted out of the ceremony. I made house calls to expectant mothers, but for the most part, I wanted them to be here in the birthing room.

It was neither an everyday thing, nor an every week thing. It was however, enough to keep me busy. I was trying not to take so many pills, or smoke as much weed. I wanted to be alert while I took care of Nana, and I had made her a promise.

I took a little less each day, to help with the cravings my body would feel. Lana was telling me almost daily now that she was leaving town soon. I was aware that she was waiting until Nana was gone, and I loved my friend more for staying with me through this.

I knew who would sell me what drugs if I wanted them, when I no longer had Lana running for me. When she would bring up leaving, I would ignore her, not being able to think of anything but Nana right now.

Nana was a little worse each day. I couldn't stand the thought of her leaving me. In May, the doctor sent a nurse to the house who hooked her up to a morphine drip. This kept the worst of the pain from Nana, and I could see just moving was excruciating. I hated for her to have the needles in her, but took comfort in her not hurting as much.

At the end of the month, my graduation came and went without me. I had not been to school since the night at the ER. Instead, I received my license to practice as a certified midwife. Nana beamed with pride, knowing her life's work would continue through me.

I did not bring up the not being able to have babies because when I told Jean-Paul this news he simply smiled and said, "Well, I always wanted my bloodline to end with me anyway."

I thought this odd, but he was odd to me in general, so I didn't dwell on it. He hugged me, and told me we could adopt.

One night, I talked to Nana about the cold feeling Jean-Paul gave me from time to time.

"I guess that will change when we become intimate?" I asked, hoping she knew the answer.

"It may. Do you feel love for him?" she asked, knowing the answer.

"I like him an awful lot. I'm not sure what love is, Nana. I know I loved Matthew, but I don't think I can love anyone else like I did him."

I wanted to cry and steadied myself. There it was. I was still grieving over a dead guy. I feared ever loving again. I feared never loving again. The very thing I swore I wouldn't do, I was doing.

"Friendship grows and trust grows, but love is evident from the beginning. It will grow ever stronger and deeper. Love is not something to hope for, but what is." She looked at me, worried. "You don't love him." She shook her head. "You will love again, and it will be evident from the start. There is no substitute, Piper." She said this very matter-of-factly.

I didn't love Jean-Paul. I thought I did, but I only loved what he could give me. He was kind to me and could provide for me the kind of life I would accept in substitute for what I couldn't have, now that Matthew was dead. What a mess. We talked a little longer, and then Papaw was ready for bed. I hugged and kissed them both.

As usual, I listened to their muffled voices well into the night. My head wasn't so fuzzy, and the sharpness was beginning to fill my heart with dread. I had to feel, to live, and right now I didn't want to feel anything. Yet I fought the urge to step outside and smoke or drink.

Finally after what felt like hours, I slept, uneasy with my newfound understanding. I woke after what seemed like only five minutes of sleep. I sat up sweating and breathing heavy. I felt Daniel's hands on me. Someone said my name. I listened hard to make sure I wasn't dreaming.

"Piper?" Papaw was saying from the hall.

"Yes?" I called back shaking all over now.

"Piper, honey, come. She's going."

I jumped out of bed, my mind chanting *No. No. No. No. No. No. No.* I got to the room and saw Papaw lift Nana's hand to his face. He looked up at me, tears streaming.

"Get your brother," he said, in a still, quiet voice.

Nana's eyes were open, and her breathing was labored. I flew downstairs to the living room.

"Nathan!"

He didn't answer. I saw him asleep by the light of the TV.

"Nathan!" I screamed again, but got no answer.

I hit him in the chest hard.

"Nathan!" He finally stirred. "Nana's dying!" I screamed and headed back upstairs.

I heard him fumbling to get up the stairs behind me. The scene in the bedroom had not changed. Papaw still sat, holding Nana's hand to his face. My throat squeezed shut. I put my hand to my mouth so as not to scream. One thing I had heard many times in the last few weeks. When it was time, it was time. We were not to rob her of a peaceful exit.

I shook, standing by the bed, trying to control myself. Nathan held me to his chest, as I quietly sobbed. Lana came in the door. I absently thought she must have either been with Nathan or in my bed without me knowing. I held out my hand to her, as Nana lay motionless, her breath rattling. Lana cried with me. I stood on one side of Nathan, and she on the other. Papaw was statue-still, weeping without moving.

We stood, the family Nana loved so dearly. Papaw stroked her hair, and a tear slid from her eye.

"Be at peace, my darling. Be at peace. I will see you soon," Papaw whispered.

Nana tried to grin, but the muscles around her mouth no longer cooperated. Then she slipped away. Her eyes slightly parted. The trace of her tears was still visible, and she was gone, gone to be reunited with my dad, gone to my dead baby, gone to Matthew, gone to be with Jesus. Gone from me forever.

CHAPTER SIXTEEN

Ryan ~

I was wasted. That much I was sure of. That was about all I was sure of. Sixteen straight hours of filming and a bottle of fine whiskey promised a good night's sleep. Sheldon was on the sofa still playing guitar with Nathan. I loved my best friend, but I also wished he'd go home every now and then.

Of course, home was his posh London flat with his wife, Beatrice, and three daughters, Sophia, Rakhel, and Libby. Now that I thought about it, time at my place might be the only peace he got.

Sheldon and his wife had more money than anyone I knew, yet he lived like a bum when he was with me. One of the things I loved about my friend was that you would think him normal, or close to it.

Honestly though, Beatrice was related to royals, and hers was one of the oldest families in England. Sheldon was one-third heir to a shipping company. Mix the two, and you had wealth beyond measure. I knew this, but most of the world thought of Sheldon only as my sidekick.

He was that as well, but the guy was smart, funny, and one hell of a musician. Most nights I loved him, just not so much tonight. I could hear the high pitch of his laughter, no matter how loud I turned up my music. I jammed a finger at the iPod to shuffle but still heard the pair of them.

Sheldon and I spent most of our youth roaming the street of streets of West Hollywood trying to make money with acting to support our blues "band" which was me on the guitar or piano and Sheldon on bass. After meeting by chance at the same commercial auditioning, Sheldon and I have rarely apart.

On a wild hair one night I left my hometown of Elko Nevada and rode in the back of a pickup with four other teenagers to Hollywood simply because I was bored.

The girl I was with at the time was sixteen, and at fourteen, I could not say no when she asked if I'd go while she tried out for a small role in a TV. movie. While waiting a receptionist asked if I had ever acted and would I be interested?

Twenty minutes later, I walked out with two hundred and fifty dollars and Sheldon as my new costar and best friend.

I was born Robert Thomas Pierce, but legally changed that to Ryan Knox as soon as an agent told me it was a much cooler. I am a Ryan and try daily to forget any other existence before. After that first commercial I never looked back to the life of poverty in Elko.

The broken life of a little sister killed by hit and run as she followed me across the street. The tragedy caused my mother to abandon me and my father. I spent several years being blamed for my sister's death and cannot recall a life before I was a fault. My father spent day and night sipping beer from the moment my mother left without warning so when I was invited to Hollywood I jumped at the chance to escape.

I didn't count on the possibility that I would act beyond a hair commercial, except to fund our band. I found myself starring in a movie that next year and the band took a backseat to the sudden demand of film making.

Sheldon was an incredible musician and lived the rebellious opposite his parents intended. Tattooed and grungy with all-night jam sessions is what he preferred to years at Oxford.

That's been several years ago and my music abilities are no longer a factor as my film career has taken over my life. I'm passed the point of ever being able to do anything else now. Not that I don't like acting, it just wasn't what I set out to do and now I don't feel I can do anything else.

Nathan laughed being me sharply out of the daze like sleep I was about to enter. I rolled over pushing my face into the pillow. Why did I not just stay at hotel while they were both in town?

I'd met Nathan Mitchell a couple of years before on location in Nashville. He was visiting the set with Sheldon, and we became instant friends. Nathan was an extraordinary musician. He recorded a couple of pieces for the film, then came and went like the seasons.

Sheldon acted in small roles, but only because he liked it that way. He said acting took too much of his time, and he could not "invest" in the demanding roles that flooded his unanswered inbox. He drove his agent crazy.

I was envious of Sheldon's talents. I had to work many years to achieve the kind of fame that came so easily to my friend. Right now, he was using his God-given talents with Nathan's God-given talents. The combination was amazing. They would be sleeping, then they'd head off to some venue singing the blues tomorrow, and I'd board a plan to LA in the morning.

I didn't know how I got here, and certainly couldn't find my way back. Would I if I could? An accidental actor just goofing off to pay for my band? Now I was in too deep to do anything else.

Finally, somewhere between the Stones and Elvis, I slept hard. At five in the morning, Viola was shaking me awake.

"Hurry, man! Get your ass up!"

I slowly opened a heavy eye. She was throwing clothes in a bag, grabbing this or that off shelves, not paying any attention to the condition of the garments.

I pulled myself up knowing Viola would have no mercy on me.

"At least I don't have to dress," I said, trying to make her happy about one thing. I failed.

She waved her hand back and forth.

"Jesus Christ, it smells like you've been eating a hippopotamus ass all night. Brush your teeth before you kill somebody!"

That shut me up, and put me in a foul mood.

I grudgingly brushed my teeth, threw a hat on my head, and headed for the door, Viola fussing all the while. I glimpsed Nathan and Sheldon passed out on my couches. I wanted to be one of them, just for a day.

"Okay, put this on," Viola demanded.

I put on the jacket she tossed me, and followed my five-two-in-three-inch heels, black-haired, tatted-up assistant into the elevator.

"Tell me again why you live in this shit hole?" Viola asked, holding the rail as we went down four floors in the wobbly elevator.

"Because it's cheap and private," I said, from the depths of my bad mood.

"Here." She handed me four Motrin and water. "You look like you were beat with an ugly stick. Roger will have your ass if you're late again."

I swallowed the pills as the elevator opened. We got in a cab, and headed to the airport.

"Molly is already there, waiting"

I snorted, "Good for her."

Viola ignored me.

"Here's your schedule, and tell me what you want for breakfast."

I glanced at the paper, and folded it down to a two-inch square.

"Whatever. I'm not hungry," was my reply.

It seemed all I did was fly from state to state, and eat—other than acting in major motion pictures, that is. I had yet to get a lead role. I was always attached to some other actor, and I was sick of it. These swooning teenage dramas. I wanted to do something besides make the studios richer. At twenty two I was more than ready to do a lead mob style film, but was told repeatedly I was too pretty, or too baby faced.

"What crawled up your ass and died?" Viola did not appreciate my lack of interest in her goings-on. I looked at her squarely.

"Tell me again, why do you work for me?" I asked her this at least once a month.

"I don't work for you, and you couldn't afford me if I did," she said, with that ice-covered tongue.

In spite of how annoying she was, I couldn't do anything without Viola. Twenty minutes later, I scrambled to get out of the car. I turned to look at her.

"You're not coming?" I asked, disappointed.

She smiled sweetly, acid nearly visible on her lips.

"No, sweetheart. I will fly in tonight. I have to work a real job and can't babysit you every day." Then shut the cab door in my face.

God, I loved her. Not in any way sexual, but she was sharp, and the best "handler" there was. She worked for Roger, and was assigned to me. Roger was my manager—Roger Mitchell, a second cousin to Nathan, an Italian-American whose grandfather was from the old country, and who had sailed to the States many years ago. I heard that often, usually after at least three glasses of the finest Scotch.

His history was important to him, that was for certain—although if you asked about his parents, he'd go to great lengths to change the subject. Those of us in his circle, however, were aware of the mob-rich genes that he came from. Combine that with Hollywood roots, a showgirl mother, and you got the rich personality of Roger.

He was raised in California, by an uncle in the business. Although he had many reasons not to be, the guy was loving and legit to the nth degree.

I wouldn't make it without Roger; of this I was perfectly aware. If I needed anything at all, he was a phone call away. I wasn't sure why he took pity on me. I was just another nobody, looking to make fast money to buy my band their eats and booze as we traveled. At least that was the initial plan.

I was content for now with my role in life. I hoped to write, and maybe direct, someday, but for now it was another stop, another set, another rehearsal. I made it through security without being recognized. When I climbed aboard the plane, I saw Molly sitting with her legs crossed chewing gum while flipping through a magazine.

Roger managed us both, but Molly was his pride and joy. He and his ex-wife adopted Molly when she was three, but Molly did not use the Mitchell last name opting to use her grandmother's maiden name of Rowland. I flopped down in my seat in front of her.

"It's way too early. Wait till we are four states away to start talking," I told her.

Molly just blew a huge pink bubble and flipped the page.

This was our second and last movie together. That much we agreed on. Though I loved her as one of my closest friends, I had to try and find my own identity. The tabloids loved us and made up ridiculous stories about us. A little known fact was Molly was gay, and only her dad, her occasional female lovers, and I knew that. The only reason she did not make this public was that she refused to be a lesbian poster child.

I tried to sleep on the plane but found it impossible. I drank coffee and read Molly's magazines.

Molly moved to the seat beside me.

"Three months, then you're off to Louisiana for your big break," she said, placing her arms around mine, and laid her head on my shoulder.

"No contract yet," I said, not wanting to get my hopes up. I looked out the window for something to do. I was nervous I would not get the part. They liked me, but so had many others who had passed on me.

"You will," she teased.

I pulled my face back to look at her.

"You know something I don't?" I asked.

"Well, I heard Viola and Dad saying some paperwork was coming FedEx today, and I heard Viola would be presenting it to you tonight."

I held my breath. This part would open many doors for me. My fragile heart couldn't take the rejection if it fell through.

I couldn't back out of acting now. I was in too deep, but I'd go crazy if I kept filming these sappy dramas forever. This was something Roger and I both were well aware of and were trying desperately to change.

After we landed, we rode to the set in our waiting limo. A few paps were around, but after a few shots, they left us alone, waiting for someone more famous. Molly and I headed for makeup, and soon were on set. We filmed for seventeen hours and finally got to the house around midnight.

The next day we would do it all over again, but for now I chain-smoked, and snorted coke with Molly until I heard from Viola.

Even the coke didn't take the nervous edge off. I was a wreck. What if this didn't work? What if I was stuck in this position forever? I'd be some loser actor on a stage in Texas, working for my dinner. Not that the idea was not somewhat appealing, but I highly doubt I would be accepted as a musician now that I've been acting. The public seem to find actors amusing when both careers are attempted.

It was just the images of my dad that crept into mind at the thoughts of failure, his skin yellow from liver damage, from years and years of alcohol. I touched the tips of my fingers and imagined the calluses he had in the same spots from playing guitar.

I refused to think I was anything like my father. He spent to majority of his time in a recliner smoking and sipping beer day and night. There's no life there and when he did decide to speak to me it was mostly about how my mother left because I killed me sister. I had to shake the thoughts from my head before they carried me down low.

It was three in the morning before Viola got to the house, the one Roger allowed us to use when we were on the West Coast. He purchased this specifically for Molly, for safety reasons, he told her. Molly tried to refuse, but often failed at not accepting Roger's gifts. She wanted a name for herself. Most likely she would always be known as the Mitchell heir.

Viola lit a cigarette. She thumbed bright red, talon-like nails through a file. Blowing smoke out of the side of her mouth, she placed papers in front of me.

"It's yours for the taking. Just don't screw it up," she said, without preamble or an ounce of humor.

My heart hammered in my ribs. I felt Molly rub my shoulders.

"Ah, Ryan, this is excellent!"

I thumbed through the contract. The details were unimportant. I could see the important things and lawyers had combed through details such as what I would make. This would be the pivotal point in my career.

I would either do great, or I would fall on my face in front of millions of fans. Not my fans, but the fans of the novel on which this film would be based. I hugged Viola a little too hard. She did not protest. All business, she showed me where to sign and had to guide me back to the present as I drifted off into my own thoughts.

"I mean it, Ryan, you screw this up, and we will be sharing a boat paddling down shit creek," she told me sternly.

I was starting to get a complex.

"Don't you believe in me, Vi?" I asked, a little offended now.

Stuffing papers back into their proper places, she looked into my eyes, piercing me.

"Ryan, if I didn't believe you could do this, I'd be in my bed watching *ER* right now, but instead I'm here." She gestured around her in disgust—not at the house, but at the whole West Coast. I understood.

"It has nothing to do with your ability as an actor, Ryan." She paused, and for a split second, she looked unsure of what to say. "It has to do with your ability to handle things when the lights go out. If you make the shit mags and kill the film before it's released, I will cut off your balls, understand?"

I narrowed my eyes at her.

"I will behave. I swear it. I'll make you proud, Vi, you'll see."

I hugged her and kissed her cheek. She waved me off, and, after she packed up her papers, she left.

Viola was never one for many words or affection, but from time to time, I knew she loved me, just because she wasted words on me. Now to party. I did more coke and drank more to celebrate. I didn't sleep, so needless to say, the next morning I had bags under my eyes that made the makeup artist curse repeatedly.

Molly and I shared Roger's five-bedroom house in the hills for the duration of the film. There was much anticipation over our current movie together, a sweeping love story set in the thirties. We both hated it, but it was a stepping-stone to the next big thing.

Molly had started acting at the age of six. She had a constant flow of scripts and was a decent actress. She was my best friend, most of the time.

We snorted lines of coke together, popped pills, and often passed out in the same bed. We had a functioning relationship

We met each other's needs while together, but it never went further than mutual respect and loving friendship, and love her I did. She was better than most guy friends. We shared hours eating and enjoying old movies. We fought over the best kinds of music and writers. It was as close to normal as I'd ever got.

Our friendship started when I was in a low budget film as her supporting actor—aka lover. I can't complain. It got me noticed at least. We had a complex drinking and drug-induced relationship.

We simply supported each other's habits. Molly experimented with things I was still nervous about. She loved Demerol and had tried heroin. I favored coke and Jack Daniels which I did a lot of during the days of filming *Sunset,* which we finished filming in record time.

CHAPTER SEVENTEEN

I said good-bye to Molly as I headed south to Louisiana and she, far north to Vancouver. I met up with Sheldon and Nathan at the airport in Dallas. I'd been to Louisiana only once, and briefly.

I had a rare free week before I had to report for duty, or rather rehearsals, so I planned on hitting the clubs with my buddies. Maybe karaoke if I was lucky. I had a swanky studio provided apartment, and we planned to stay there together.

Sheldon would come and go, as he was a married man and had responsibilities, like going to Disney World and Florida beaches with his wife, four-year-old daughter, and two-year-old twin girls. For the most part, their marriage was a match made in heaven. As long as Sheldon and Beatrice stayed faithful, they agreed to continue their careers that had them in separate locations at times.

Bee, as we called her, was one of the wealthiest women in Europe. She maintained control of her parents' boutique shops, and successfully so.

Choosing to spend most of his time in London, Sheldon traveled to the States every few weeks to direct a video, or cameo a show. The guy was multitalented, to say the least. The funny thing is that *he* was supposed to be the movie star, and I the musician.

Life made our choices for us, or at least for me. Sheldon turned down some of the most sought-after major motion picture roles of recent years, choosing instead a life of family, music and travel, while a board of men and women ran his portion of the company.

We spent the next couple of days in New Orleans. I met some girls and hung out at the local pubs, listening to Sheldon sing while Nathan played guitar. Nathan, I had heard, had a beautiful girlfriend, Lana. I got the impression the movies Lana starred in were of the adult variety. I refrained from asking Nathan too much about it as he did not bring it up himself.

I do know Lana worked different hours all the time, but would only be in the same place for a week at a time. If I had to guess, the movies she was working on were probably cheesy soft porn. Sheldon never said this for sure, but I would bet on it.

Sheldon was slightly shorter than me, and was solidly built—not bulky, but strong. He would be an extra in the film with me. I loved it when he took these small roles, as we had more time to goof off and have jam sessions.

Sheldon and Nathan often called me a toothpick, because they said I was as skinny as one. I was six foot three and lanky. Wardrobe often complained I was too thin. The coke didn't help with that. They didn't need to know that detail though.

I was heavier than I had been before. *Sunset* had required I put on muscle for the seminude shots. I loved the feeling, but the workouts were pure hell. Add the food I had to eat every two hours, and the result was lean muscle that took me a while to get used to.

After a few days to relax, it was time to start rehearsals and filming. We were on a pretty tight schedule as the studios pushed for us to be done and the faster the better.

I had read the script at least ten times and had long since memorized my lines. I was ready for the big time. Hopefully anyway. Our apartment was clean enough and stocked full of booze. We ordered take-out and played music when I wasn't due on set. Sheldon would leave to meet his girls at Disney, then return to film his scenes.

This left Nathan and me, roaming the city without our chaperone. Sheldon kept us in line, but I had made a promise to stay out of the tabloids, and I was convinced that Viola would follow through with the castration if I got into any trouble while filming.

Nathan and I mostly stayed in and played music when he was not with Lana. We would drink and write songs that would never see the light of day—thankfully.

With only a couple of days left on our filming schedule for Louisiana, I'd given up on meeting interesting people from the South. Every girl I met was doe-eyed and looking to be "found" by Hollywood. None had a clue, and I got tired of trying to explain it to them.

Sheldon returned tanned and happier after being with Bee and the girls. A new tattoo was still bright pink and healing on his already covered arms. This time it was an angel, and Beatrice was her name. I rolled my eyes at the cheesiness of it, but I had to admit I was jealous he had the love of his life, money, looks, and beautiful little girls.

When he got back that night, we headed out for a party that Nathan and Sheldon had been booked to play. It was Friday night, and I had the next day off. We were due to wrap, and move on to Mexico to finish filming the following Monday.

The filming so far had been going great, but there was something in me that was sad, no matter what I did. It was always there—when I woke up and again when I would go to sleep.

My intentions for the night were to listen to good music, get drunk, and sleep. When I woke the next day, I would do it all over again for my day off. So far, I was more than halfway through my list for the evening, when I walked right into a wall. I smacked it, face first. Seeing lights for a second, I thought it best to have a seat, as Nathan began to play a new set. My head spun, and the ramblings of strangers were beginning to work my nerves.

I was still blurry-eyed when I caught sight of her. At first glance, I thought I'd imagined her. As my line of vision cleared, I found her again. She was standing off to the side of the room, picking at the label of a beer bottle, looking bored, obviously uninterested in the party.

She had milky, peach-colored skin, and long strawberry-blonde hair. She wore no makeup and reminded me of a hippy. I guessed she was around twenty. I was used to trying to guess a girl's age, because I had to be careful not to end up in bed with a minor.

The girl looked from person to person intensely and, I thought, with a little fear. Someone was talking in my ear about my Oscar-worthy performance from that day. I nodded, but paid him no attention, and kept watching the girl, intrigued by her out-of-place state.

I found myself drawn to her, and I began making my way to the beautiful stranger. I wasn't sure of what I would say when I reached her, but I was certain I'd come up with something.

After years of practice with women, you would think me a pro, but this girl made my insides clench. A dark-haired girl reached her first and handed her a set of keys. I paused and watched as the two giggled and conspired about something.

Sipping my beer, I watched as the dark-haired girl returned to where Nathan sat playing. The strawberry blonde girl's eyes flicked toward Nathan. The light in her eyes left as the dark-haired girl walked away.

She was the saddest thing I'd ever seen. Not in looks but in the defeated way she appeared. Finally, I gathered myself and walked straight up to her. I said the first thing that came to mind.

"You're in Lana's films?" realizing the dark-haired girl must be Nathan's girlfriend.

I could have kicked myself.

The girl looked affronted, and I couldn't blame her. Dark, ebony eyes looked back at me. Damn, she had the deepest brown eyes I had ever seen. I was instantly transfixed. I had momentarily forgotten what I had asked. I realized she had spoken, and I hadn't heard.

"Excuse me?" I said, bending my ear to her lips. Her breath brushed my ear, and goose bumps formed on my arms.

"Go. To. Hell." She spoke very slowly, as if I couldn't understand English.

I pulled back, feeling all interest leave my body. Most girls would recognize me, at least enough to be taken with me. It was one of the downsides of being me sometimes.

I would have enjoyed a conversation without the girl knowing my face or wanting to make it in Hollywood. Boring and pathetic girls, in other words. I looked at the deep brown eyes squarely to make sure she was serious.

She was.

I turned and walked out the door, pissed at myself for being so stupid. I should have just asked if she sucked cock for a living. I didn't blame her for being offended by my question. It's not normal, I suppose, to be asked if you do porn.

I saw Nathan's car parked in the shadows of the lot. I had used all my coke but had a few pills left. Sick of the party, and hurt by the girl's rejection of me and my stupidity, I climbed in the backseat. It smelled like Armor All.

The guy worshipped this car. Why? I didn't know. I'd heard him brag about it being a classic, and blah blah blah. I swigged down the pills and the rest of my beer, and hoped I wouldn't be found till morning.

Tomorrow, I was off the whole day. I planned on sleeping as much as Sheldon would let me. I covered myself with my jacket and fell asleep. I could have walked back to the apartment, but in my drunken state, the car seemed a good place to be left alone.

I had only been out for a few minutes, or so I thought, when I woke to the sound of crying. I realized that I was moving, but momentarily forgot where I was. Opening my eyes, I saw lights passing overhead.

I sat up, trying to get a grip on my situation. How much had I had to drink? The girl behind the wheel screamed and nearly did a donut in the middle of the road.

"Whoa! Whoa! Whoa!" I said, as we skidded off the road.

When we stopped, she leaped from the car like a scolded dog. I looked out the window, and watched her stop fifteen feet from the car and look back at me, breathing heavy. It was the sad girl from the party.

Her chest was heaving, and panic was on her beautiful face. I opened the door and exited the way a person being arrested would, hands in the air.

"It's okay! It's just me, Ryan." She took no comfort in the words. "From the party?"

She placed a hand over her heart as if to steady it

"What the hell are you doing?" she said.

I put my hands down, not used to anyone but Viola speaking to me this harshly.

"What am I doing? What are you doing, stealing a car?" I yelled back.

She knitted her brows together and almost laughed at this. I tried not to notice she was beautiful even when doing this.

"I didn't steal anything. What are you doing in the backseat?" she asked, a little less angry.

"I was knitting a sweater. What do you think I was doing? I was trying to get some sleep." I turned and kicked the door shut. I was mad, but had no idea why. "Where are we anyway?" I demanded, looking around.

The sky was black. My internal clock gave me no indication of what time it was. I wasn't sure I even cared. When the girl didn't answer, I looked back at her. She seemed to be thinking.

"I was going to the shore to watch the sunrise. I wanted to be alone. Get away," she stated simply.

I blew out a heavy breath and looked around again for something to do. There was no traffic, and we were on a road without lines. There was vegetation around, but not much.

I decided we were not far from the coast, but definitely far from anywhere I was familiar with. I'm not sure what made me do it, but I thought I'd play along.

"Well, you're just going to have to take me with you."

I gave her my best camera smile.

She looked at me with sarcasm in her dark eyes.

"I don't know you. You could be a murderer," she said.

I put my hand to my chest and acted injured.

"I should be hurt you don't know me, but I'm not. This time next year, everyone will know me," I said in mock arrogance. Sheldon would be proud. "For now, I'm just Ryan, and you are?"

I held a hand out for her to come forward and shake. Honestly, I just wanted a reason to touch her.

Something came over her eyes just then, as if she were slipping into to a character herself.

"Livia," she said, taking a few steps forward, and shaking my hand lightly.

Electricity ran through me at her touch. What was wrong with me? I smiled politely, as if nothing had passed. I wasn't sure if she was being honest, but I nodded.

"Nice to meet you," with a bow. "Now Livia, may I drive us to the shore to watch the sunrise, or shall we return to that dreadful party?"

Livia looked down the road, deciding.

"Come on. Time's wasting," I said, with a smile.

I had the feeling I was getting creepy with it now, but I wanted nothing more than to be alone with this girl. I needed to make a decent second impression.

Finally, she just tossed me the keys and got in the car, making sure not to brush me as she did. I caught a whiff of sweet perfume, laced with a hint of flowers. It was intoxicating.

Light-headed I got behind the wheel, a little self-consciously. I wasn't a great driver, and now I had my nerves to deal with.

"Where to, love?" I asked looking over at her, truly lost. It was dark, but I could see her delicate features turn sad in the dashboard lighting. "You okay?" I asked, genuinely concerned.

"I'm fine," she said softly. "Just straight ahead till we reach the shore. It's not far."

We drove maybe a half hour. I talked mostly, and Livia stayed tight-lipped. She was not cold, and I knew this was an act. I sensed she was fragile in most ways, but there was a hard exterior about her, keeping her from relaxing with me.

She wore no wedding band, and when I asked, she said she had no boyfriend. She sat in stony silence, hands pushed tight between her thighs as if I was going to rip one from her body at any second.

I stopped at a gas station, and bought a dozen beef jerky, chips, water, cheap beer, and a dollar ninety-nine rose. This got me a small laugh. She took it from my hand, as I held it up to her.

"I love roses," she said.

She held it to her nose, eyes closed, smelling the fragrance.

I drank her in. There was a childlike quality, innocence, about her as she did this, as if she'd never smelled a rose before. It left my head buzzing.

We arrived at a deserted beach in the middle of nowhere. I parked the car and got out. The air was nice and clean. The sound of the waves crashing against the shore was hypnotizing.

I walked to the front of the car and looked around to see if we were alone. There was nothing as far as my eyes could see.

When Livia did not follow, I walked around and tapped on the half-open window.

"Is this what you wanted?" I asked, a little confused.

She looked at me, then the surroundings, then back at me. I thought she looked scared.

"I shouldn't be here," she told me.

I sighed, bewildered.

"But don't you want to be here?"

She twisted her hands nervously, and I opened the door, taking her silence as a yes.

"Isn't this where you are supposed to be?" I asked.

She grinned and unfolded her long body from the car.

When she stood and looked at me, I guessed she must be five-nine, or five-ten, judging by the models I had dated.

"Hey, you're not a model are you?" I asked, teasing.

She didn't laugh.

"No. I'm nobody." She said.

This struck me as odd. People normally did not reply in this way. She walked to the trunk and got out a blanket.

"I'm afraid to think what and who has been on this, but it's what we have," she said, apologetically, then strode past me to find a place to sit.

She moved like fluid. Delicate and graceful. I watched her with my hands in my pockets as she spread the blanket and sat cross-legged, waiting for the sun. I turned off the headlights, tossed my shoes in the back, and walked to join her. We sat in silence as the sun rose.

The sky turned different shades of dark blue, then light. The water was dancing to the dawn, putting on a show for its audience of two strangers.

It was majestic and beautiful. I sat a little behind Livia, just so I could watch her and not be noticed. I couldn't guess her age, but she was young. Her face was like porcelain, smooth and lineless, except a thin scar just under her right eye.

Her profile was perfect, the strong line from the bridge of her nose to her pouty lips all in perfect proportion. When the sun was fully up, a tear threatened to fall from the corner of her eye, but she quickly wiped it away. I touched her shoulder.

"You okay?" I asked softly.

She jumped.

"Sorry," I said.

Livia wiped her eyes.

"I'm fine."

I knew that was a lie. This girl was anything but fine. She obviously had the weight of the world on her.

I knew I had to seize the opportunity in front of me. I did not want to go back to the apartment complex just yet. I wanted to keep her here, and find out more about her, see if I could maybe get her to like me. I stood and started to undress. She looked up at me, shocked.

"What are you doing?"

I unbuttoned my jeans, and she looked away blushing.

"You ever skinny-dip?" I said, unashamed of my body, knowing the workouts and diet I'd been following were paying off.

"No. I mean, yes, when I was a child and foolish," she said, looking down the beach so she wouldn't see me.

I began walking to the water, and when I was waist-deep, I turned to her, throwing my hands up.

"This is life, Livia. Don't you want to live it?" I asked as if I knew the secrets to life and this was one of them.

I thought she would get up huffy and mad. I thought she would demand we go back now. I did not expect her to stand and begin undressing.

I stood still, watching her. Waves tried to knock me down, but I stood perfectly still, soaking up both the new sun on my back and the stranger before me.

I was taking in every movement, the elegance of her arms and legs, then the roundness of her breasts and hips. The soft places in between.

She walked, knowing I was watching her. I was focused on her beauty. Her hair flew playfully in the wind. Her nipples rose hard and alert as her feet hit the water.

I had the desire to reach out and take her. I didn't. She dove like a swan into the salty drink. I followed. When we surfaced, we laughed like kids, swimming here and there.

"This is crazy," she said, breathless and happy.

"You're beautiful," I said stupidly.

She grinned at me, embarrassed. I wasn't sure, but I could almost feel the wrappings holding her together loosen.

She said nothing, but turned to swim further out. I stayed within arm's reach of her, feeling like any given moment she would disappear, and I would wake up in the back seat of Nathan's car, stiff and hung over.

"Got any beef jerky left? I'm starving!" she asked, flashing me gorgeous white teeth.

I grinned.

"Yeah, about a dozen. I bought all they had!"

We made our way back to the blanket after a few minutes of swimming. I tried to be respectful and not stare. I wanted to look at her and melt into her. I just knew she would dress, and I wouldn't see her flesh again today.

I made my way to the car and grabbed the goods along with the now warm beer. When I turned to walk back to the blanket, Livia surprised me again. She was lying on her back with her arms on her forehead, still nude.

I had seen many women naked. I had never seen anything as beautiful as this woman. She was slightly too thin, like she worked too hard or was sickly, but that was her only flaw. I drank her in as I slowly walked toward her. I stood looking at her in the sun.

Her arms were over her closed eyes. She reminded me of a bird, or some small animal warming in the sun. She had goose bumps from the wet. Her nipples were hard and standing.

She had a small pool of water in her belly button. I fought the desire to bend over and suck it out. There was a deep scar just above her trimmed pubic hair. There were small scars on her torso here and there that reminded me of cat scratches.

I drank her in like old wine, savoring every inch of her. I stood erect and in awe. She must have felt my presence, because she moved her arm to look at me.

"What?" she asked innocently.

I cleared my throat, hoping the bag hid my obvious mood.

"Nothing," I lied easily, just as innocent.

I was drunk, but hadn't had a drink in hours. I knelt on the blanket, and began to sift through the bag. Livia propped herself up on her elbow and looked in the bag with me.

When I looked up, saying something about the warm beer, I met her eyes. Damn. I was falling hard and fast through deep rivers of chocolate. She didn't look away.

She drank in my face and licked her lips absently. I swallowed nervously. I was never nervous with women. What was wrong with me? Wasn't I immune to naked, beautiful women by now? But here I was, acting like a schoolboy being examined by a hot teacher. I forgot the bag and put my hand to her face, leaning close to her wet lips.

"May I?" I asked in a hoarse whisper, every breath breathing deeper into hers.

She did not protest, and I bent to kiss her.

I found her breast with my free hand, and ran my other through her long hair. I laid her back on the blanket, not wanting to go too fast, but unable to control the now raging desire I felt running through my body. I pulled away from her mouth with great difficulty.

I began to kiss, lick, and softly bite her collarbone, then her breasts. Small seductive noises came from her throat. I made my way down until her legs were parted and my mouth on her. She shook under my probing tongue, making soft, incoherent sounds of pleasure.

After she shook from her release, I made my way back up her body, pausing for only a moment at her breasts. Her hands were all over me, crazed as much as I was now.

When I entered her she bit at my wrist, which only fueled me further. I kissed her frantically. I did not want to stop. Her legs tightened around my waist, I arched my back, and pounded her into the sand. Making beastly sounds of my own, finally I collapsed in exhaustion on top of her.

I could feel her heartbeat, and I'm sure she could feel mine. After I caught my breath, I rolled over beside her. We lay in the sun for a long moment breathing heavy.

I was not drunk. I was not high. I was fully in the moment with one of the most beautiful women I'd ever met. I wanted to soak it up and never leave this spot. The movie be damned. The world be damned. I had found bliss on earth.

We slept intertwined in the morning sun. When we woke, we made love again, then ate our convenience-store goods, then swam the day away. We lay on the blanket, talking quietly to one another, exhausted from sex and the sea. When she dozed with her back to me, I looked for what I'd felt in the water. When I saw the roughly healed scar on her left upper shoulder blade, about six inches long, I thought it odd.

It was a bad injury, and it had healed poorly. I traced it with my fingers, wishing to smooth its surface, knowing whatever made this scar must have caused her great pain. I hadn't noticed her open eyes and was caught off guard.

"It was a burn," she said, and offered no further explanation.

I bent my head and brushed the scar lightly with my lips. I held her and did not want to push the subject now, not while we were drunk on each other. I would ask later.

I ran my fingers down the curves of her body, tracing her ribs. There were light bruises there, and a faded black bruise on her hip. It was unspoken, but I knew in my heart someone had put these on her purposefully and probably the burn scar as well.

She lay silently, watching the fading light as the sun set, and allowed me to touch her. I laid my head on hers, and watched the last sliver of orange disappear from the sky.

We packed silently and drove in silence, not wanting to spoil the air with idle, meaningless chatter. I was paranoid about love, so I'd never known what it was. Was this love, or merely a deeper form of lust?

I looked over at Livia. She was looking out the window. I could see a reflection of sadness on her face when we passed under a streetlight. I pulled her to me and kissed her hair. This was not lust.

Yes, I was overly attracted to her, but beyond the physical elements, there was a magnetic pull toward her, an energy I'd never known, and I was nearly certain I would never feel it again.

Livia curled up like a cat beside me as we drove to the apartment complex. I stopped and parked where the car had been the night before.

"Nathan will probably have called the car in stolen by now," I said, and Livia smiled.

"I'm due on set at three in the morning," I told her. "Can I see you when the shoot is done?"

Livia looked up at me and reached to kiss me.

"Meet here at the car, or if Nathan takes it, here in this spot, agreed? At six this evening?"

I noticed I sounded like I was begging, but I didn't care.

Livia nodded. There was a distance in her eyes that made me weary. I wrapped my arms around her middle, inhaling deeply the sweet perfume and salt of her hair.

I spotted Viola's rented Pontiac in front of my apartment.

"Great," I said sardonically, allowing my unwilling arms to release her.

"What?" Livia said, following my gaze.

I shook my head.

"My pain-in-the-ass handler is here." I put my eyes back to hers. "Here? At six?"

Livia nodded.

I kissed her again, and watched her go in the opposite direction. When I could no longer see her frame in the dim lights, I made my way to the unit I was staying in.

We would be leaving in three days, and I planned on spending every one of my breaks with this beautiful and mysterious woman. I looked back to where she had left me. A ghost in the night.

CHAPTER EIGHTEEN

I looked to see which direction Livia had gone, dumbfounded that I hadn't asked where she was staying. I would find out, and I could always ask Nathan or Lana. When I got inside the apartment, Viola started on me without warning.

"Where the hell have you been? You think you can just disappear for twenty-four hours? You do not have a life when a studio owns you. If there are any drunken bar fights in the tabloids tomorrow, I will personally kick your ass."

I shut my eyes and shook my head.

"Jesus, Viola," I started, but this didn't help her mood.

"Don't you bring Jesus into this. He has nothing to do with anything we are talking about," and on and on she went.

It lasted at least ten minutes. All the while Sheldon sat, still in makeup from filming earlier, smiling at me.

When Viola had appeared to be finished with me, he said, "Sure you want this life?"

Viola shot him a nasty look.

"Don't you add to this. You, with your tiny bits in movies. You could've won an Oscar by now, but no, Mr. I-Don't-Want-To. You're wasting my time and energy. Did you wrap today?" she added for clarity.

"Sure did. Two takes, and done," he told her, grinning

Viola nodded, returning to her professional self.

"Now," she said when she saw me narrowing my eyes at Sheldon. "You will be on set in an hour. They have bumped our flights to Mexico for early afternoon..."

I held up my hand.

"Wait, what?" I demanded.

Viola turned an icy stare on me.

"Did I not speak English?"

I stared back just as hard.

"We don't start filming Mexico for another four days," I said, pissed off now.

Viola closed her heavily lidded eyes with what I thought was annoyance, but her voice was like speaking to a child about how yes, one plus one does equal two.

"You did not read your schedule. We have to be ready and waiting in Mexico by mid-week. We have to check in and do rehearsals and test lighting. Come on Ryan you know the drill by now."

I gaped at her trying to take in what she was saying.

After going back and forth for twenty minutes, I got in the shower, fuming now. I let the hot water wash my anger away. I would leave a note at the car, and explain that I would be in Mexico for two or three weeks tops, then after that it was Rome for another four weeks. I would leave my number and my New York address. And apologize profusely. And hope Livia would not think she was a one-night stand.

I ran my hands through my hair, flashing back to the way her skin felt in the sea, the way the salt tasted on her body once on the beach. I opened my eyes and tried to clear my head.

No matter what I did, I was worried I'd never see her again. A feeling that was brand new to me. I liked it, but my heart felt heavy.

Viola opened the bathroom door.

"Let's get a move on, hotshot. We leave in ten minutes." She closed the door again.

With the heaviness in my chest, I hurried out of the shower, and into the same clothes I'd just taken off. I didn't bother looking in the mirror. Hair and makeup would shave and clean me up. I wrote out the information I would leave at the car as quickly as I could, thinking I would tell Sheldon to be on the lookout as well.

When I yelled for him down the hall, Viola sighed heavily.

"He's gone already. Let's go!"

Following an irritated Viola to her rental, I muttered for her to wait.

"Please give me one second."

In frustration, Viola growled at me. I ignored her and headed to the Camaro, but it was gone. I looked around me. It was nowhere in the lot. Viola pulled up beside me.

"Let's go," she demanded.

I looked around the complex, and the car was nowhere in sight. An ambulance and police cars were parked a building away, but no Camaro.

"Damn it!" I screamed.

Viola said nothing, just kept inching forward with each step I took, frantically looking for a car that wasn't there.

I stood in the middle of the parking lot. I had no last name, no apartment number, no nothing. I kicked the side of the Pontiac as I made my way to the passenger side. I threw open the door, got in, and slammed it shut. I was in a black mood, and Viola knew to say nothing to me.

On the way to my trailer for makeup, paranoia crept up. What if I was the one-night stand? Livia did not care for me one bit. In fact, I had to talk her into going, and I talked her into everything else.

I smacked my forehead, and said, "Idiot!"

A guy carrying a boom mic muttered, "Sorry," and hurried away as if I'd been taking to him.

I stomped up the steps, feeling like a used postage stamp.

Hours later, Sheldon came to watch. He stayed back, away from everyone, chewing on his already short nails. When we finally wrapped, he told me Nathan had been shot and was in the hospital.

"What?" I said, shocked, thinking of the police cars.

"They think Nathan and Lana had an all-night drug binge with one of her suppliers. Things got ugly. Lana was shot in the neck. Nathan fought them and was shot. It was pretty bad. He had surgery and it looks like he's going to be okay now. He's with his sister at the hospital," Sheldon told me.

I called as soon as I was in my trailer, and the set was being torn down. An operator connected me to Nathan's room. A woman answered, and I had to pause.

"Livia?"

My heart stopped.

"No," she said calmly. "This is Piper, Nathan's sister."

Her nose was stopped up, no doubt from crying. My heart started back up, but the heaviness returned.

"Oh, I'm sorry. Is Nathan able to talk? This is his friend, Ryan."

Silence, then muffled voices, and then Nathan got on the phone. He sounded terrible.

He assured me all was well, and that he would be staying with his sister and her husband for a while in Tennessee. After I hung up, I looked for Sheldon. When I found him cracking jokes with the stage guys twenty minutes later, I didn't hesitate.

"Do you know a girl, a friend of Lana's maybe, or Nathan's, named Livia?"

We walked toward a waiting Viola.

"No bro," Sheldon said. "How come?"

I shook my head.

"Damn it." I explained very little as to why I was asking.

I would find her one way or another. I headed to the airport with mixed feelings of dread and uncertainty. I tried to sleep but was too distracted. I did some coke and drank bourbon slowly, allowing the warmth to take over. By the time we reached Mexico, I was stoned and pissed off at the world.

Days flew by, and no word from Nathan. I couldn't reach him either. When I finally spoke to Roger, he explained that Nathan was staying with family in Tennessee.

"Nathan is getting clean. It might be best if you gave him some time to sober up. He'll return your calls. Just give him time to deal with the withdrawal, and get stronger."

I agreed this was the best, and left it at that.

I thought of Livia day and night. When drug-induced sleep would finally find me, I closed my eyes, hearing her voice. Tasting her skin. I could not locate her. No one could find a Livia who stayed at the apartments.

Darkness was settling in my head and heart. In no time, Viola, Sheldon, and I were off to Rome. As we took off, I looked out the window of the plane, wondering if somewhere down there was a girl I was for sure in love with.

I sighed a heavy sigh and tried to sleep, listening to Sheldon tell me about Beatrice meeting him with the girls when they landed. They would stay for a while and might even look at some property. I tried to be happy for him, but he knew me well.

"What's up, bro?"

I kept my eyes closed, and shook my head.

"Nothing. Just tired."

"You act like you're in a funk. Better snap out of in or you know Viola will have your ass."

"Just let me be Sheldon. I'm not in the mood to be lectured," sounding every bit the asshole I was.

Sheldon left me to my thoughts.

I only saw him twice in Rome. I returned to filming and drowned myself in booze every chance I got, trying to keep hope alive that I would see Livia again, and maybe she could understand that I didn't leave by choice, and I didn't have control of my own life. I rolled my eyes thinking of just how dumb that sounded.

CHAPTER NINETEEN

The shoot in Rome took longer than expected, as shoots often did. I could not join Molly on the red carpet for the L.A. *Sunset* premiere. She called to tell me it went great, and numbers were rising in the States by the day. "I'm being followed day and night by the paps. Just wait till you get back. It'll be the same for you. I'll bet you we'll be married in two weeks, the way they're talking!" she laughed.

I went along with her numbly. I did not believe it would be the same with me of course. Molly was a somewhat higher priority, considering her film career and her notoriety.

"Hey, listen. They're running old pictures of us hanging out. They're trying to make our on-screen love a reflection of our blossoming off-screen love." She laughed. "Just be prepared," she added, more serious now.

I had to do a media tour in the States when I got back. I had done this a few times before, but never on the hems of a big-budget movie. I was excited. Maybe I would be noticed a little more.

Roger called the next day. This was strange. He never called while I was on location. I was immediately on guard. He got right to the point.

"I'm sending Viola tonight. She will help guide you through the frenzy. There are teenagers everywhere. I don't know who is worse, them or their moms. Anyway there will be a guy by the name of Josh Logue waiting for you at the airport. Nathan recommended him, and so far he is excellent security. He's a little young but great at what he does."

I couldn't get a word in, but agreed with the occasional, "Okay." Finally, when he took a breath, I said, "What? Security? Why? How's Nathan?"

I hadn't talked to him, but Sheldon was headed to Tennessee to see him, with his girls. He had told his daughters they could visit Dollywood and ride pretty ponies while they were in Tennessee, and that they might even see wild eagles.

"He's doing good. Being sober suits him. I'm headed there for Christmas. We'll work out your schedule, but I believe you and Molly both will be in France. Maybe we can meet up for New Year's. You've hit the big time, kid. It may not be with the movie you thought, but that just means the next will be even bigger. You know what they say? Be careful what you wish for."

If he was proud, I didn't hear it in his voice. He sounded almost sad.

"You'll be in Tennessee for Christmas?" That was all I had gathered from all he said. "Why?"

I asked, not knowing what would possess this avid New Yorker to travel to the hills for Christmas.

"Nathan and Piper are my cousins. Well, their dad was my first cousin anyway. I've never told you that our granddads were brothers?"

I stupidly said, "Huh?"

He continued. "Yes, our great-grand pop came from the old country and settled in Cosby, Tennessee. Bought up a bunch of land and married a local gal. My dad was much older than the senior Nathaniel, but my dad sought adventures away from the sticks, while Nathaniel went to the war, and came home a hero, and brought a wife with him too. Dad never returned, and after their dad passed, Nathaniel inherited most of the land he'd been helping to work. Granddad always kept a piece set aside for my dad, but when he died, it went to Nathaniel. Anyway, we reconnected not long ago, when I found Nathan playing here in the city. It's been wonderful getting to know my family all over again. I go home, as I call it now, every chance I get. Listen to me go on and on about this stuff."

I listened intently, wishing I were somehow kin to Nathan and Roger too. I was an only child, with a mother lost to me and a father who had wallowed in self-pity since the moment she left him for another man.

Sheldon, Molly, and sadly, Viola were my family. Roger too, but we mostly talked business. I loved Roger, and considered him a surrogate father.

"Be careful, Ryan. Some of these crowds can be a little overwhelming. You'll like Josh. Get some rest, and I'll see you soon." He hung up, not waiting on me to say good-bye.

Viola arrived and stayed the remainder of the shoot. She was on the phone constantly or else watching the news. When I would ask what was going on, she would say, "Nothing. Just concentrate on your acting."

I couldn't reach Molly. I assumed she was doing the media circuit, but it was making me nervous. We finally wrapped in Rome. I felt confident in my first big role. The main actress wasn't well known, but she was nice enough.

The film would have me in emotional states I hadn't known I had. If I were honest, I would admit it was due to the woman I left in Louisiana. I couldn't think about her without guilt and frustration.

I headed back to the States, not knowing what wave of crazy I was about to get slapped with. Viola handed me Valium, vodka, and a stack of tabloids on the plane. She explained the craze that surrounded this tiny movie Molly and I had shot together.

Every magazine was covered with my picture, accompanied by Molly. With a jolt, I saw the front cover of one magazine, a small player in the market of tabloids, but they had clearly hit the jackpot without even knowing it.

I sat naked on a blanket in broad daylight with a long-limbed beauty straddling me. It was a grainy photo, taken from some distance away, but you could clearly make out my face. Livia had her head tilted, and her face was half-shadowed by mine. My head whirled, and for a second I wondered if I had actually been there with her. I touched the slick cover with my finger, willing her to know I was still looking for her.

The little magazine had no idea what they had captured, but I was a hot topic and they ran with anything right now. All the other magazines were splashed with my and Molly's secret wedding. We were either arm-in-arm, as we often walked like this, or laughing, talking close to each other.

We were painted as lovers. We were not. Molly was like my sister, pure and simple. To have our innocent relationship distorted in this way made me feel ashamed. Besides, had no one noticed she was gay? Then again, she was a good actress.

We arrived at JFK airport. I was met at the terminal by a beefy man with brown hair and a deep, tropical tan. He introduced himself as Josh. By the time I had reached JFK, *Sunset* had crossed the three hundred million mark and was still climbing.

"Ryan?" Viola said sharply, turning to me in the terminal. "Stay in front of me, and stick to Josh, understand?"

For the first time I was worried.

"Okay," is all I said, knowing better than to question her.

Josh walked me through what was about to happen. The more he said, the more my stomach clenched. I was going to freak out, right there in front of everyone.

"Remember, do not stop. Keep your head down, glasses on. The flashes will blind you. Just watch my legs and feet. Do not slow down. Keep directly in pace with me. Viola will be behind you, not for security, but for damage control. Do you have a favorite song?" He looked at me seriously, as if guessing I was going to melt down.

"Um, yeah, guess so." I took the cap he held out for me—a black Yankees hat. I put it on, not caring.

"Good. Keep singing it as we walk. Not out loud, but in your head. It will help you stay calm."

I was scared now. What was going on? I looked back at Viola. She shrugged, and gave me a pitying look. Did she really feel sorry for me? If so that would be a first.

Before I could breathe, we were off and nearly running. Josh's long legs stayed in my sights. When I heard screaming, I forgot for a second, and looked up. I wanted to be flattered, but I was horrified. My ears nearly burst. Flashbulbs were going off quicker than I could blink. I lost sight of Josh, and nearly got swept away by the current of what must have been hundreds of screaming girls.

I felt Viola's hand on my back, pushing me to keep going, Josh got a handful of my jacket and pulled.

A girl was screaming, "Please take me home with you! You would love me."

I wanted to pass out. The crowd was swelling and crushing me. I couldn't breathe. I couldn't think. The screaming was deafening. I was picked up off my feet more than once. Josh pulled me so hard my jacket cut into my neck. I paid no attention to it.

I tried to start singing in my head, but then I forgot the song. After what felt like twenty minutes, we climbed into a waiting Suburban. I'd never been more thankful for anything than I was for that car. Viola was already in the front seat when Josh and I got in.

I took several deep breaths before.

"What the hell is going on?"

Viola looked back at me smiling, "Welcome to the movie business, kid. You're a star." And she winked.

We were flying down the streets at breakneck speed, Josh looking here and there, making comments. I felt stings on my neck and hands, little tiny scrapes from fingernails.

We were on Fifth Avenue before Josh spoke. "You did good, Ryan, and I think we are good at the Plaza," he said.

I frowned.

"The Plaza? I wanted to go to my apartment," I said, now looking at Viola.

She ignored me, if she heard me at all. Josh shook his head.

"No can do, padre. Maybe tonight when the crazies are worn out, but it's a bees' nest at your place."

This pissed me off. As nice as the Plaza was, I was ready to go home and veg in front of the TV, in my underwear, with food that was bad for me, and maybe make a few calls to try and locate Livia again. I wasn't going to give that one up.

"Shit," I said, disgusted.

Over the next few days, it only got worse. Paps and girls found my hotel in the city, and then someone published the address of my apartment in SoHo. Molly was staying with me by now. All we did was drink, snort coke, and pop pills.

I watched the streets, frantic and anxiety-ridden. I watched the tabloid news obsessively.

Molly and I were always the first story of the night. Though she thought it was crazy, it didn't seem to bother her like it did me. I had nightmares of being chased. Josh stayed day and night, and though it wasn't said, I had the distinct impression that some of these people would easily hurt me if they got to me. I was a prisoner for weeks.

Finally, I was escorted to my apartment in the dead of night. A few paps were camped out, and I was paranoid as hell by the time I got inside and dead-bolted the door. The next few days, I did business on the phone, and Viola was in and out of the apartment. She never commented on the amount of drugs or booze I was consuming.

I was having a nervous breakdown, and this is how I dealt with it. We never spoke about it. Someone I did ask about was Molly. She had begun shooting Heroin every day, and the tabloids were tearing her apart. A photo of Molly and a young girl kissing at a party surfaced and spread through the news like wild fire.

"Vi? Do you think Molly is okay?" I asked Viola, as she read over a memo.

Her business guard was down. Her dark hair still silky and professional, but she had taken off her shoes while she read and sipped wine from a plastic cup. Had I not been concerned for Molly, I would have found this sight amusing.

Viola didn't answer at first. Instead, she finished what she was reading, then looked at me long and hard. Finally, shrugging, she said, "Depends on what you call okay. Are you okay, Ryan?"

I sighed, annoyed with her.

"Vi, I'm serious. Molly hasn't been herself since I got back. Has something happened I don't know about?"

Viola sipped her wine, and said, more seriously this time, "I think she is having trouble with…you know." She paused, searching for words, a weird thing for Viola. "With a girl," she finished simply.

"Molly has a girlfriend?" I asked shocked.

Viola looked at me a little sadly.

"Yeah. For a while now. Maybe a year, but she's not willing to be seen with her, and it's just a strain on their relationship. Then you add to all this mess with the tabloids, and the studios having a shit fit," Then she stopped short.

"Hold on," I said, trying to wrap my head around this. "Molly has a girlfriend? Why didn't she tell me? You're saying that…" Then it was my turn to pause. Molly was definitely off lately, but I blamed the stress and the drugs. "What are you saying? And what about the studios?"

Viola began to explain that Molly had been showing up late, and sometimes not at all. Other times she was so stoned, they would have to shut down for the day. Molly had been replaced recently, because the producers felt she was not fit to work with. The media, of course, was told Molly herself backed out of the film because of other commitments.

"So, in short, no, Molly is not doing good. Roger is getting fed up with her," Viola said, as she wiggled her feet into her shoes.

I could see the businesswoman in her returning now. Catch-up was over, and now it was off to work.

"Why wouldn't she tell me? We share everything," I said, a little hurt.

Viola stood and began to gather her things. "You've got your own problems to worry about, and besides, it'll probably blow over. Roger is trying to get her into Betty Ford quietly, but so far Molly isn't willing. You can't force a person to take care of herself, you know? Molly is an adult, and rebellious, to say the least." And with that, she wished me good-night and was gone.

Josh and I did become big buddies. He stayed in the apartment with me in the evenings sometimes, by my request. I hated to spend night after night just watching the news. Josh and I began to play five-card draw. He had to teach me, but I caught on quick. He cursed when I finally began to beat him.

"Damn it," he would say in disgust.

"Where are you from Josh? Your accent, it reminds me of Nathan."

Josh smiled.

"Probably because Nathan and I grew up about two miles from each other. His baby sis was my best friend all through my childhood."

I stared at him.

"You serious?" I asked in disbelief.

"Oh yeah, I'm serious. We all grew up together, but Nathan left home rather early. Yeah, man. Piper was going to be my sister-in-law, but my brother had an accident." Josh stopped to take a deep breath. "He didn't survive. It was really hard, but Piper took it especially hard. I don't think she ever got over it, even after she married. The baby might help. She's due in a couple of months. Man, I swear I've never seen a more gorgeous pregnant woman in my life! Mercy, that girl is an angel."

I laughed. Everything with Josh was bigger than average.

"This is Tennessee? Where you're from? I thought you were from Florida?" I asked, and began to shuffle the deck.

"I lived most of my life in Tennessee. Then after my brother died, we moved." Josh shrugged. "I played some football, and gave that up after I blew out my knee. I tried the military, but my leg was shot. Figuratively speaking, I mean. A friend told me about security, and since I'm as big as a house, I tried it, liked it, and now here I am with you." He smiled at me.

"Exciting isn't it? Fighting off twelve-year-old girls?" I asked sardonically.

Josh chuckled. "I'm more worried about their mommas."

CHAPTER TWENTY

After weeks of insisting, Molly finally came to stay with me briefly, and took the back way out of my apartment building, through an alleyway, when she had to leave. She was much easier to hide. She was due to start a new film and had to be in Vancouver for the next four months. I had things to do, but didn't.

We canceled all media tours, deeming them unnecessary since the movie was flourishing on its own. We expected the craziness to pass once the DVD was out, but it didn't. If anything it got worse. I flew to Vancouver to be with Molly for her wrap up. My drug buddy and adviser always made me feel better.

She was my best friend. Sheldon wanted no part of the madness that surrounded me, and I missed him. The crowds were not as bad in Canada, but the paps were. I noticed a change in Molly while I visited. She wouldn't talk about relationships and was too stoned to talk for long.

I was concerned she had begun to shoot heroin regularly. She did this in her leg to hide the puncture marks from the cameras. I stayed with my coke and booze. I had more money, but couldn't go anywhere to use it. I could afford to buy a house but had no desire to stay at one place for long and I was actually fond of staying in hotels when I traveled.

I flew to Los Angeles to stay with Roger for a couple of days when Molly finished her filming, and to prepare for the L.A. premiere of the first *Scott's Eye*. I was also getting ready to shoot the sequel to the detective film. I played Elijah Scott, a detective, and I loved the role. The sequel took me to Florida to investigate a serial killer.

My contract for this film was the biggest I had signed to date. I felt like a star then. I had people at my beck and call. I did nothing on my own anymore. I had a runner for everything.

In Los Angeles with Roger, I had a good time. The paps followed me, and there were always fans, but it was far more tolerable than in New York. The premiere was incredible as I spent the evening with some of the famous actors and producers alive.

Josh and I were a team. He kept the crazies off of me, and I stayed glued to him, watching his feet, singing my songs with my head down. I would've gone crazy if it were not for Josh.

When I was alone, I would think of Livia. Did she see my face on magazines? Did she believe all the stories of my supposed wild ways? Did it bother her when romances were reported?

I drank her out of my head every night, but she was always there the next day when I woke. I did have the occasional fling with an extra. I remained unattached, and hated the thought of being in a relationship with anyone.

Sheldon brought his family out to stay with us for a while on the West Coast. I loved them all. Bee was great, and the girls called me Knoxy, a name Sheldon had often called me when we were kids.

They told me stories of the pretty lady, Piper, and horseback riding, and about the little girl who lived in Tennessee. It seemed Nathan had stayed home for a while, and Sheldon had been in and out of there every few months.

I was jealous he had all this family—not just Bee and the girls, but his parents in England and now the family he had joined in the mountains of Tennessee. My mother had left my father, and me for another man when I was eight.

I didn't remember much about her, but the loss of her after my sister was killed, left my father a bitter and broken man. I sent him money and called on his birthday and holidays. He was incoherent most of the time.

I looked around me. Molly, Roger, Sheldon, Josh, and even Viola were my family now. I would add Nathan to that list also. We were misfits for sure.

I finished up in Los Angeles. Roger and I headed back to New York. I had new contracts signed and money in the bank. When I arrived at my apartment, a crowd waited for me to make the mad dash from the car to the door.

Josh led the way. It was crazy to me. Honestly, the fame was flattering, and I was grateful to the fans, but shouldn't these people have jobs? Or children they are taking time away from?

Doesn't the teenagers have school? What was wrong in their minds that they spent day and night hunting me, only to get a distorted picture of me running behind my bodyguard?

Molly was in the apartment when I got there. Josh left at my request, as I dealt with the messed-up state I found her in. I picked her filthy body off the floor and put her in the tub, clothes and all. I ran the water as she babbled on and on.

"They won't leave me alone!" she screamed in my face, her eyes bulging in their sockets. "Why won't they go away, Ryan?"

Her arms were tracked with needle marks. I was in no shape to take care of her myself. I would call Roger tomorrow. He didn't even know where she was right now.

They had had a huge argument a couple of nights before, and she let it be known she wanted space. She thought the pressures of being his daughter were too much to handle. She set out to make her own money and name, yet the fact that she was Roger Mitchells only child added to an already chaotic life.

Seemed every person that came in contact with Molly asked for something. Sometimes it was to meet me, or if she could get them in the door for acting jobs.

I looked down at the filthy water filling up around small frame.

"When did you eat last?" I asked her.

She looked at me, noticing my presence for the first time.

"Hey, Ryan," she said, and began to close her eyes.

I got her undressed and re-filled the tub with soapy water. I let her soak, checking on her every few minutes to make sure she hadn't drowned. I made grilled cheese sandwiches, stepping on a needle and nearly screaming in the process.

All I had to drink was wine, so that's what I gave her once I got her dressed and in bed. Thunder and lightning were moving in the city. The sky was turning black, making the apartment dreary.

Molly didn't eat much, and naked, she looked like a skeleton. Her body was like that of a thirteen-year-old, underdeveloped boy. She was pathetic. I cleaned the needle marks as well as I could, and then left her in the bed. Best to let her sleep now.

Josh called to let me know he had to leave because of an emergency back home. I was not going anywhere for a few days so I told him to go, and that I hoped everything was all right.

I did some coke and drank the wine. Around half past three, I heard something and discovered I'd been sleeping on the couch. I got up and went to check on Molly.

She was propped up against the headboard, eyes closed. The tourniquet was tied tight, and blood poured from the needle still in her arm.

I grabbed a shirt from the floor. My head spun from the wine. I took out the needle, tossing it onto the nightstand. I pulled off the tourniquet, cursing.

"Why the fuck are you doing this?" I yelled at her.

She mumbled, eyes rolling. She reached for me to lie beside her. I made up my mind to call Roger first thing in the morning.

"Make 'em stop, Ryan," Molly said.

I lay beside her and held her to my chest.

"Make who stop, Molly?" She didn't answer, and I shook her shoulder. "Make who stop, Molly?" I asked again.

She fluttered her eyes, "The voices, the phone calls. They never stop."

I watched her pitiful, gaunt face and kissed her head.

"I'll make 'em stop, Molly, I promise."

I lay there, making sure she was breathing okay. Eventually I fell asleep. Then, after what felt like only a few minutes, I woke to something cold on my face. It was still dark. I swatted it away, and squeezed my eyes tight.

"Wakey wakey."

Something tapped me twice on my cheek.

"Molly, let me sleep. I'm exhausted." I swatted again.

Cold metal touched my temple, and then ran down the length of my face to my chin. Then fear hit me hard, for I knew what it was. I sat straight up, terrified. The bathroom light was on, and I could plainly see the gun in Molly's hand. She laughed at my reaction.

"That better be a prop." I said the first thing that came into my mind, hoping she had taken a fake gun from a movie set.

She shook her head.

"Nope," she said, in her mocking, baby voice.

I reached for it.

"Don't," she said, dead serious. The living room TV flickered colors across her face, and in that instant, I knew she was beyond my help.

"Molly. Give it to me," I said, like I would speak to an unreasonable child.

Again she laughed. She pointed the gun directly at me.

"Bang!" She teased.

I fell backward to the floor. She laughed harder. I spoke from behind the bed, keeping it between us.

"This isn't funny! Put it down before something happens!"

I glanced at her over the top of the bed. She wasn't laughing.

"I thought about taking you with me."

She was crying. At some point during my sleep, she had put on globs of mascara, and now it was running. She had dark pools under her eyes, and long black tear-streaks. She shook her head.

The pretty young star I knew as Molly was nowhere in this room. The only things here were the ugliness of the drugs, and her coked-out BFF.

"Molly." I started toward her, and she opened her eyes wide, pointing the gun at me.

"NO! I don't want to hear it, Ryan Knox! I know everything you're going to say, and I can't listen." She put her hands over her ears.

"Okay. Okay. Okay." I frantically ran through thoughts in my head. I came up with nothing. I stood up, thinking I'd just catch her off guard, and wrestle her for the gun. I held my hands up, to show I was harmless. She looked up at me and smiled.

"Love you, Ryan. You were always good to me."

I knew what was about to happen, and if I had been just a little quicker, I might have even got there in time.

I lunged at her, scrambling over the bed, as she put the gun in her mouth. Before I could reach her, brain matter and blood splattered my face. I got off the bed, but there was nothing left to do or say.

Molly's head hung forward, lying on her chest, a gaping hole in the top of her head. I dropped to my knees. I heaved, and threw up the wine I had nursed all evening. I cried and sobbed.

"Molly, why did you do this to me?"

It was a selfish question. I should have said, "Why did you leave me alone?" It was an equally selfish question, but that's what I was at that moment, like I had been when my mother left, and again when my sister died.

Alone. My body shook from the sobs leaving me. I couldn't remember ever crying this way before. After a few minutes of this, awareness took over. I ran to the window.

It was still raining, thank God. No paps. No crazy fans. I took one second to look at Molly's body, and then dashed out the door, making sure I left no bloody handprints anywhere. I ran through the alley behind the building. I ran twelve blocks, behind apartment buildings and businesses. I blessed the sun for staying down.

I ran through the city, through the cover of the dark, splashing water. I made it to Roger's office building just before the first light of dawn. I took the stairs two at a time to the twenty-second floor. I pushed the code on the keypad, and softly shut the door behind me.

I bent in half, heaving and sobbing. After I got control of myself, I walked to Roger's desk and sat in his oversized leather chair. I stayed perfectly still, my hands resting on my knees, touching nothing, controlling my breathing, waiting until he arrived, promptly at seven as he always did. I watched the sun rise over the city, as the rain cleared.

A bitterness rose in me at the realization that this was the first sunrise I had watched since lying on a deserted beach, months and months ago. It felt like another lifetime now. She had left me too. Probably never looked for me.

Everyone I knew and loved left me. I was worthless to everyone, except the studios, and to them, I was a face on the screen. I did some coke that I found still stashed in my pocket and began chain-smoking. I waited, no longer crying, but mad. There was a hole in me that would never be filled.

At seven, Roger came through the door, coffee in one hand, paper in the other. I stood a bloody, wet mess. My face was caked with dried tissue and blood. Roger took one look at me and dropped the coffee and the paper.

Walking toward me fast, he searched my face, and said in an emotionless whisper, "Molly?"

Without changing expressions, I told him about the last twenty-four hours, the binge she was on, the filthy, skinny mess she was. I held nothing back.

Roger just looked out of the window as I told him everything. When I had finished, I sat and waited for questions like, "Why did you let this happen? You know it's your fault, right?"

But Roger spoke in a hoarse, controlled voice.

"Take a shower, Ryan. You were never there. Understand?"

I began to question what he said, but then he turned his manic brown eyes on me.

"Molly destroyed her life." He hit the top of his desk with his fist, hard. "I'll be goddamned if she takes you down with her!"

I was scared of Roger then. I took in his crazed eyes and didn't even think of protesting. A hurt expression crossed his face, but only for a second, and then it was all back to business.

"Ryan, please. Allow me to handle this. I loved my daughter, but she was a grown-up. She left a mess for you and me to clean up. Please shower. I will have clean clothes waiting for you when you finish."

He pointed toward the bathroom behind us. I walked toward it, numb and dead inside.

I couldn't think of the brain tissue or bone fragments that covered my upper body. I washed as hard as I could, wishing I had ammonia to scrub the images out of my head.

When I emerged from the shower, my ruined jeans and shirt were gone. In their place were a shirt and jeans I would have likely picked out for myself. Black Nikes sat on the floor. A new razor and toothbrush were on the sink. I absently did as I was expected to do, only stopping once to throw up. When I was shiny again, on the outside at least, I walked back to Roger's office.

I found him in front of the window, looking out over the city, lost in thought. His face was unreadable. I stood beside him, looking out as well, not looking at him. He and I grieved for Molly, before the world knew of the tragedy that awaited them. Neither of us could absorb it all, and it would be a long time before we were ever normal again. Whatever normal is, as Molly would say. Would have said.

"The jet is on standby. You're going to Malibu. Wait in the house until I call. Speak to no one. Do nothing. Josh is on leave, but we should be able to avoid exposure right now," Roger said softly.

He hugged me for a long moment, Roger comforting me instead of the other way around. I couldn't stop it from coming and sobbed on his shoulder like a child.

"I couldn't stop her. She just—"

But my mind caught up with my words. No one knew how many days she had binged, how long her self-destruction had been going on. We held each other.

"I'm sorry, Ryan. I'm sorry, and glad it was you with her in the end. She loved you very much," Roger said, his voice muffled by my shoulder.

I wanted to say, then why did she leave me? Like everyone else? But I didn't. Roger turned back to the window, placing his hands in his pockets. If he shed a tear, I didn't see it. I was dismissed for now. I was to wait for further instructions.

I placed a hand on his shoulder for a moment, sorry for him, and then turned to leave him in peace to mourn the loss of his wild child. Molly would leave a hole in both of us. I was both furious and confused, but every few minutes the image of Molly's blood splattering the wall shocked me to the core.

I boarded the jet twenty minutes later. Viola sat, for once not moving. She was looking out the window and barely glanced my way when I came through the door. I sat opposite her, and stayed quiet.

After we were in the air, I slept. Restless, I fought waking more than once. When we were somewhere over the Midwest, the news broke. A maid, staged by I assumed Roger , found Molly's body in the apartment.

They had no idea where I was, but stated that I had left around ten that night, as stated by my representative, heading to my next location. I would not hear details, or be bothered by anyone for the next three days.

I had my drugs delivered to me by FedEx. I sat poolside day and night, as Viola worked out of the office of Roger's Malibu house. I slept for hours and hours, wishing I would drift away and never return. Eight days later, I returned to New York for the memorial service.

I spoke with Josh and Nathan. Sheldon stayed at my side, protective of me. I was grateful, but I also knew he was there to keep me calm. I thought I caught a glimpse of Livia in the crowd, but when I started toward her, she was lost in the sea of black.

For a split second, I forgot where I was, and all that mattered was reaching the woman who haunted my thoughts daily. When I realized I must have imagined her there, I came crashing back down to earth, and the dead.

I sat with Roger, and both of us stayed quiet as we listened to the minister talk about heaven and Jesus. He said Molly was at rest now, and we should take comfort in that. I stood, angry at Molly for doing this.

I stormed out of the church, and was greeted by a sea of cameras. I headed to my hotel, ripping buttons from my shirt, trying to get out of the suit that was suddenly strangling me. I began to drink, and I stayed drunk for days. Stoned to the max. I would not answer the phone. I would not answer the door.

Everyone knew where I was, and I only acknowledged Josh's presence after he threatened to kick the door in. I asked to be left alone. I told him to tell the others I was not suicidal, but just needed to be by myself. If I was not out of my room in a few days, they had my permission to come in and get me.

Everything in life be damned. I tossed socks and shirts over any clock I could see. I had food, drugs, booze, and cigarettes delivered to my room. I slept, and smoked the days away. I eventually emerged and took a cab to the cemetery. I drank for hours, picking at the ground, pining for my closest friend.

"Are you at peace?" I shouted at the concrete. "I'm not, you bitch!" I screamed like a crazy person. "Look what you have done! Look what you did!" I threw my half-drunk bottle of Jack, breaking it against the words, "Beloved daughter and friend."

I fell to my knees, and cried. I was picked up off my feet. I was half-carried to a car by huge arms.

"Put me down. I wish to die."

No reply.

"I said, put me down, goddamn it!"

No response.

My head wobbled on my neck.

I looked at Josh's face. He wasn't even breathing heavy from carrying me.

"Asshole," I said.

He chuckled at this, "You ain't dying today, Ryan, not on my watch."

He proceeded to the car, and tossed me like a sack of potatoes into the back seat.

I dried up, mostly, over the next few days. Roger was in contact. I assumed it was he who sent Josh to me. I was to begin filming in a few days. The crowds tapered off, but whenever I was forced out of my bed, girls and cameras continuously surrounded me.

As long as I pretended Molly was away filming, I was okay. The moment reality came back to me, I would go on a binge. This was, I later realized, the beginning of my downward spiral.

CHAPTER TWENTY-ONE

Over the next ten years, I would film sixteen movies. I would visit countless locations, win dozens of awards, sleep with hundreds of women, yet none with a face or a name I cared to remember. I would drink many gallons of vodka, Jack, and straight whiskey.

I began using heroin when the coke no longer gave me what I wanted. Yes, the very drug that swept Molly away from me. I grew to love it. The needles I so feared no longer bothered me. The pain just meant I was still breathing, even though I'd been dead inside for years.

Dozens of women called, saying they were my mother. I never answered them. My father died quietly and alone in his bed. He was as yellow as a filter from a smoked cigarette from liver damage. This had no effect on me.

I buried him and flew to Paris to film the same day. I was honored at many different awards ceremonies. Sheldon came and went from me, not understanding why I was so different or why I could not snap out of this.

Nathan knew. He had used for years, but now seemed a different man. Nathan won an Oscar for his music. He was not a rich man, but he had priceless things. He was always talking about home, and his niece. I tuned him out when he did this. The less I connected with anyone, the less it would hurt once they were gone from me, and because they would all leave me.

Neither Hollywood nor the world knew my habits. They were transfixed by my "art," not knowing the misery and the anger I had on screen was the real deal. The acting I did was my everyday life.

Viola went on to be big time. Roger gave up most of his clients, with the exception of me, Sheldon, and Nathan. We were his focus, when he had one. His once black, shiny hair grew dull and grey. The outside of him was a reflection of the inside of me.

He tried to talk to me about what I was doing, but I'd shut him down. I would stop talking to him for weeks, when he tried to talk to me. I knew this hurt him, but I had to keep him at a distance so I would not die from the pain of it all.

The year my chronic lifestyle finally came to a screeching and sudden stop, I took some time off. It wasn't a long time. Just a couple of months, but I was talked into it by Sheldon and Nathan, who promised a big concert Halloween night.

"Drinking, girls, the clean air of the mountains. It'll be a blast," Sheldon promised me.

I was going in October to Nathan's family home in the sticks of Tennessee. Maybe it was curiosity that got the best of me, to finally see the place I'd heard so much about. Either way I was going. Before I left New York, I arranged for my FedEx deliveries to Nathan's country home. I followed Josh through the airport, and headed to Cosby, Tennessee.

CHAPTER TWENTY-TWO

Piper ~

I was a bundle of nerves. I didn't know what I had been thinking, going off with a stranger in the middle of the night to a deserted beach, and then skinny-dipping with him! And not to mention the sex. Oh, man, the sex!

I nearly ran back to Lana's apartment. Would she be able to tell anything was different? Would Jean-Paul? Lord, help me, Jesus, I would be a dead woman. He didn't even know I was here, and hopefully never would. If Papaw had not absolutely insisted on me taking a Greyhound bus down here, I'd be at home, and would have never met Ryan.

Ryan Knox. The name would be a permanent tattoo in my head. I came by bus and would ride back home with Nathan on Monday. Jean-Paul would be none the wiser. I wasn't sure what Papaw's motive was behind wanting me out of the house, but I jumped at the chance to get away.

I was in a miserable situation with my marriage. I hid as much as I could from Papaw, but he was smart and knew me well enough to know I was not blissfully in love with my husband. I would have settled for just liking him.

We waited for our honeymoon until after Nana died. We got a chateau in Gatlinburg, high on the mountainside. It was nice. I accepted I would never love anyone as I had loved Matthew, but I would try to be a good wife.

Jean-Paul was different in many ways. He was not a warm person. He was polite, like he knew all the right things to say, but there was no emotion behind his words or actions. He was strong, and I had my arm squeezed till it was black if I mouthed off to him, or gritted teeth in my face if I did not agree with something he said. The extent of what he could do was hid from me until the honeymoon.

Away from Papaw's protection, Jean-Paul revealed the beast that slept within. After making love on that first night, I prepared sandwiches for us to share in front of the fire. I had stupidly forgotten Jean-Paul hated mayo. After the first bite, he spit the food at me, disgusted.

"What kind of a wife are you, if you can't even remember what your husband eats?" he screamed at me.

I reached to quickly take the sandwich away, but I made my second mistake.

"I understand, but you don't have to get nasty about it. Here, I'll make another."

Jean-Paul's big hand slapped me hard across my mouth. I lost my balance and fell to the floor.

"Are you crazy?" I shouted back at him.

I should have shut up, but I just had to say it. I wore no clothes and had been wrapped in my blanket. Jean-Paul picked me up by the hair, and slammed me on my belly in front of the fireplace. I was pinned, with his foot in the middle of my back. I kicked and tried to get free, but his weight was crushing me into the tile floor.

"I'm sorry, okay?" I said just to get up at least.

Jean-Paul moved his foot closer to my neck, holding me in place, paralyzed.

"You're going to learn to shut that smart mouth of yours. Didn't your dead daddy ever teach you respect?" he screamed at me.

I tried not to beg, but my pride left me as self-preservation kicked in. I knew he was going to snap my neck, if he pushed any harder into me. I saw from the corner of my eyes a white-hot poker, fresh from the fire.

I screamed, but as soon as it touched my flesh, all sound ceased from the shock and pain of it. Jean-Paul laid the poker down my left shoulder blade. It was a sensation I'd never felt before and a pain I thought I would die from. The breath came back to me, and I sucked in raggedly.

"Stop, please!" I screamed.

I heard the poker being tossed back in the fire. Jean-Paul grabbed my hair, and pulled my head back so he could hiss directly in my face.

"Best you learn now, bitch, I will not tolerate disrespect. That's just a taste. Next time it will be your face. If that doesn't work, I'll gladly remove your tongue." And he let go, only to kick me between the legs.

He left, slamming the door behind him. I lay where he had tossed me, for a long time in shock. The words that Daniel said to me came back so clearly.

"You will never be loved. Who would love you?"

I wept, only allowing myself a moment for that release.

Nana's care of me the last few years gave me some strength to carry on. When I got myself to a mirror, I was horrified at my disfigurement. The burn was deep and jagged. I thought of the searing I'd seen done to cattle and horses, before owners had switched to tags. I was now branded like an animal.

I should have gotten out of there. I should have run, but in that moment, I only thought, well, at least no one would see it. I cleaned it the best I could.

I put on a T-shirt and lounge pants, and cleaned up the mess. I placed the poker back in its holder. I made fresh sandwiches and waited on the couch, numb all over.

I began to go over everything in my mind, never knowing I was sick there. I thought of our family land, and the house. Jean-Paul was the only way I would be able to keep it up and afford it. I had to make sure Papaw was taken care of.

I could bear this cross. It wasn't so bad. I would just make sure I was good, and knew exactly how to make the sandwiches Jean-Paul expected me to, and most importantly, watch my mouth. I was dirty and ruined. Jean-Paul was the best I was going to get.

The only love I ever would have was cold and dead in the ground. This was what I deserved. When he returned after midnight, drunk, I was still in the same spot on the couch. I stood and began apologizing immediately, promising to be better and kinder. Jean-Paul kissed me. And I willed myself not to recoil. "Don't make me hurt you. I don't want to hurt you, Piper." I promised again to be a good wife. I tried being what he wanted as a wife.

Later, I only "made him" hurt me a few times if you don't count the hair pulling and shoves. I had become a master at hiding things. Papaw tolerated Jean-Paul, but he wasn't crazy about him. When he found a bruise I'd failed to cover up on my collarbone, Papaw was furious. I tried to convince him it was not from Jean-Paul.

"Papaw, I'm serious. I ran into a branch. That's all, I swear." I lied easily. He narrowed his aging eyes at me.

"I'll be goddamned and cold in my grave before I let some son of bitch Cajun put his hands on you, Piper. I'll kill him. Where's my shotgun?" Cane and all, he began marching from the kitchen.

It took me twenty minutes to convince him it was not Jean-Paul. We didn't speak of it again, but Papaw was up to something. I found him in deep conversations on the phone. Then a few days after Jean-Paul left for work, Papaw came to me and demanded I board a bus the next morning.

"Why?" I asked. "What's going on with you?"

Papaw sat at the table sipping his morning coffee.

"Nothing," he shrugged. "You need to see your friends. Get out of the house. If Jean-Paul calls, I will cover for you," he said winking.

"I can't leave you alone, Papaw. Who will look after you? Who will help with your medicine? Feed you?"

He shook his head.

"I'm not senile yet. It's only for a few days. Go see your brother. I'll not take no for an answer."

The battle was lost. I would do as he wished, not only because he wished it, but also because I was dying to get away from Jean-Paul controlling what I wore, what I said, what I ate. A few days of freedom sounded like heaven to me.

Then Papaw told me in passing, "Roger is coming to visit, so I won't be alone, and there's no need to check on me. Go. Have a good time. Be young," he said sternly. Then smiling, he added, "There ain't nothing going to happen that me and the Lord can't handle."

In spite of my mixed emotions about leaving him, I was excited to see someplace different. I hugged him twice and kissed his rough whiskered face. I rode the Greyhound bus through east Tennessee, across the state of Alabama, and finally reached New Orleans twelve and a half hours later.

Nathan picked me up and took me to dinner. He looked bad, but was in high spirits. I would stay with him and Lana in her apartment. Getting to see my brother and best friend felt like someone had lifted a huge weight off of me.

I was enjoying my stay and dreaded going back home. My only complaint was the constant partying. It just wasn't for me, and I longed to see the beach before I went home. Last night, the sudden urge to see the sunrise led to a day full of passion and great sex with a stranger. I guess I'd done exactly as Jean-Paul thought I would if I were out of his sight. I didn't regret it in the least.

Right now my head was buzzing from Ryan's cologne. I knew in the darkness, walking back to Lana's apartment, I was blushing and grinning like an idiot, thinking of his touch on me. His lips on mine, on my neck, all over me. I never knew making love could be this great. Matthew was kind and gentle. I loved him still, but we were kids, inexperienced at love-making.

The last near twenty-four hours with Ryan was almost animal-like behavior, and the word "ravish," took on a whole new meaning. I laughed out loud as I began to climb the steps. I would do it again tonight, and then I would have to explain that I was actually Piper, and that I was married and only after the sex. My face split into a wide grin. I was totally unashamed of myself. This would be my secret.

I began to worry a little. Would anyone notice a difference in my appearance? If Lana did, no big deal, but if Jean-Paul did then I was dead. Literally dead. Then who would take care of Papaw?

As he had warned me hundreds of times, Jean-Paul would cut my face off or burn me beyond recognition. The image left me cold inside. Yes, I had done a very bad thing the last twenty-four hours. I spent it making love to a gorgeous man on a beach, but damn it, I was alive inside for the first time in forever.

And I made plans to do it again that evening! I was on fire inside. I had lived two years with a man who criticized my every move. Who had burned me with a poker on our honeymoon. I was slapped in the mouth for having a different opinion, shoved and punched for not responding quickly enough.

I crept up the stairs to the apartment, wondering why I had given Ryan my first name, and not my real name. I guess I'd wanted to be someone different, if only for a day. I hadn't planned on anything happening with him, but he said the very thing I needed to hear, nearly identical to words Nana would say, and I couldn't resist. Plus, he was gorgeous.

I got to the landing of the apartment, and noticed the door was cracked open a couple of inches. I thought, *odd*, for a split second, and walked in, unprepared for what was inside. My brother was laying half in the hallway and half in the living room, as if he had crawled there.

I walked into the dimly lit room and said, in a teasing voice I often used with him, "Nathan, what are you doing on the floor?" Then I noticed he was naked, and covered in blood.

I screamed, loud and long.

I began to shake him, screaming.

"Nathan!"

I put my face to his nose and mouth. Soft, hot breath hit me.

"Thank you, God! Hold on, Nathan." I ran to the kitchen and jammed a bloody finger on 9-1-1. I have no idea what the operator said. I gave the operator the address and apartment number.

"Please hurry!"

Slamming the phone down, I turned down the hall, screaming for Lana, never considering someone was in the apartment still.

"Lana!"

No answer.

I flipped the light on in her bedroom. Things were scattered everywhere, and blood covered the bed, but no Lana. I ran from room to room, checking on Nathan in between.

I ran back to the bedroom and took in the room again, as I heard the ambulance approaching in the distance. I looked over the bed carefully. Willing myself to think, I followed with my eyes the trail of blood. I walked around the bed where there was a small gap between it and the wall.

She was there on the floor. Her eyes stared wide. She, like Nathan, was naked. Blood covered her entire body. One of her hands was on her neck. I knew as I fell to the floor on my knees, she was dead.

Under the hand holding her neck was a gaping hole. The congealed blood around it told me she'd been there a while. I shut her eyes, and brushed her jet-black hair from her beautiful face.

An officer had to carry me screaming from the room. My best friend had lain there alone and died. I hoped she'd said a prayer. I hoped Jesus came and took her.

Lana, who was so understanding of my screwed up life, in many ways saved me from myself. Never judging, never failing me. Always there to cheer me on regardless of her circumstances. She was dead. Dead like my baby. Dead like Nana. Was I as good a friend to her? How could I be? I left her, and while I was on a beach with a man, she was here dying.

Did she call for me, and I didn't answer? The thought tore at my insides like claws. I heaved and sobbed until I was throwing up. Eventually I was sedated.

I fought the paramedics and the police. I had to be restrained. Absently I noticed Sheldon was there. He tried to calm me. He promised he would follow in Nathan's car. I clawed at my face and pulled my hair until the drugs took over. I was a zombie when a doctor talked to me about my brother's condition.

Sheldon was there, helping me, holding me up. Beatrice arrived not long after.

I was told that Lana and Nathan were most likely part of a drug deal gone bad. Nathan was lucky to be alive, they said. I called Papaw, and argued with him for at least half an hour about his traveling to the hospital.

Only after agreeing that Nathan was out of danger, and that I would drive us home as soon as he was released, did Papaw agree not to come. Papaw then told me he would tell Jean-Paul when he called that I left to go to Nathan, but he would lead him to believe it was after Nathan was shot. I didn't disagree.

"Piper, honey, I'm sorry about Lana. She was a sweet girl, in spite of where she came from. She don't have to worry about nothing no more," Papaw said in his all-knowing voice.

Tears fell from me, and made puddles on my shirt. He was right, but I couldn't think of that now. I slept in a chair while Nathan recovered. Lana was cremated. I disagreed with Nathan's choice at first, but had to agree Lana would never want to be seen displayed in a casket.

I cleaned her apartment and gave most of her clothes and personal things to a women's shelter. I kept a blanket Nana had given her years ago. It only had small spots of blood on it, and I could get those out. I wouldn't wash it now though. Lana's perfume was still on it. Yet, like Matthew's jacket that I still kept in my old bedroom closet, time would carry away the scent of the person I loved. Lana's scent would vanish as well, in time. For now at least, I had her with me.

Jean-Paul arrived in Louisiana. He was his usual presentable self. Nathan called him Pompous, but never criticized my choice to marry him. Nathan, of course, was oblivious to what Jean-Paul really was to me.

When Nathan was safe to move, we made our way home. He only remembered being shot. His last memory of that night was laying down with Lana, then the gunshot, then pain. He had no idea who did it.

I brought Lana's ashes home with me. When Jean-Paul left again for work, I climbed to the cliff where we would always go and sun ourselves, or skinny-dip. I dropped her ashes into the water below, making her a permanent resident of a place I loved.

Lana had no relatives I knew of. Her grandmother was in a nursing home, long since lost to Alzheimer's, or maybe she was dead now. Lana never knew her father's family. The baby I had delivered years ago never knew her.

I grieved, as did Nathan. We stayed quiet most days, as he sobered up from years of drug use and healed from the gunshot wound. He and Papaw would sit and have deep discussions about God and life. I would listen, mostly knowing the answers already from years of Papaw's guidance.

"I'll tell you, and I ain't ashamed of it, but it nearly killed me to bury your daddy," Papaw said to Nathan. "I believe with all my heart God has blessed us with one another. When it's said and done, I hope I've done some good in my life. I hope I've loved you kids enough."

He looked from Nathan to me with tired eyes.

"More than enough Papaw," I said, and hugged him. "You're the greatest."

Papaw used a red bandana he kept in his back pocket to dry his eyes.

"Nathan, I'm mighty pissed off about your condition. God gives you life, and this..."

He gestured to Nathan's bruised and scabbed arms. They were much better, but still the damage was visible.

"This is what you do with it? This is how you repay Him for your God-given talent? Nathan, please don't do this no more," Papaw said, in a small helpless voice I'd never heard before.

I looked at Nathan and was surprised to see he was crying now. Papaw squeezed my hand and let it go. He took Nathan in his arms, like he was holding a child. Nathan wept for the pain he caused us all, the loss of Lana, the years he spent doping and drinking that he couldn't get back. He reached out for me, and we three wept together.

I fought the coldness in my heart. I wanted to believe all was okay, but dread and despair consumed me. I went into a state of oblivion in my mind. I felt nothing. I heard nothing. I just walked aimlessly around.

I did what I had to and nothing more. I often thought of Ryan, and whether he was looking for me. I decided he wasn't. It was inconceivable that a man would want me around for anything other than to be used. I felt different with Ryan though, I felt wanted, desired. I would shake those thoughts off, knowing they were just my imagination.

While Nathan recovered from his wounds, he recovered in his mind. Losing Lana, probably the only girl he ever loved, took its toll on him.

He sobered up. Nathan was determined to be healthy. It wasn't long until he was ready to go back to Nashville.

"For nothing else but to finish what I started," he said.

Nathan had started a soundtrack for a movie. The movie people told him they would wait for him to recover, since they were delayed in filming anyway, and should still make their timeline.

My life with Jean-Paul did not change. He refrained from hitting me, while Nathan was there at least, and when I hugged my brother, who was now twenty pounds heavier than he had been, I thought to myself that at least I had a little peace, if only for a little while.

Papaw's mind was beginning to slip. I helped him the best I could, when he let me. We danced some nights after dinner, the way we did when Nana was still here. I know he longed to be with her again. Papaw never again saw the abuse I endured. Jean-Paul was very good at placing the blows on my body, and not my face or arms.

Then, when Papaw moved to the small room off the grand room, giving us his and Nana's room, he was too far away to hear the goings-on in the bedroom, where I got most of the beatings, and if I made any noise, I would be beaten worse.

There were many times Jean-Paul would threaten to kill Papaw or Nathan, if I did not shut up or do as I was told. Sex with Jean-Paul was torture. When he was home from work, he insisted I take part in things I didn't think anyone normal would do.

He loved to choke me to the point of me passing out. Other times he would say horrible things in my ear, causing me to gag. He had a strange fixation with holding a knife to my throat while on top of me. It was horrible, and I did everything I could not to show just how sick he made me.

I secretly began to plan my escape, but how? I'd been assured of my death or my brother's if I did anything wrong. Also, Jean-Paul was the financial thread that held my family together. When Nana died, her insurance would not pay once they found out she refused treatment. I was a midwife, but babies did not come every day. What money I made I tried to save.

We closed Papaw's veterinary office when he began forgetting things. Time, little by little, was taking him from me. With each passing day, he stayed on the porch a little longer, watching the sunset.

Nana often told me her favorite time with Papaw was watching the sun rise or set from their bed. They would talk of things new, and things from years past. He was comfortable and peaceful. His body was not betraying him like Nana's did, but his mind was unconcerned about the present.

I found Papaw sleeping late one morning. I thought he was just tired, but when I returned to him an hour later, he was gone. Lying there, still sleeping, he had slipped away, gone from me to be with Nana. A part of me accepted that after Nana went, he no longer wanted to be here.

Selfishly, I would have kept him with me forever. I went to the funeral home to cut his hair and shave his face. I traced my fingers along his eyebrows, never wanting to forget how animated he could be. I imagined this would be how my dad would look at this age.

Bitterness tried to enter my heart at the thought of not having my dad with me. I couldn't keep the feeling; Papaw would hate me for it. Now father and son were together, and I hoped by the grace of God, I could be forgiven and join them someday.

We buried Papaw beside Nana. That was the lowest I'd been in a while. I'd resisted drugs, trying to remain clean, as I had been since Nana's death, but I began cutting again.

When Jean-Paul saw the marks, he beat me and said I was evil and going to hell. He said I must have a demon in me. I believed this to be true. I was always fighting it, but the demon always won.

I was alone in the house after burying Papaw. Nathan had gone again after the funeral. I lay in the birthing tub, feeling sorry for myself, adding up all I had lost. I thought of Ryan, and wondered if he thought of me as well. He also was lost to me. I had Papaw's straight razor I used to shave him with. He preferred this to a more modern disposable.

I'm not sure what led me to this moment, but as I added up my losses and thought of the stacks and stacks of unhappy things, I began to cut my arm, knowing I'd pay for it later. Jean-Paul would most likely kill me this time.

Instead of the nicks I carved in my flesh for relief, this time I took the straight razor, and slit at least a ten-inch opening in my forearm. The blood gushed from the wound, quickly turning the water bright red.

I thought, "Well, that was easy," as I watched the flow.

I was accepting of my decision. I hated to leave Nathan, but he had a life and would go on. I wished I could see Ryan again. Nana always said I'd know love when I saw it, and I swear it was one day on a beach, and I saw it. I mourned the life I would never have with him. I was to the point of giving over to death, when someone burst through the kitchen door.

"Piper!"

I jumped up, wrapping my arm in a shirt, and throwing on a robe, all in quick succession.

"I'm here," I called back, running through the birthing room, and nearly colliding with a frantic Elisabeth Hatchet.

She was breathing fast and holding her swollen belly.

"It's coming!" she screamed.

I helped her to the table and barely got her on it.

"He's coming! He's coming!" she said again.

Two pushes and he was here, Elisabeth's fourth child with her high-school sweetheart, Cooper. I cleaned him up and gave him to her.

"Matthew." She breathed the name.

I sucked in a breath when I heard it. Elisabeth looked at me, smiling. I returned the smile through tears. I stood in a robe, touching my forearm. Was it a coincidence my death was interrupted by Matthew? No. It was exactly something he would do. He saw me, and sent an angel my way, as if to say, "Something better awaits you. Just hold on."

I cried myself to sleep after sewing up my arm that night.

The next day, I explained to Jean-Paul that I fell as Elisabeth was calling to me, causing the cut. He didn't question me. I had become an Oscar-worthy actress. It would be another three weeks before I thought of my missing periods.

Sure enough, Jean-Paul and I would be celebrating our miracle baby, who we thought would never come. Daniel had not won. He had not destroyed all of me. I inwardly said, "Take that, you bastard."

CHAPTER TWENTY-THREE

Jean-Paul was kind to me during my pregnancy, returning to his gentlemanly ways. I actually thought a baby might help us. He brought a middle-aged woman, Maria, home to help with the housework when I reached my sixth month, afraid I would harm the baby if I did too much. I was grateful, but a little perturbed that the woman only understood Spanish and did not speak at all.

Maria went about her cleaning and lived in the room Papaw had slept in before he died. Late winter we welcomed our baby girl into the world. Jean-Paul allowed me to name her Ellie Grace, Grace after Nana.

Maria was a huge help to me. I had to have the baby in a hospital. I was considered high risk, and at one point, Ellie tried to come too early. I was scheduled for a C-section, and ended up having a full hysterectomy. My uterus had given me all it could and had to go. Daniel had done more damage than anyone knew.

Maria and I bonded quickly over the baby. She was learning to understand English, but still would not speak. I wondered at times if she couldn't speak, or whether she could and just refused to.

Nathan came and went, healthy and happy. He won an Oscar. He also carried tremendous debt, but he refused to file for bankruptcy. He worked tirelessly to try and make up for his drug-riddled past. It pleased me that Roger was trying to help him. As for me, I knew I was being abused, but I had no idea what that actually meant until Ellie was four.

Being hit or slapped I healed from rather quickly for the most part. I knew to stand perfectly still, and to be attentive to every word Jean-Paul threw at me. When the Scotch took effect after an hour, I dared to nod, and say, "I'm sorry. I'll do better from now on," keeping my eyes averted.

It went from the receipt order to how much I spent on laundry detergent. After being told what an overspending, stupid cow I was, I was then instructed to perform oral sex. It repulsed me. I got on my knees, as he began to unzip his trousers. I began thinking of other thoughts to keep me sane.

Had I acted like I didn't want to or showed any sign of displeasure I would have suffered physically. So I did as he wished. He pulled at my hair and bloodied my lips, but I stayed on my knees as he instructed.

As I later watched Ellie sleeping, I thought I would kill the man that ever tried to force her into anything like I had been forced into. I would kill him and not blink an eye.

It dawned on me for the first time ever that the sexual abuse was minor in comparison to the names I was subjected to, or the constant put-downs. I realized at that moment, touching the splits on the inside of my lips, that I was sick of feeling bad. I was in a dark place in life, for not only Ellie but for myself. I would crawl out, and then I would run like hell. I had to, or die this way.

I began trying to find my way out. I had to be stealthy about it, or I would end up dead, and that would leave Ellie with Jean-Paul, an idea I could not stand.

Sheldon came at least three times a year with his family. Ellie had playmates, and I had adult conversations. This did not sit well with Jean-Paul, who was becoming more aggressive each time he was home. I was a great actress, but it now seemed just my existence annoyed him.

I had a healing broken wrist when Roger next came to visit. He stayed in my old room, now the guest room. On the night before his departure, I cooked a huge dinner. Roger had been walking the horses around with Ellie. She was growing at a rapid pace. The marks on the wall were measuring her taller than I was at seven.

When they came in the door, Ellie was telling Roger stories she was learning in school. Roger winked at me and sat at the table as if there were nothing better in the world than listening to Ellie.

"You know, Ellie, you might grow up to be a producer. Make your own movies! Or be an actress, because you are so pretty with those great big blue eyes. If I didn't know better, I'd think you were kin to my friend, Ryan Knox," and Ellie laughed at the thought.

I laughed too, for just a second as this sunk in. I kept up with the tabloid news on Ryan when I was allowed to, as Jean-Paul disapproved of it. I couldn't allow my thoughts to wonder about Ryan too much, because it made me so sad, and I had a little girl who depended on me.

I was at the sink, drying a plate and lost in thought. Once the idea of what Roger was saying had firmly set in, I dropped the plate, staring at Roger in horror. I was trying to do the math in my head. I couldn't keep up.

"What? What is it?" he asked, frantically running to me.

I bent over double and dry-heaved, trying to keep my dinner down. Maria helped Roger get me to the couch. Ellie was saying, "Mommy! Mommy! Mommy!" Truly scared.

"It's okay, baby," I told her, but it was anything but okay. It was unbelievable.

I looked at Ellie, placing my hands on either side of her face, and there he was.

Ryan, the same eyes, the same mouth. She was Ryan in miniature female form. How had I not seen this? How would I not know? With burying my best friend, nursing my brother back to life, Papaw dying, and getting my hair ripped out every other night by my husband, and then trying to die…Matthew.

Matthew saved me from killing myself and my baby. Matthew, always saying that there was something better, and to just hold on. Matthew.

I laughed then, like a crazy person. I laughed till I cried. And cried and cried. The realization and irony of this was just too much. Maria took Ellie to bed, and I calmed down.

Roger placed his hand over mine.

"Can you tell me what it is?"

I wanted to so bad but was afraid.

I shook my head. We sat in silence, sipping wine until it was time for bed. I left him at the stairs. I lay in bed still in shock.

When I was still awake at two in the morning, I made my way to my old room where Roger was staying. I knocked softly, and he answered.

"Come in."

He was on the phone. I waited until he finished and set the cell phone aside.

"Sorry. I operate on West Coast time."

I nodded and shut the door. Roger had a bottle of Johnnie Walker on the dresser, a half-full glass beside it. I walked to it, and swallowed it down.

"I need to tell you something, but what I need to tell you could cost me my life, and maybe Ellie's as well. It's not that I don't trust you, because I do." I eyed him nervously. "Distract me. Tell me some of your secrets until I can get calmed down.

Roger thought for a moment, and then began to tell me about his daughter's death. We never spoke of Molly. I knew of the suicide, as did everyone else, but Roger never wished to speak of her, so I left him to whatever feelings he had about the tragedy.

He told me of the planning it took to remove the man from the picture. He never mentioned a name, but I had a feeling I could narrow that list down to one. Ryan.

When he'd finished, I could appreciate his confidence in me. I dreaded involving him in my secrets, but I was ready to tell now. I went to my old window and then onto the roof outside.

Roger followed, and I began to tell him everything. From Daniel to Jean-Paul to Matthew to Ryan to Ellie. I left nothing out. I talked about the daily abuse I received, cringing at the thought of being labeled a victim. To say he was shocked at my admission would be an understatement.

We watched the sunrise, and in the morning hours, we had a plan. It would take some work, but we were co-conspirators now. We had to get Ellie and myself out of the dangerous situation we were in.

Now, to act on what I thought I already knew. We had to have a DNA test done to prove what I was already sure of. Nothing would be said to Ryan until the truth was confirmed. Roger knew if this got out, I and my daughter would be dead, and we would never be found. Jean-Paul promised me that all the time.

I acted as I always did, like I was an actress in my own movie. Roger said the test would take several weeks, so I waited impatiently. I was already sure of the results but needed the confirmation.

Ellie turned eight and got a new saddle from Roger. Finally, in May, Roger called with one word.

"Positive," is all he said.

I was not at all surprised, and I grew more and more in love with Ryan through the daughter we shared. I began to look forward. If something did happen to me, then Ellie would go to Ryan, and Roger would make certain that happened.

I began to notice Jean-Paul watching me, closer than normal. When I was on the phone after he left for work, Maria came to me looking frightened. She was twisting her hands and looking around. I touched her hands to stop her. Maria pointed to the phone, then to her ear.

"You need me to call someone?" I asked, never knowing her to call a soul.

Jean-Paul said all of her family was in Mexico, and could not be reached. Maria shook her head, and then pointed to the phone again, but this time she took both hands and extended pinky and thumb like a phone, and placed both hands to each of her ears.

"Someone is listening," I said, my stomach turning. "For how long? Since when?"

Maria shook her head and shrugged. Dread filled me. Had we spoken of Ellie? Just the previous week, Roger and I agreed a private investigator should follow Jean-Paul when he left to drive his truck. Roger felt like we needed to know his habits, and find out if he was doing anything illegal.

Roger said he would be coming with Sheldon on July fourth. He also wanted to know Jean-Paul's schedule. I told him he would be gone that week. We said good-bye until the fourth. Now as I saw the fear in Maria's face, I wondered if we were in danger at this moment.

"Watch Ellie. I'll be back in just a minute, okay?"

I didn't wait for her to answer. I left and drove Papaw's old truck as fast as it would go to the grocery store. I jumped out at the pay phone and pushed a half dozen quarters into it.

I was in near panic when Roger picked up.

"He's listening to my phone conversations at home. Maria just told me."

I looked around me, paranoid I was being watched.

"What?" Roger asked in disbelief. "Why would he do that?"

I took a deep breath and tried to think.

"He likes to know what I'm thinking all the time. He doesn't trust me with anything." That was a fact. "He doesn't want me going to church if he isn't with me, because of my talking to other men, and having my own thoughts without him guiding them."

I was rambling now but couldn't stop. I was in full-blown hysterics now.

"Roger, what if he knows. Have we said Ryan's name? Oh my God, Roger!" I was breathing hard now, thinking. What nagged at me? It wasn't just this. There was something else that bothered me.

And there it was. The pieces of a jagged puzzle slid into place.

"He killed him," I said, not listening to what Roger was saying. "He killed him!" I said, louder now.

"What? Killed who? Piper, what are you saying?"

I placed my hand over my mouth, and tears blurred my vision.

The scene of Matthew's body, with no helmet in sight when I knew he always wore his helmet, because Matthew was the most responsible person I knew, and did what was expected of him.

"Roger, a couple of years ago I found Matthew's helmet in our garage. It was hid back behind some decorations. When I asked Jean-Paul about it, he said he found it while he was hunting and couldn't remember where."

I paused, sickened by my own stupidity.

"Roger, Matthew had a horrible head injury, an injury that would have left a mark on the helmet he never went without. When we got him from the wreck site, his helmet was missing, and I searched for it myself, along with his family."

I closed my eyes remembering.

"Matthew's helmet, when I found it in the garage, was spotless. No marks. Jean-Paul killed him because we loved each other, and had made plans to get married after college. At my party, I remember Jean-Paul was there, and he seemed agitated and weird to me. And I had seen someone in my woods."

Roger listened as I let all this stuff out I'd been holding inside.

"Piper, there's something I need to tell you, but quickly. The investigator I hired to track him? He was found dead on the side of the highway. He had to be identified by dental records. He was burned beyond recognition," Roger said in a rush.

I nodded numbly.

"He likes burns," I said in a hoarse whisper, and as if mine was fresh, it stung to remind me how much he liked them.

"Get Ellie, and get to the airport. I will have two tickets waiting for you there. Pack nothing. Tell no one. Understand?"

I agreed and hung up. I sped home.

CHAPTER TWENTY-FOUR

On my way home, I passed Ellie happily waving at me from the back seat of her school friend's car. I skidded to a stop.

"Damn it! I forgot I told her she could go today!" I yelled at my steering wheel.

The girls had wanted to go for ice cream. If they were not back in thirty minutes, I would go get her. First, I had to do something about Maria. How could I have forgotten about her? Roger said two tickets, so he forgot her too.

I would go home and talk to her. I would give her some cash I had saved and tell her to drive to Knoxville and get lost in the Pigeon Forge tourist motels. I found her in the grand room, sitting stiffly in one of the high-backed chairs. She was white with fear. When she saw me, she shook her head frantically. Dread filled me.

"Is Jean-Paul here?" I asked almost in a whisper.

Maria was looking out the window behind me. She took my hand in her cold one and shook her head again. Her eyes went wide trying to convey something I was not getting. Then it dawned on me.

"He's in the woods?"

Maria nodded. I began to pull away, but Maria squeezed my hand tight. I gave her my attention, though my mind was racing.

"Yes?"

Maria pointed to her mouth. I didn't understand.

"Maria, what is it?"

She continued to point, and then slowly, she opened her mouth.

All these years, I assumed Maria didn't speak because of the language barrier, but now, as I looked in horror into her mouth, I got it. Where her tongue should be was a small nub. It was obviously not removed with precision or care. Though healed long ago, it was ragged. Tears came to Maria's eyes as I began to rub her arm.

"Will you tell me?"

She shook her head, scared.

"Would you tell Roger? He can help you."

She shook her head even harder, grey hair shaking.

"Jean-Paul?"

She didn't answer, but I was positive that if Jean-Paul did not do this to her, he knew who did. One thing was sure, Maria was afraid of Jean-Paul in the worst way. I made a promise that she would be okay. I turned to go.

"Come on, let's go" I was saying to Maria, when I saw him standing in the doorway.

His boots were mud-covered, and he was layered in dirt and sweat. He gave me a disgusted look, as if I'd spit on him. I put my hand on my stomach, willing it to be still.

"Jean-Paul, I wasn't expecting you," I said, hearing my voice shake.

He was big and mean. Jean-Paul placed his narrowed eyes on me, then Maria, but said nothing. I was crossing over into territory that would surely bring about my death, but at the moment I didn't care. In the years I had been married to this bully, I thought this was the best chance I'd ever get.

Daniel had ruined me so thoroughly, I knew I'd never be worth anything ever. So when Jean-Paul hit me, I took it, thinking it could always be worse, knowing I'd lived in a dog collar.

I had finally seen how much worse it could be. I did something I didn't know I was capable of. I launched myself at him. All the anger I had bottled up poured out of me. I wanted to kill him. I wanted to watch him bleed. I hit, clawed, and bit my way through his blows.

He threw me toward the kitchen, and I landed flat on my back. The breath was knocked out of me. I didn't have a second to lose, as I tried to run. I wasn't running to get away this time. Oh no, I was going to get a weapon.

A knife or my shotgun. He pushed me down, and Maria jumped on him. In a split second, Jean-Paul had her by the throat, strangling the life out of her. He threw her, and her breaking neck echoed though the room.

I fought harder, but each time I hit at him, he punched me with his closed fist, blurring my vision. I collapsed on the floor defeated and near passing out. He grabbed a handful of my hair. I felt strands separate from my scalp.

"No!" I screamed, as I elbowed and kicked at him.

Jean-Paul had my head held back, as if to slit my throat.

"You stupid bitch," and he punched me in the kidney.

The pain took my breath away. He was forcing me to the steps. I fought like a wild animal, reaching back to pull his hair or claw his face. We got to the stairs, and he pushed my face into them. He began ripping my clothes, taking time in between to punch my ribs or my face.

One of the blows landed on my temple, and I momentarily saw black spots. I could do nothing to stop him. I kicked and screamed, but he sodomized me with little effort.

"How's that feel?" he was saying, nearly laughing now, pushing further inside me. "Think you're going to fight me, but look at you now, bitch. You ain't so tough now, are you?"

I couldn't breathe. The shock and pain of it was carrying me away. He had forced me before, but never this kind of evil. He pumped into me, and I begged him to stop.

I just screamed and screamed. My insides were being torn apart. I went away in my mind, as I did with Daniel. I couldn't stay in this place. It was too much. My face and neck were being crushed to the steps. I knew in a minute I would be dead.

Jean-Paul pulled at my breasts ripping my flesh. I was floating away. I didn't want to come back. Roger would make sure Ryan got Ellie. Sheldon and his family would help raise her. I could no longer take this life. It was too much.

I heard a blast, but it sounded like it was somewhere far away. When I felt Jean-Paul's body lift off of mine, I stayed still, anticipating my death. I turned to look and I saw my daughter holding a smoking shotgun.

"Ellie!" I was stunned and crumpled on the floor.

I reached for her, and she came to me. She was crying. I looked down, only seeing out of my left eye. Jean-Paul was spread-eagled, dick hanging out, bleeding from different places on his face, chest, and arms.

He was not dead. He was blasted with buckshot from Papaw's old gun, buckshot we used to scare away a wandering bear or hog. Not to kill, but to sting.

I got Ellie's hand and ran to my room. I was on the brink of passing out. It felt like there was great damage done to my face. I stumbled into the room and shut the door.

I called 911, and got a .357 out of the gun case I kept under the bed. I loaded it as I told the operator what had happened. She tried to keep me on the phone, but I hung up. I tried to sit, but that was impossible. I knelt on my knees in front of Ellie. She was no longer crying.

"Maddie's mom dropped me off. I thought he was killing you," she explained.

"Shh, shh, quiet now. You saved my life, and that makes you an angel." I tried to smile, all the while listening for footsteps.

Blood poured from my bottom. I pulled a blanket to me, to spare her the sight.

"Momma, you're bleeding," she said.

I kept the .357 in my hand, ready if Jean-Paul came to find us.

"Listen to me very closely, baby," I rubbed her arms to try and comfort her. "They are going to separate us. I'll probably go to the hospital."

Not probably. I had to. I felt the blood continue to leak from my lower half and also from my face.

"Don't be afraid. Tell the policemen what happened. You did nothing wrong, understand?" She nodded.

I thought for only a second before I decided to tell her the truth.

"Ellie, this is going to be hard, but I need you to understand."

She nodded again, looking dazed.

"That man downstairs?" I was whispering now. "He's not your father, baby."

I was crying now, thanking God that Jean-Paul had no claim to my child.

"He's not?" she asked innocently.

I shook my head.

"No baby, he's not. You haven't met your daddy yet, but you will."

I crossed my heart and smiled at her. She looked happy at the thought. I hugged her.

"He's a handsome man who is kind and loving."

She nodded in my hair. I felt dizzy and tried to hurry before I was swept away in the current. Adrenaline was leaving me, and I was beginning to sway. I put the gun on the nightstand and got a pen from the drawer. I took Ellie's hand and began to write Roger's numbers, office and cell, and then Nathan's and Sheldon's numbers.

"You call them as soon as you can, or let one of the officers call, okay?" She might have said yes, but I slid to the floor then.

"Mommy!" she said, scared.

I touched her face. So much like Ryan. I wondered again why I hadn't seen it.

"I'm okay, baby. If he tries to come in, I want you to use the gun, okay?"

She nodded. She knew, as I had at her age, how to use a gun. Living in the woods, it was a must.

"I'm going to close my eyes for a moment, but don't be scared. Everything will be okay."

I lay, trying to stay conscious, until I heard the police and ambulance coming in. Relief flooded me, as I was carried out on a gurney. Ellie rode to the hospital with me, and I gave over to sleeping, holding her hand, praying to God all would be all right.

I woke hours later to Roger pacing the room.

"You didn't sign up for all this, did you?" I said and tried to smile.

He came, and sat beside my hospital bed. It was night, I noticed, as I glanced at the dark sky outside my hospital window.

"You're going to be okay," Roger said in a whisper.

Nathan was asleep in a chair, along with Ellie on his lap.

"Is she okay?" I asked of Ellie.

Roger glanced at her, then back at me.

"More than okay," he smiled. "She's something, that girl. They have Jean-Paul. He had a few stitches and a head wound, but he'll be in county lockup till tomorrow, then I'm hoping the big house by next week. Listen, we've got to talk."

Roger's voice turned serious and dark. He lightly lifted a chair to scoot in closer to me. I tried to sit up but found it too big a movement just then. Roger raised my bed slightly. We glanced at the sleeping pair every few minutes, to make sure we were not overheard. Roger told me all he'd learned.

"We were not able to find out much, but what we do know is not good. Jean-Paul and his family ship people from South America into the States by way of various trucks and possibly ports. The individuals pay good money to lie flat in the upper parts of a truck's bed, hid from anyone who doesn't know the compartment is there. They only hauled maybe ten at a time, and only once a month. Jean-Paul oversaw this part of the operation, as did his father, Maurice, before he went missing a few years ago."

Roger glanced back at Ellie and then returned to me.

"It's rumored Maurice fled deep into Mexico, but no one is certain. This was a highly sophisticated operation. After

Maurice disappeared Jean-Paul was treated like a stepchild by his brother, and uncle."

I tried to shift to a more comfortable spot. I felt numb, and I noticed a sharp pain in my belly. Roger placed a hand on my shoulder to keep me from moving.

"Relax," he warned me. "I believe Maurice brought Jean-Paul to Tennessee to try and give his son a different life. I don't think Maurice was aware of the extent of Jean-Paul's evil ways."

Roger sounded almost sorry for Maurice.

"They have a high-end brothel in Louisiana. This is where Jean-Paul stayed most of his life. The women there are mostly immigrants from South America, working off debt to bring their children here. They never work it off. Most die there. I was told that Maria was one of them and tried to escape. Instead of doing away with her, they made an example out of her. They gathered all the girls in a room and cut out Maria's tongue. She nearly died from it. A few years later, Jean-Paul brought her to you, knowing she couldn't speak." Roger finished this with disgust, tossing a glance at Ellie and Nathan again.

"She's dead, Roger," I said in a numb voice. I put the hurt away until I could deal with it. Roger nodded.

"Matthew," I said, and my heart ached. "Roger, Jean-Paul killed my boyfriend, or caused the accident that did. I think he used to watch us, while we were together in the old blue barn. Looking back now I think a lot of things that didn't add up about his behavior."

This thought made me sick. Matthew and I were so in love, and so innocent. Our time together was the best of my life, and now it would forever be tainted with the thought of Jean-Paul watching from the shadows.

Roger nodded.

"I'm afraid there's nothing we can do about that, Piper."

I closed my eyes, and spoke quietly. I truly felt beaten, inside and out. We talked well into the night. I couldn't bear the thought of leaving my home, but Roger insisted we come to stay with him in New York for a while.

"You will have to testify. You can come home long enough to do that, and then return to New York, at least until he is put away. Agreed?"

I reluctantly agreed. We made arrangements for someone to check on the house and horses. I was so thankful for Roger. I tried to convey this, but the words came out choked from my swollen lips. I reached up to wipe my eyes, and gasped from the pain. I felt a long line of sutures just under my right eye. Roger took my hand from my face.

"You'll heal," he said, close to tears himself.

"How bad?" I asked, now doing inventory on my body.

Roger looked down at my feet as if talking to them would be easier.

"There's twenty staples in your scalp. Your elbow is broken. You have sixteen of the smallest sutures, placed by a skilled plastic surgeon under your eye there," he said, indicating the place I had touched. "Your ribs are badly bruised, and you have some other bruising here and there, but the biggest concern was from…" Roger stopped and swallowed.

"From the rape," I finished for him, in a dead voice I was all too familiar with.

Roger nodded sadly.

"Risk of infection, but you're on good medicines and strong antibiotics. We can continue your care in the city. Piper?" He said my name in a stern voice, to make sure I was listening. "This is a very bad guy we are dealing with. Do you understand?"

I looked into his eyes, the same color as mine and my dad's.

"Yes, I understand," I said.

Roger brought his face down to mine, speaking softly so only I could hear him. "There's a very good possibility that Jean-Paul is responsible for murdering your friend Lana, and nearly killing Nathan."

I was stunned silent. That thought chilled me to the bone. Lana's murderer had never been found.

"Roger?" I said, desperate and terrified at the thought. "Does he know? About Ryan? About Ellie?"

Roger looked down at me sadly.

"I don't know."

CHAPTER TWENTY-FIVE

We buried Maria in our family cemetery. Someday, I wanted to find her children, if I could, and let them know how sweet and wonderful their mother was. Nothing like the monster my mother had been.

It was a quiet and private burial. I said good-bye to the lady who had cared for me and my daughter so lovingly. So kindly. I stood, leaning on a crutch for a long moment, and felt the breeze that carried the smells of the pines down to where I stood.

I had suffered, but I would not allow anyone to call me a victim. Things had been done to me against my will and I, by the grace of God, still stood, even though I had been knocked down by people who were supposed to love me the most.

I was brought up short by the knowledge that I had been murdered in different ways, but still I breathed. I swore by the trees and the sunlight I would not be knocked down again. I would rise from the ashes and be wiser, stronger, and live with all my heart. I placed a hand on Nana's stone.

"I screwed up, Nana, but if the Lord lets me, I'll make it right."

I raised my head to the heavens, and prayed silently for strength. For guidance. For forgiveness. For comfort. For Ryan to be healthy and accepting of Ellie.

"And Daddy, if you can hear me, I miss you something awful."

I laid a rock at each of my loved ones' gravestones, saying a prayer to receive each of their strengths. I wanted Daddy's pure love of life, Nana's accepting mind and thoughtful spirit, Papaw's incredible strength and knowledge, Maria's kindness. I said a prayer for my dead baby and turned to join my waiting family. I would begin again with a song in my heart.

"I might be down, but I ain't out," I said to Papaw's stone, as I walked away. I swear, when it was at my back, as I turned to go, I could almost hear him say through the breeze, "Atta girl, Piper."

The city of New York was a little overwhelming when compared to my country home. I'd never leave Cosby. It was in my blood, but this was a nice change. Roger spoiled Ellie rotten. While he worked, Ellie and I would walk the streets to do some window-shopping, and we would eat something new every afternoon. We loved the mix of different cultures and religions.

Ellie was right at home in this city. It both made me sad and excited me to think how fast she was growing and how she was showing an interest in life I never had. Roger talked me into allowing him to enroll Ellie in a school of arts.

After only a month she went from playing Chopsticks on the piano to much more complex forms of music. I was so proud. Sheldon and his girls visited, as did Nathan. I got to spend time with Josh, who couldn't tell me who he was guarding. I figured he was a great bodyguard. He laughed when I tried to guess.

"Donald Trump? Liza Minnelli? One of the Olsen twins?"

He would shake his head, smiling.

"I couldn't tell you if I wanted to. I love you, but give it up."

Josh and Matthew were so different when we were younger, but now we were entering our thirties, I saw pieces of Matthew in Josh—the mannerisms I loved so much, the knit in the eyebrows.

"I still miss him, Josh," I admitted to him.

Josh wrapped me up in his big arms.

"Me too, Piper. Me too."

We shared the loss of a kind and gentle spirit. I figured we always would.

I had to go home and testify against Jean-Paul a few months later. The police had botched some evidence which caused some charges to be tossed out of court. He was sentenced to two years in prison. His lawyer pled him down to lesser charges, and since he had scratches and marks on him from me and Maria, Jean-Paul pretty much got away with murder.

I found out we were never married as Jean Paul did everything to stay off of any legal documents. We were never legally married. I hated the thought of my old pastor taking a bribe, but he was dead and gone now, so there was no use in holding a grudge against the dead, because they could care less about our problems anyway.

I was ready to return home. I loved the big city, but I wanted my mountains. Ellie begged and pleaded to stay.

"But Mom, in Europe all kids go away to school," she whined.

I couldn't bear the thought of leaving her. A report from the prison holding Jean-Paul changed my mind instantly. Jean-Paul had corresponded with some of his relatives and was going to try and have Ellie taken from me and sent to live with his family.

I was horrified. It scared me to the point of agreeing to whatever kept her most safe. It hurt me deeply to admit she was safest away from me. Jean-Paul was told of Ellie's paternity, or his lawyers were. Not who her real father was, but that he was for certain, not her father.

Ryan's identity, though important and inevitable, would be a secret until he was well. Roger and I had plans to help Ryan, but we would need Sheldon and Nathan in on it— them, along with a good doctor.

I was frightened of what would happen next. I felt I would be keeping Ellie safer by separating myself from her. She would remain in New York, and with a heavy heart, I agreed to go home alone.

"You know how to use your video chat, so it will be like talking from the kitchen to the grand room," Ellie said, far wiser than her age. Ellie was born with wisdom and acceptance, just like Nana.

"I guess so," I said, trying not to make her sad.

I returned to my Cosby home. I would visit every couple of weeks, and Ellie would come home for long weekends and holidays, if her schedule permitted it.

Nathan returned home with me. He, Sheldon, Roger, and I conspired to try and help Ryan, as Ellie stayed at school with Beatrice and the girls as they split their time between London and New York. It was not going to be easy. I wanted Ryan to know of his child, and how wonderful she was. But I wanted him to be healthy when he did learn of it.

Ryan was scheduled to be off for a few weeks. Sheldon would bring him to Cosby in hopes of getting him clean and sober. I reluctantly agreed to this, fearing Ryan would hate me for tricking him. I also feared seeing him after all the time that had passed. I thought of him, but would not allow the thought of being with him to take root.

I was still the dirty, diseased girl Daniel had ruined so long ago. Roger wanted me to prepare the house for a long absence, in case Jean-Paul was released early from prison, a possibility that made my blood boil. I set out for home, with my brother in tow. He surprised me two days later by saying he wanted to bring his girlfriend home, at least until after Halloween.

I knew Nathan was popular with women; most musicians are, but after Lana he was careful with who he was with, fearful he would relapse. I admired his strength and gladly agreed to meet this mystery woman.

When his girlfriend arrived I was overjoyed. She was a tall, dark-skinned black woman, with a whip-like tongue and a huge, kind heart. She was exactly what Nana would have picked for Nathan. Her name was Deedra, but, "Everybody calls me Dee Dee," she told me.

She came with leopard-print luggage and a baby English bulldog that Nathan called Dixie, his "pride and joy." I often came to the kitchen to find Nathan singing to Dixie while cooking. Dixie would watch him with droopy eyes, waiting for falling crumbs from her master. I loved her. She slept with me most nights, and I felt safer with her.

I was counting down the days till Ryan came. I was a nervous wreck by the time that day came. I decided to be as normal as I could, choosing my jeans and T-shirt for the day. I didn't want to give the impression I was dressing for him.

No matter how I felt about him eons ago, and I still had little butterflies in my stomach when I thought of him, there was no way a man of his popularity and money would go for a country bumpkin from Cosby, Tennessee. And even if he did, I could never let him into my messed up world.

Still, when I heard Sheldon yell, "We're here!" from the front door, I quickly checked the mirror, to make sure I was neat and as pretty as I could be.

The scar on my right cheek was a shiny, thin line and was on top of the one I already had from climbing a tree with Josh when we were little. It was only noticeable in bright light.

I made my way out of my room in a daze. Would he remember me? Had he ever thought about me? Who was I kidding? Ryan Knox dated supermodels, at least four to five different ones every year.

I was the girl with the tragic past and the psycho non-husband who tried to kill me, even if at that moment, I felt like the girl on the beach. I had to steady my breathing as I made my way downstairs.

CHAPTER TWENTY-SIX

Ryan ~

I was in the middle of some hick town, because my best friend talked me into it. I didn't want to be anywhere, especially not at an old farmhouse in a place that doesn't register on most maps.

I had to admit though, as I took in the place, it was nice. It was three, maybe four stories, on several hundred acres of breathtakingly beautiful land. There were woods as far as the eyes could see. The mountaintops looked like they were covered in thick white smoke. Hence "smoky" mountains, I thought with a snort.

I was with Josh and Sheldon. Nathan and Dee Dee were there already, with Nathan's sister, whom I'd never met.

"If this girl asks for an autograph, I'm out of here," I said to Josh.

He shot me a look of disgust.

"Dude, get over it. Piper's not like that."

Yeah, right, I thought. In the end, they were all "like that." We got bags from the car and climbed the porch stairs in front. There were pumpkins and scarecrows here and there.

Even in my bad mood, I felt instantly welcome.

"What kind of name is Piper anyway?" I said wrinkling my nose.

Sheldon looked back at me, dead serious, and said, "It's an angel's name." Then he smiled and added, "You'll see," and followed Josh through the door.

At the entryway, Sheldon shouted, "We're here!" tossing down bags and taking off his shoes, revealing his big toe poking through a hole in his sock.

"You got more money than a Saudi sheikh and you can't buy decent socks?" Josh teased him.

Sheldon shrugged, not caring what his socks looked like. I did as he did and looked around. It smelled like warm apples inside the house.

It made my mouth water. On the left was a great big room, with a baby grand that sat in the corner. At this, I brightened.

I loved piano, and had my acting career not swallowed me whole, I would have taken a chance at playing professionally. In the middle of the room were three couches set in a semi-circle, with an old wooden table in the middle.

Over the top of an ancient fireplace was a television, placed so as to be easily viewed from the couches. It was a cozy room, with huge floor-to-ceiling windows that covered the east side of the room.

I glanced to the right and saw a dining room table that sat at least twenty, maybe more. Roses and fruit bowls were the centerpieces. This went through to a brightly lit kitchen.

Everything I'd seen so far was charming and comfortable. It kind of reminded me of an old bed and breakfast, but much more personal. The entryway was directly in front of a wide staircase, which rose in a curve to the next floor. Beyond the first flight of stairs, I couldn't see.

Nathan and Dixie greeted us, followed by Dee Dee. Sheldon had already gone to the kitchen. He always complained that he gained at least ten pounds from Piper's cooking when he visited.

I was in the middle of asking how far we were from anything, when legs caught my eye. They were connected to a frame I watched walk slowly down the stairs.

It was as if everything was moving in slow motion. I saw the jeans, then the grey Rolling Stones T-shirt, then the light, strawberry-blonde hair, and finally the face. It was the face I'd dreamed about since my time in Louisiana years before. I stood with my mouth open, mid-sentence, watching her walk our way.

Following my gaze, Nathan turned to the woman.

"Piper! Bout time!"

Playfully, she bumped his stomach with a small fist.

"Piper?" I said stupidly.

"Yes," she said smiling. "Ryan? It's so nice to meet you."

I knew I was frowning in response. I put my best faux face on.

"Nice to finally meet you," I said, playing along.

I wanted to say, "What the hell?" Did she even recognize me? I'd memorized every inch of her, and could recall it vividly, no matter how wasted I got at times.

Piper hugged Sheldon. I was instantly jealous.

"You all hungry? I've got chicken casserole in the oven."

"Starved!" Nathan said,

"Woo-hoo! Me too", added Sheldon sounding as if his mouth was already full.

"Sure," I said still deflated at the less-than-warm reunion.

I don't know what I expected, but it wasn't this. Piper? Her name was Livia, or so I thought. I was suddenly aware of my appearance. I was grungy, and my beard was thick and itchy. I should have shaved, damn it.

I asked to use the restroom, and took my backpack with me. I only had a little blow left, until the overnight package arrived tomorrow. I would make it last till morning, or early afternoon.

When I was done I was more relaxed and could sit without twitching at least. We all ate and laughed. I watched the beauty I'd fallen so hard for. When I thought of her name and how different she was, I had to agree Piper was a better fit for her than Livia.

Later we watched *The Postman Always Rings Twice*, with apple pie topped with vanilla ice cream. When it was late, we left Sheldon asleep on the couch. Piper showed me to my room. Nathan said, "Good night," and followed Dee Dee to a room down from mine.

"I'm just there," Piper pointed to a door across from me. "If you need anything, just holler," she said lightly and turned to go to her room.

She stopped and turned back to me. I perked up, hoping she would acknowledge who I was and our time together.

"If you smoke, make sure you open a window," she said, and I deflated again.

"No problem," I said sourly, going into the room.

"Ryan?" she called.

I stuck my head out of the door.

"I'm really glad you're here," she said simply.

I watched her open her door and enter her room.

"So am I, Piper," I said, but my voice was so low I wasn't sure she heard me.

Over the next few days we all laughed, ate, and watched movies. It was family time. I'd never had time like this, and I noticed quickly how much I loved it. Bee and the girls could not make it for Halloween. When I inquired about a baby picture in the living room, Piper said she had a daughter away at school.

"Ellie," she said sweetly.

I thought she was uncomfortable talking about her, so I asked no more. Most of the time Piper was warm and friendly, but other times we would all sit and talk, especially in the living room, and she would wander off in thought. A sad expression would creep over her beautiful face.

I fought the urge to ask what was wrong or to put her in my arms. The truth was the drugs kept me satisfied and numb. I began to resent my addiction, for the first time in years. I relied on it to function now.

Halloween night was here in no time. Sheldon, Josh, and Nathan had the barn loft open and were doing sound checks for that evening's concert. By the sound of it, everyone in the county was coming. There were two horses hooked to a bed of hay, I supposed for hayrides.

The people would bring their own drinks and blankets, and sit in the yard. I said I would watch from the porch of the house, knowing, as always, my face would cause a stir, and the last thing I wanted were strangers gaping at me, or the paps to find me and start hunting me, taking pictures.

I got a surprise when Piper presented me with a Zorro costume, mask, hat, and gloves. I would be unrecognizable. Piper came downstairs, glittering in a halo and white dress with wings. The outfit was so fitting for her.

Sheldon walked up behind me.

"See? I told you so," he said so only I could hear and walked away, scratching his multicolored Afro wig. He was right. She was an angel. I followed everyone out to the yard. People were everywhere now.

At least a hundred had already arrived. Some stood to the side, some lay on their blankets, all had a beer in their hand. I took a beer for myself, and stood with Josh, as Sheldon and Nathan began the show.

Sheldon was a genius. He sang Brittany Spears, Loretta Lynn, Kid Rock, and Uncle Kracker. There wasn't a song he couldn't sing, or a song Nathan couldn't play. They performed in perfect harmony, as only two people with a long history together can.

The crowd hooted and hollered like true hillbillies. I kept a watch on Piper. She gave candy to children, danced with old men, and spoke to everyone, the perfect hostess.

The darker the night got, the more people showed up. Sheldon asked that everyone stand for a slow dance before he and Nathan took a break.

"We're gonna slow it down, and let the lovers come forth for this one," he said, and nodded to Nathan to begin.

He sang with precision, "Let It Be Me," by Ray LaMontagne. Couples all over were dancing now. I set my beer down, and strode confidently over to Piper before anyone else could. Josh started to say something, but I ignored him and stayed on course.

I didn't speak when I got to Piper. I just took her hand, and pulled her into the swaying crowd. I took my hat off and tossed it, not caring where it landed. I was still covered with a skullcap and eye mask.

Piper blinked and looked around like she was ready to run. I remembered how reluctant she was on the beach, and I recalled the words I'd said, standing naked in the water.

I bent to her ear, "This is life, Livia. Don't you want to live it? Are you living, Livia?"

I felt her body stiffen, and she tried to pull back from me. I kept my face to her ear, glad I had shaved.

"No. Please stay."

After a moment, she relaxed into me. I traced her face with my lips as Sheldon sang the befitting song for us. Piper breathed onto my neck, and I moved my lips down hers. She smelled of the same sweet perfume I remembered from so long ago.

I kissed her collarbone, and made my way back up to her ear. I rubbed the side of her face with mine, much like a dog would your hand. I didn't care who saw me. I'd wanted this girl for years, and now I had her in my arms. For just a second, Piper laid her head against me. This small movement had me breathing heavier.

I bent my head to whisper in her ear.

"I've wanted this for years, Piper. Don't you remember me?"

She neither answered nor moved. As the song ended, I kissed her mouth softly, feeling her body turn rigid from fear or repulsion,

I didn't care. She parted her lips and kissed me back. I felt my own body respond. I couldn't have written a better scene for a movie.

Piper pulled back and quickly walked away from me. I stood, watching her go. Sheldon was telling everyone they'd be back in fifteen. I didn't see Piper the rest of the night or at all the next day.

I should have been watching where I was headed, but being doped and desiring a woman, who obviously did not desire me, clouded all the signs that were there all along.

I was about to crash without a parachute. I had to hand it to them, my misfit family. They pulled it off perfectly.

The night after the party, I found Piper in the kitchen, laying out thick slices of ham and roast beef. Fresh homegrown lettuce and tomatoes. Fresh baked breads and sour pickles. There were chips and tea.

I began to apologize for kissing her Halloween night, but she waved me off.

"No, it's okay," but once she said this, I felt worse about it. It wasn't okay. I had wanted her, so I'd put her in a position that she did not want to be in. That was not okay with me.

Roger came to be with us a while. This should have raised a red flag, but I greeted my mentor and father figure as always. He brought his girlfriend, Rebecca, with him. Rebecca was a pretty, forty-something, Wall Street somebody. She wore diamonds everywhere and reminded me of a brunette version of Zsa Zsa Gabor. After dinner, Nathan asked me to stay and help him clean up. Piper went with Sheldon, Josh, and Roger into the living room.

The rest said good night and headed up the stairs. Still, I was ignorant about what was coming. I helped Nathan put things away and piled dishes into the sink. We were talking about my schedule when we got to the living room. Nathan motioned me in first, and I heard him slide the heavy wood doors closed behind me.

I might have felt something, a warning bell, but it was the FedEx package on the coffee table that brought me up short. I looked at it, then up to Roger's unreadable face. Piper had her back to the room, looking out the window. Josh and Sheldon sat on the couch opposite Roger.

"Ryan, please, have a seat," Roger said in the voice he normally used for negotiations.

Nathan came and sat on the back of Roger's couch, looking down at the floor and wearing an unmistakable expression of pity. I had a couch all to myself.

Alone, as always. Symbolic, but my reality. Roger leaned forward, placing his arms on his knees, and began to talk.

"Ryan, we are all here tonight, because we all love you."

I involuntarily glanced at Piper's back.

"We have one purpose, and that is for you to be well," Roger was saying.

A movement behind me caught my attention. I turned to see for the first time two men standing by the wall. I'd never seen them before, and the sight of them made me nervous. Roger tapped the FedEx box to get my attention. I began chewing on my nails. I knew what was coming, and I resented the mutiny of it all.

"You have choices," Roger was saying.

Apparently, they had concocted a plan. If I did not stay, at least through the New Year, and get clean, with the help of a "world-renowned doctor," and he gestured to the older man behind me, I would go to jail, charged with the federal crime of having my drugs shipped to me. He waved a hand toward the other man I assumed was here to carry out my arrest, were I to choose the latter. When I tried to speak, Roger held up a hand to silence me.

"If you do not get and stay clean once and for all, I along with Josh, Nathan, and even Sheldon..." I glanced at Sheldon. He had his eyes on the floor, refusing to meet mine. "...will cut off all contact with you," Roger finished.

My face screwed up in rage at this.

"You're serious?"

I looked from Roger to Josh to Nathan to Sheldon, who said, "As a heart attack, bro," looking me square in the eyes this time.

I searched his face for humor, or a glimmer of something that said anything but what I'd heard. I found nothing there but defiance and truth.

"You're godfather to my girls, and you stood stoned at my babies' christenings," Sheldon said, obviously hurting. "I love you man, but this shit has gone on long enough. Time for change before you force me, force all of us, to bury you."

I hurt inside like I'd never hurt before. I glanced at Piper's back again, wondering what her role in all of this was. She couldn't stand the sight of me.

I stood up and looked at each one, wanting to shoot them one by one for making me feel like a reject. Roger stood and tried to touch me. I pulled away like an angry child.

"Stay here, Ryan. Get yourself well, or if you wish, I can arrange anywhere you would like to go," Roger said, sounding sad and weary. "Piper and Nathan have opened their home to you. At least here you would be able to stay out of the news." Roger continued, almost pleading now. "Ryan, if we'd known, we might have saved Mol—" he started.

"Don't talk to me about that!" I screamed at him, and I actually covered my ears, unable to stand hearing her name.

Closing my eyes, I could hear the gun shot, feel the splatters of her blood. I stormed from the room and out the front door, slamming it behind me. No one tried to stop me.

I walked down the driveway and down the narrow path these people would call a road. I didn't care where I was going. I was getting away from this place. I ripped my pocket trying to pull my cell phone out. I jammed a number in, and nothing. I tried again, and still nothing. I threw the damn thing into the trees somewhere, and kept walking. Viola was probably part of this shit too.

"Traitors!" I screamed at the night. "You're all fucking traitors!"

I walked on, not knowing where I was headed. After a few minutes of this, I couldn't see the house, or anything that looked remotely like a road. There were things moving in the woods.

Birds made noises, and I realized it was cold. I stood looking around, and then I began to think about what they had just said to me.

I admit, I liked my drugs, but I was ready to rid myself of my reliance on them, and if I was completely honest with myself, I just didn't want to be told how easily I'd be tossed away because I had a problem. I thought of my father and of dying alone, the way he did.

I don't know how long I sat in the cold, lost in the boonies, but I was now numb. I leaned, tired, against a fencepost, craving a hit. I laid my head back, and stared in amazement at the sky. Above me was a blanket of stars.

I'd stayed in brightly-lit cities for so long, I'd forgotten what this looked like. A car came slowly down the road and stopped in front of me. I walked to it, recognizing Nathan's old Camaro. I flung the door open and crumpled inside, defeated. Piper sat behind the wheel, looking out the windshield.

"Want me to take you to the airport?" she asked, not looking at me.

I tried to dry my eyes, not wanting her to see my weakness.

"Or back to the house?" She took my hand, and said, "It's your choice, Ryan, but either way, I need you to be well."

I didn't understand what she was saying. Why would she need me to be well? That didn't make sense.

I looked back at her and told her to take me back to the house. Roger was still sitting on the couch. Nathan, Josh, and Sheldon were gone from the room. The doctor remained, but the other man was gone. I sat beside Roger and listened as Piper climbed the stairs.

I wanted to ask what she meant when she said she needed me to be well. Roger began to talk, and the doctor joined in to explain how to become drug-free. I sat numbly and nodded in understanding.

It was late by the time we finished. I was to start right then. All drugs were gone. No drinking. No nothing. The doctor would treat my withdrawal as much as he was able, but I would work toward being completely off that also.

"With hard work and commitment, you will be successful," he said, and so I agreed that I would confront my drug use, the abuse of my body.

I was given two pills, and told to go to bed. Tomorrow was the first day of the rest of my life.

Roger looked at me sadly.

"Do you want this?" he asked me.

I nodded.

"No, Ryan, listen to me. Do YOU want this, or do you want to be found dead by a maid someday?"

I winced at the memory of Molly. A pain shot through my chest at the thought.

I nodded slowly.

"Yes. I'm tired Roger. To the bone. I am weary of this life. I can't be everything to everybody anymore. I want to cut back, and maybe write some, when I'm through this, I mean." I looked at my old friend, and saw tears in his dark eyes.

"Let's get you better, and then I'll help you any way I can," he promised, wiping his eyes.

CHAPTER TWENTY-SEVEN

I woke to a nearly empty house. Everyone had gone, except Piper and Nathan. Dixie was there, but I didn't count her. I hurt all over and went through hell. Piper came to wash my face, and hold the trash can as I threw up.

At first, I refused to let her see me this way, but she demanded I allow her to help. She told me about the pill and coke habit she had had. She said she just quit one night, wanting to live a way her grandmother would be proud of.

She talked about her daughter, and it soothed me some to listen to her voice. The doctor came and went, but didn't stay long. I couldn't grasp time. I spent my detox freezing and throwing up. I started out the pale color of corn and faded to a chalk white.

Piper kept at me until I ate at least once a day.

"You must, you must," she would say until I gave in.

I would watch her face stay empty while she shaved me with a straight razor. I wasn't concerned as she placed the blade on my neck. After each stroke, she would wipe the hair and foam across a towel on her shoulder. I was so weak, shaving was the last thing on my mind.

"It is a fact. You feel better when you are clean," Piper told me.

As she sponged my face and neck, she would tell me stories of her dad or of her time here in this room. I loved the attention she gave me. I looked forward to watching her face as she talked to me. I reached up once, and traced her lower lip with my thumb. She took my hand and gently kissed the palm, closing her eyes as she did this.

It was such an intimate thing, yet so simple. I felt cherished for being me, and not the star I'd been morphed into over the last almost twenty years.

Just before Thanksgiving, Piper and I took the horses through the woods. I had taken riding lessons for a film years ago, and returning to a saddle after I'd swore I'd never do it again was a strange sensation. We slowly climbed a mountainside. I looked in wonder at the varying colors of the leaves. This truly was a magical place.

We paused at a bend where Piper laid flowers. I watched, not asking whom they were for. After she returned to her horse, we began to descend back around the mountain. We returned to the house as the sun set on our backs.

I helped with Thanksgiving dinner that week. I hadn't celebrated this way before. I got a kick out of the turkey and pie Nathan insisted were his recipes. I did enjoy it though, and this was the first time everyone would be home to see me and the progress I'd made since Halloween.

As they arrived one by one, they each showered me with complements on the healthy state I was in. I was down to two of the doctor-prescribed pills a day to help with the cravings my body still felt. I thought about using all the time like a piece of me was drifting and I couldn't quite grab hold yet.

Though my want of drugs was still with me, I was becoming more accustomed to be alright without them. I was eating all the time. I ran with Nathan to keep my weight in a good range. We celebrated our family.

All the while, Piper got thinner before my eyes. Worry creased her forehead. When Roger was there, I often found the two of them in deep discussion. When I entered the room, they would go silent. Whatever it was that was causing her discomfort, I hoped it wasn't me.

Piper began hanging sheets on the walls and draping them over the furniture in parts of the house we were not using. When I asked, she told me that she was going on a trip after the New Year. I found I looked at the calendar a few times a day.

By Christmas, I was dreading leaving. My color was the light mocha it had been when I was a child. Piper wanted me to tell her about my life. We never spoke of Louisiana. I feared losing the deep connection I had with her.

As I did on the beach, I felt a magnetic pull toward her. We could sit in silence or chat like old friends, sipping coffee on the screened-in porch, watching deer come and go in the distance.

On Christmas Day, we all ate a huge breakfast, with chocolate chip pancakes, bacon, sausages, eggs, and potatoes. We were stuffed and happy when we sat down to open gifts. Piper gave me a Perez Hilton T-shirt that was the brightest pink I'd ever seen. I wore it proudly. He'd been a fan of mine for years, so I was glad to support him in this simple way.

A dinner fit for royalty was served and almost entirely consumed. When all was quiet, and we had finished watching *It's a Wonderful Life*, we began saying our good-nights, and I asked Piper to stay with me for just a moment. We sat in front of the fire.

I don't know why I was so nervous, but I was. I gave her the box I'd carried in my pocket all day. When she saw it, she smiled.

"I'll never forget what you have done for me. My time with you, and I mean all my time with you, will live in me forever." I said this so she knew I meant Louisiana, as well as here in Cosby.

She started to say, "You shouldn't have," but I stopped her.

"Can I appreciate you, for just a moment, please?" I said.

She opened the box slowly, eyeing the necklace inside as if it were the Hope Diamond. She read the inscription on the white gold pendent, dangling from a shiny white gold chain.

"For where we have been, and to where we are going, my love."

I watched several different emotions cross her delicate features. Landing on one her dark brown eyes filled with tears. She put her hands over her face and cried. I immediately began to apologize.

"Here, it's corny I know. I can send it back," I said, reaching for the box.

She shook her head, wiping her eyes.

"No, no, no. It's beautiful." She snubbed like a child.

I patted her knee awkwardly.

"Then what is it? Why has this upset you?"

I gave her a moment as she wiped her eyes and calmed slightly. I was afraid she'd start crying again so I stayed quiet so not to trigger anything.

"Oh, Ryan, I'm so sorry."

"Piper, you have nothing to feel sorry about."

She dabbed at her eyes with a Kleenex from the coffee table.

"Just tell me, Piper, it's okay," I assured her, not having a clue as to why she was so emotional. She just stared at me for a long moment as if searching for words.

"I couldn't meet you," she said, picking a random thought, I assumed. "I couldn't meet you because-"

Piper was breathing fast, almost panicky.

"Lana died. Nathan was shot, and there was blood everywhere, and I was married at the time, or I thought I was, and I had to come back home, and then I slit my arm open, I don't know if I wanted to die or not, I think I did, but then Matthew showed up."

She took a deep breath and closed her eyes.

"I couldn't meet you-," she said again in a soft voice.

My thoughts tumbled around, but then clarity came.

"Because Nathan got shot?" I finished.

She nodded.

"I was going to leave a note at the car, but it was gone when I left that night. I remember," I said.

She nodded in understanding.

"You were married?"

She looked up at me helplessly in obvious internal turmoil.

"I never was. I thought I was, but it wasn't legal."

I tried to follow her, but she was talking so fast, on the brink of hysterics again.

"It's okay," I said, but she stood, still holding the box, all of everything but okay.

"Don't you see, it's not? It's not!"

I stood also.

"Well, spit it out then, damn it. I don't understand."

She bit her lower lip, and shut her eyes again. Placing a hand on my chest.

"Soon we must talk, but right now I'm tired, okay?" she said sadly.

"Piper, can't you talk now?" I asked slightly annoyed.

"I promise, we will soon. I just can't think right now. Give me a little time? Please?"

"Of course," I answered, and then I asked, "Soon?"

Piper nodded, and I kissed her forehead

"Everything's going to be okay. Okay?" I asked, unsure myself.

She nodded again, looking at the floor. I placed my finger under her chin. Reaching down to the coffee table, I picked up a small branch of mistletoe, and I placed it above my head.

She grinned at me as I leaned in to kiss her. Her lips sent waves of electricity through me. In a matter of seconds, we were kissing heavy, mistletoe be damned.

Breathless, I pulled Piper into me hard. Abandoning her mouth, I went for her throat. Her arms were locked around my neck, and she was responding with just as much need and desire as I had. I laid her down on the couch, my mouth back on hers now.

We didn't need to talk tonight, this was much better anyway. I placed my hand on her side, working up to her breast. She reached down between us, feeling the bulge through my jeans. I groaned in agony.

"Excuse me?"

We became perfectly still locking eyes.

"Shit," I said, as Nathan knocked on the coffee table.

I moved off of Piper, placing a pillow from the couch over me. Piper scrambled to pull her shirt down, and sat up.

"Phone," Nathan growled to Piper, neither amused nor embarrassed, but rather cold as ice. Then he walked from the room.

I watched him go, shooting daggers from my eyes. Piper hurried from the room, throwing me an apologetic look as she went.

I fell asleep on the couch alone. Piper must have returned at some point, because I woke at three in the morning with a blanket on top of me and Dixie snoring beside my face.

I fought the urge to sneak into Piper's bed. Nathan would probably shoot me thinking me an intruder, then I thought he might shoot me for fun after catching me with Piper.

I understand to whole "big brother thing" but he seemed really protective. I wondered absently if it was my unstable history with random women over the years. That's enough to cause any brother to feel a little hesitant with my involvement.

I made a mental note to share with Nathan that Piper was not some fling I would have while I'm here. I actually want to be with Piper. *Be with her how?* I thought. *BE with her, Be with her.*

I didn't know the first thing about relationships. I mostly dated models that were readily available to me at every turn of my career. We did our drugs, had our fun then I moved on to the next city and next model.

Sure there was a few that wanted relationships with me but I learned quickly it was the younger ones that took extra precautions to not get pregnant. In return I would make sure they were my date at various events in Hollywood giving them exposure to the public by way of cameras or tabloids. It was always good for them in the long run and good for me at the time.

I suppose this did make me a bad candidate to be with Piper in Nathan's eyes. One thing's for sure, Piper desired me just as much as I did her. The years hadn't changed that about us.

The next day I got the cold shoulder from big brother. Nathan made sure to stay with one of us never giving us time alone. I got the impression he was waiting for something, but what, I had no clue. Whatever was going on with him made him moody and protective with Piper. I dismissed this as the big brother thing.

I was waiting on a word to indicate exactly how he was feeling. I didn't have to wait long.

"She ain't one of your throw-always, Ryan," he told me in a low voice, almost sounding threatening when we alone in the kitchen.

"I know that," I said, just as threatening.

I was more than a little hurt that he thought I would use Piper like an extra on a film set, but on the other hand, Nathan had witnessed and participated in many nights with countless, nameless females—throw-aways, as he called them.

"I know that," I said again, understanding now. "She's unlike anyone I have ever met before. I've spent years trying to find her."

Nathan looked confused at my admission. "Years?"

"We met in Louisiana. You remember? I had no idea she was your sister, obviously."

Nathan's face became dark. I knew he was thinking of Louisiana and Lana. I did not push the subject further. I left him in silence to think.

New Year's Eve came, wet and freezing. Fortunately, Nathan was playing a private gig that night, and I was watching the clock until it was time for him to go.

The intensity that surrounded Piper and me was palpable. It pulsed in the air when we were together. So it was no surprise we were intertwined in each other as soon as the door shut behind Nathan.

"Wait," Piper said, breathless

"Why?" I asked, between her lips.

"He might come back," she said, pushing my arms off, but not leaving my mouth. "Oh, I know," Piper said, wide-eyed, pulling back from me, and leading me to the room I knew she delivered babies in.

I had her shirt off before we walked through the door. Piper kicked it shut with her foot and locked it without looking. She pulled at my jeans, and I worked off her bra.

Her mouth was enough to drive a man insane, but add her warm body, and I was in orbit. She bit at me teasingly. I sat her down on a bleached white sheet, and became reacquainted with her topography.

Sucking on soft flesh, kissing her inner thighs until she panted like a puppy. She quivered beneath me, and then turned to lay me down as she worked her way up and down my body.

My hands had to touch her. My mouth had to stay in contact with her. She gave in as I pulled her on top of me. I held her as she began to rock.

The hunger she had drove me crazy, and when she began to tense with orgasm, I gave in as well. I collapsed back on the bed, taking Piper with me. We lay still until our breathing was normal once more.

"This is the birthing room then?" I said and she giggled from under her hair.

"Yes, it is, this is my favorite room in the house, and I have a birthing tub. Would you like to see?"

She sat up smiling, ruddy in the face.

Ten minutes later, we were submerged in the tub, chest deep in bubbles.

"Ah, if we only had candles," Piper said, straddling me.

"Please, no. That would be too cliché, would it not?" I said, as she was running her fingers through my hair. I watched her breasts dance in the water.

"I suppose," she said, smiling.

I placed her hand on my cheek and closed my eyes.

"Where have you been, my love? Where have you been all these years?"

Piper said nothing.

I pulled her face to my chest, cradling her like a child. I searched, and found the scar on her shoulder blade that had me puzzled so many years ago. I trailed a finger down her spine and then raised her face to touch the scar under her eye. I leaned forward and kissed it. Piper traced my face like a blind person would do, memorizing every detail of every line on its surface.

One of us hit the plug, and water began to drain. We took no notice, but continued this form of making love. Only suds covered us now as our hands searched the more delicate parts of each other.

The tips of Piper's hair were wet and stuck to her body. I could not imagine anything more beautiful. Piper's eyes were dark from her mascara, and given her deep-set eyes, she looked wild in the brightly lit tub. I probed her, and she responded favorably to the touch of my hands between her legs.

I guided her to lie back, and allow me to have my way. She watched me as I began to find the places that pleased her most. Greater than any high I'd felt, I devoured her flesh.

She began to whine and pull at me to enter her. I traced her nub before I entered, setting her legs to shaking. Her back arched, and I joined her in climax, once more wishing this could go on all night. If I had my way, we would do just that.

CHAPTER TWENTY-EIGHT

"Piper? Are you in there?"

I jumped, startled by the pounding on the door. We had fallen asleep, and the light outside gave no indication of what time it was.

"Ryan? Piper? Open the goddamned door, or I'll kick it in!"

Nathan was yelling like the house was on fire.

Piper jumped up off the bed.

"Just a second!" she yelled back, looking for clothes.

Giving up, Piper put on a fluffy white robe, and then tossed me my jeans. I just got them zipped when the door opened.

"Aw, for Christ sake, I don't want to see this shit," Nathan said, putting a hand over his eyes at the sight of me.

"Nathan, stop it! What's wrong?" Piper sounded scared.

Nathan put his hand down, and looked mean.

"You think it's okay not to answer the phone? For hours? After the shit that's happened, you think you haven't nearly killed me? Given me a heart attack? Damn near killed myself to get here. Thought I was going to walk in to find body parts!"

"I'm sorry. I am. We fell asleep," Piper said, trying to soothe him.

I was not about to apologize. Number one, I wasn't sorry. Number two, it didn't sound safe to say anything to Nathan at this point, he was so pissed off.

"Roger's on his way. He landed a while ago. He'll be here any minute. He's been trying to call. You've had him worried sick, but I suppose you were just too busy to answer the damn phone."

Piper placed a hand on her hip.

"Quit being a baby and tell me what's wrong," she demanded.

"Hell, woman, I don't know. He just said he needed to talk to you, and he would be here shortly. He said everything was okay now, but you should pack a few things."

And throwing me a nasty look, he turned his back on us and began to walk away. Pausing, Nathan bent over and picked up Piper's shirt. He handed it to her with a sour expression. She snatched it out of his hand and shut the door in his face.

"We better hurry," she said to the room at large.

Removing the robe Piper began putting her panties on. I looked at the nightstand clock. It was 11:59. I turned on the radio, twisted the dial, and we heard a countdown at twenty. Piper smiled, and we met each other halfway.

Locking ourselves in each other's arms, both of us with bare chests, we finished the countdown with the crowd, and began kissing before the first "Happy New Year!" was said.

We slowly swayed to *Auld Lang Syne.*

"Wherever we are going, I want to spend my time with you. Always. Never again to be apart," I told her seriously.

Piper placed her forehead on my chin. I bent my head to kiss her hair.

"What do you say?" I asked, unsure of her answer now.

I raised her face to look into her eyes.

"Piper? Roger's here," Nathan called through the door.

She kissed me long and hard, and then finished getting dressed without giving me an answer. I let it go for now, but I would bring it up again soon.

In the grand room, Roger stood waiting. He still had on his heavy winter coat. His face was white, and he looked searchingly at Piper. Roger appeared scared, and the sight of him this way unnerved me.

"Piper, we must speak but..." he trailed off, looking at me and then back at Piper. "You haven't spoken to Ryan yet, I presume?"

Piper glanced back at me and then shook her head. That drowning feeling I sometimes got before big news crept over me.

"I need to speak with both of you, but Piper, it has to be now."

Roger was stern and left a ringing warning hanging in the air.

"What has happened? Tell me. Ellie?" Piper demanded, but Roger shook his head.

"Everything is okay now, but Piper, you must speak with Ryan now, or I will."

Piper looked stunned at his words and watched him leave the room, shutting the door behind him.

"I have to go, Ryan," she said without preamble.

I frowned and walked to her.

"Piper, what's going on?"

She walked to a drawer and pulled something out.

Returning to me, I saw tears flood her eyes.

"This is Ellie. Have I ever showed you her picture?"

Confused, I took the picture. It was of a smiling little girl with huge blue eyes and strawberry blonde hair. Ellie was missing a tooth.

"She's beautiful," I said, nodding and smiling at the small face in the photo.

Piper took a step closer to me.

"Like a movie star," she whispered.

I nodded, agreeing. She was beautiful.

"Yes, she is. She's even prettier than a movie sta—" and I broke off, unable to finish what I was saying.

The words sunk in, and then I tried doing the math. How many years had passed since our time on the beach? I looked at Piper's face for confirmation. She eyed me expectantly. I looked at the photo and back to Piper again.

"Piper? Are you saying? Wait. What are you saying?" I asked stupidly.

She took a deep breath.

"Her name is Ellie Grace, and she has a God-given talent for music. She loves her horses, and makes As and Bs. I rarely ever have to scold her. Ellie is a good girl. The best," she told me, tears running freely.

My lips felt cold. I had the sudden urge to sit down as if my legs could no longer hold my weight. I took a deep breath realizing I wasn't breathing.

"But Piper?" I breathed out the name, nearly passing out. "She's mine?"

She nodded slowly, and I finally had to sit.

"Have you always known?" I asked, hoping she hadn't.

Or maybe she had, and she didn't want me to ever know.

"No. Not long ago something made me suspect the truth. Then I had it proven with a test."

Piper began to tell me her story. I understood the importance of why she "needed" me to be clean now. I got it. There was more for me, like she'd often told me the past few weeks getting sober. During those sick days when I wanted to die as my body suffered the withdrawals of Heroin and Opiates I feed it to functions.

I was not living the life I was meant to, and there was always something up ahead, if I only had the strength to seek it. The unforeseen, she had told me I understand now things which can be parallel to your everyday living, but they exist without your knowing their importance. I rubbed my eyes, feeling a little dazed.

"A daughter." I looked up at Piper, who watched me cautiously, as if I were about to explode. "We have a daughter, Piper," I said in disbelief.

CHAPTER TWENTY-NINE

No doubt this was going to take some getting used to. I didn't know how to feel exactly. Happy? I suppose. Shocked? Absolutely, but for the most part I felt weary, like I had on the wrong size shirt and it was too short in the sleeves, something that annoyed me more than I can say.

After Piper and I exhausted our conversation about Ellie, Jean-Paul, and the last few years, I understood our situation a little better, and we were ready for Roger.

He walked into the room, with Nathan behind him carrying coffee and cups. Setting down the cups, Nathan poured one for each of us. Roger began by saying again that everything was all right.

Piper interrupted and said, "You've said that before, and it sounds like things were not alright earlier?"

"There was an attempt to take Ellie earlier tonight," Roger said

Piper put the cup down with a hard thud. "What? How could you wait this long to tell us?"

Roger held up his hand.

"Please Piper, let me tell it all, and then we will discuss it together, but know that she is fine and safe with Sheldon and Beatrice. Plenty of protection."

I reached for Piper's hand.

"Protection? Where is Josh? I thought he was escorting her?" Piper asked, looking scared now.

Roger closed his eyes and sighed.

"Josh, I'll tell you about too, but let me start by saying correspondence has picked up between Jean-Paul and his family recently. One brother in particular has outright ordered him to stop this vendetta against you. But Jean-Paul is determined, and has enough hired hands to do his work for him.

There are all kinds of investigations going on, yet people keep ending up dead, and they seem to always be one step ahead of everyone else. They are very organized. You can't have their kind of power and money and not be. The one thing we have going for us is Jean-Paul does not have the resources as the others do, and his power is limited within the family."

Roger set his untouched coffee on the table in front of him. I could tell he needed Scotch, but as I'm a recovering addict the alcohol has been taken out of the house.

"This morning I received a call from a guard at the prison where Jean-Paul currently is. The guard went into great detail, explaining how for months Jean-Paul has paid to have messages delivered to and from his family. This particular guard, who called, intercepted one such message this morning. Inside it was Ellie's location and description, also a time. Taking into account what happened in the past, we wasted no time and had Josh remove Ellie immediately, taking her to a separate location and leaving whoever was coming for her to find FBI agents."

He paused and took a sip of coffee. Roger was visibly shaken. I could never recall seeing him so upset, not like this.

"No one came at the time given. I never heard back from the guard as we had arranged. It appears now that this was a trap to move Ellie out into the open. Josh let her think she was headed to the museum, a field trip he called it. We didn't want to frighten her. We had no reason to think they would be followed."

Piper sat on the edge of her seat, giving the impression she was about to run at any second. I was a nervous wreck myself, but I tried to soothe her by rubbing her back.

"They were both grabbed on the street and shoved into an SUV."

"Dear God," Piper breathed.

"Josh must have fought them hard, and I don't think they knew what they were getting into. He killed two of them outright, and the other one most likely won't live. Ellie was not harmed in any way, thank God."

I waited for the rest, but Roger seemed to be lost for words.

"Ellie is fine?" I said for clarity, and Roger nodded. "And Josh?"

Roger closed his eyes, and keeping them closed, he said, "He's hanging on. His parents are with him now."

Nathan turned his face away from us. He did not show surprise, so I figured Roger had told him Ellie was mine already. I pinched the bridge of my nose, feeling like someone had hit me there.

Piper sat beside Roger and hugged him.

"I would be dead, and Ellie lost to us had you not saved us. I'll have no pity, thank you very much."

Letting go of him, she turned and started talking about packing, but Roger pulled her back to him and said in a desperate whisper, "He knows, Piper, and he will show no mercy. He will be released in five days. There's no stopping it."

Pausing, he looked at me with deadly seriousness. "And we are all at risk."

Piper sat back, defeated now.

"It's only been a few months. We had everything planned out. Why would he get out this early? He knows about Ryan?" Piper fired off the questions one right after another.

Roger nodded answering the latter first.

"And that I'm..." but I couldn't say, "...her father."

It was too weird. Roger nodded again, understanding.

"Yes, and he was granted an early release because of the politics and money. There were issues from the initial trial as you are well aware of and it gave his lawyers a lot of things to argue for his release."

Piper and I looked at each other.

"We need to get to Ellie and see about Josh. I refuse to think anything, but that he's on the mend." And with that she hurried from the room.

Ten minutes later we were on our way to the airport. We took Roger's private jet back to New York. I knew about the man Jean-Paul. I knew there were criminal things about him, and where he came from. This could be very bad for all of us, as Roger continued to stress.

"They are a family that has limitless amounts of cash and has no issue with murder and mayhem, there are so many things we still don't know about them." Roger was telling me.

"It is rumored he killed his own father," Nathan added.

I listened as he and Roger filled me in on what we were up against. Roger leaned forward, and squeezed my shoulder.

"I'm proud of you, by the way. The doctor has told me you sleep through the night and have been completely off the meds for the last three weeks?"

I nodded and looked at Piper. She was not talking. She sat like a statue looking out the window.

"Yeah. I feel good," I told him.

I looked back to Roger, who was now looking at Piper, a sad expression on his face. I couldn't think about my sobriety right now. I was feeling so many conflicting emotions and dreaded what was coming.

Ellie being safe, Josh surviving, Piper also being safe, but selfishly, I wanted her right with me. As if reading me, Roger handed me a magazine. I didn't think it would be possible to shock me anymore tonight, but as I looked at the cover, I was just that.

"You've got to be kidding me."

Piper moved for the first time since our take off, resting her chin on my shoulder to see what I was looking at.

"Oh, no. Ryan," she said.

Splashed in bold letters on the cover of the magazine was: "Ryan has a Princess Piper," and in smaller text it read, "Mystery lady of the Hollywood hunk finally REVEALED!"

Two photos. The first was a blurred image of Piper and me on a beach years before. It was clearly me, and if you knew Piper, it was clearly her. She sat straddling me, with her long, lean arms and legs circled around my body. I had my hands on her hips, and we were obviously in the throes of a very passionate moment.

Piper's breasts were blurred, but that hardly hid the erotic nature of the photo, which was in fact the reason it was on the cover, because that, along with the headline, would make the magazine sell big-time.

The second photo was taken within the last few days. In the picture, Piper and I are on horseback. I'm in mid-sentence, and Piper is looking back at me, laughing. She was beautiful. Even now, under these awful circumstances, I was in awe of her.

"Jean-Paul must've had you watched. A local? Or maybe someone from the reservation? A little cash goes a long way. It wouldn't take much to get these, and match the old with the new," Roger told us.

I looked at Piper as she reached to open the magazine.

"It's never anything nice, love. You're better off not reading it."

She glanced at me but continued turning the pages.

"Ryan, you have commitments coming up, and I think that's for the best. This is an easy way for Jean-Paul or anyone else to track you. This way you're hunted by good hunters, and let's face it, the paps are ruthless when there's a bounty. Right now, it's a million for a photo of you two kissing. That ensures you will be followed day and night. It's smart, and it's what I would've done," Roger said, pointing at the magazine.

For the rest of the flight, we made plans. As much as I hated it, we agreed that Piper would stay with Ellie and fly to Denver for a few weeks. It was cold and remote where Roger's cabin was. Whatever it took to keep them safe, I was all for it. I would visit when I could, but I had to be cautious, as now, more than ever, I would be haunted by paps trying to get pictures of Piper and me together.

So far, and thank God, there was no mention of Ellie. I'd grown used to the attention now, but I still loathed it. I hated to bring Piper into that. Being constantly chased and shouted at, not to mention the constant flashes from the cameras isn't something I'd wish on anyone.

Nathan was snoring quietly, his head leaning against the window. Roger left us to use the phone. Piper and I sat in silence, holding hands, anticipating our future and what it held for us all.

CHAPTER THIRTY

Piper ~

Seated on the divan with Ryan on Roger's prized Learjet 85, I felt for the second time in my life that I was not in my body. How could I be? My daughter had nearly been taken today, and I didn't know if my best friend in the world was even alive. I couldn't dwell on it, or I would break, and I could not afford to break right now.

I promised myself that later, after I saw Ellie and Josh, I would allow my feelings to surface, but right now, I would concentrate on what I could control. Roger was still speaking to us about the tabloids, and how Jean-Paul could easily track us by feeding the magazines stories.

"No way did Jean-Paul know until recently about you two in Louisiana," Roger was saying.

I was barely listening now. I slid my hand down at my side. Out of sight. I watched out of the window for the lights of the city. I dug my nails into my hand, to the point of drawing blood.

I could not cut myself, but I wanted to. Ryan was quiet, watching Roger on his iPad. I wholeheartedly regretted bringing him into this mess. I wanted him well and had agreed to Roger's insistence that Ryan stay with Nathan and me to recover. I was selfish and wanted him to know about Ellie, but more selfishly I wanted to see if Ryan still wanted me.

If I had just kept it quiet, Ryan could have gone back to his life, happy and unknowing. Then, there was Ellie to consider. It was a good thing for her to know her real father. I could trust Ryan along with Nathan, Roger, Sheldon, and Beatrice to raise her if Jean-Paul did get to me.

That was a thought that grew ever more solid in my heart. Jean-Paul would not stop. He would be released in a matter of days, and he would come for me. I shut my eyes, and felt Ryan push his hand between my knitted knees.

"Almost there," he whispered to me.

I looked at him with sadness in my heart. I loved him. I knew that, but my love would cost him, as it had everyone I loved. I touched his arm.

"Daniel was right about me all along," I said not realizing I was speaking out loud.

Ryan frowned.

"What?"

Roger stopped what he was doing.

"Piper," he said sternly, as if scolding a child for saying a cuss word.

I wouldn't look at him. This man in most ways was a dad to me.

I turned to look out the window some more. It was true. Daniel told me years ago that I was unlovable, undesirable, and would never be normal, but forever diseased. At this moment, I was defeated and ready to call it quits altogether.

"Here," Roger said, handing me an iPhone. "It's ready to go and untraceable. Your contacts are stored already. The horses and the house will be tended to for a while. Let's concentrate on the positive, okay?"

I took a chance and met his eyes. He was warning me against my ugly thought. I took the phone and said nothing, but I understood he was speaking about my Daniel comment.

We arrived at the airport and entered the hanger. We all, including Dixie, rode to Sheldon's Upper East Side apartment. My stomach churned once I saw the building. I wanted Ellie. I wanted to see her rosy cheeks and smell her hair. Entering into the lavish three-story apartment I nearly ran to the girls' bedroom. They were all still sleeping.

I watched Sheldon and Beatrice's three girls and my personal angel. The sun was just coming up, and light danced across her face. I got on my knees beside her and silently wept. She was whole and healthy. I prayed to God to please let me right this life somehow. I prayed not to be delivered, but instead for the strength to do what I needed to, when I knew what that was.

I was unaware of Ryan until I felt him kneel beside me. He said nothing as he wrapped me in his arms. We stayed that way for a long while, as the relief came that my little girl was okay.

Ryan drank her in for several moments, and it was I who finally pulled at his hand to go to bed. The sun had fully risen now, and I couldn't remember the last time he'd slept. I had to remind myself that even though Ryan had done brilliantly with his recovery, he was in fact still recovering.

I was not surprised when he flat-out refused to let me go to the hospital alone.

"Josh is like family to me," he told me again and again.

So together we set out to the hospital with a huge black bodyguard named Titan.

I stifled a giggle when Ryan told me his name. Not fooled by me, Ryan grinned knowing what I was thinking. It was weird, but every time Ryan and I looked at each other I felt as if I was falling, without the danger of ever landing. A pull from somewhere inside of me was telling me I was home with him, as if space and time had never come between us.

Nathan was in the hallway when we arrived at Josh's ICU room.

"How is he?" I asked without preamble.

Nathan put his hand up in a stop gesture.

"Listen, Piper, it might be best if you wait at"

But before he could finish, someone shouted from a waiting room.

"How dare you!"

I looked around for the source, and realized too late that Mrs. Logue was shouting at me. With a manic, crazed look in her eyes, she reached back and slapped me full across the face. Ryan grabbed hold of her, and Nathan jerked me backward.

I fell on the hard concrete floor, stunned, and did not attempt to get up. Mrs. Logue was thrashing and trying to get to me.

"Are you happy now, you whore? It wasn't bad enough you caused Matthew's death, but you had to take Josh too!" she screamed at me.

Ryan and Nathan, as big as they were, struggled to keep hold of her. Frank Logue ran into the room after his wife saying,

"Imogene, hush. Hush now!" But Mrs. Logue wouldn't hush, and I sat frozen, chilled to the bone by her hatred toward me.

"Matthew should have let you rot in that ditch! You should have died rather than enter our lives, bringing your shit with you. I hope you burn in hell for this!"

At this final statement, she collapsed into her husband's arms, sobbing. Security showed up, but there was nothing for them to do now.

I got up and walked back to the elevators. Titan and Ryan caught up with me in the parking garage. I was unaware of my surroundings. Titan ended up carrying me to the Suburban. When we were seated in the back Ryan took my hands in a death grip.

"Stop, Piper! Stop!" Ryan was yelling at me.

When I momentarily came out of my daze, I realized I had clawed my arms bloody. I had scraped away at my flesh, unaware of ever doing it. I said nothing as Titan and Ryan spoke back and forth.

When we arrived back at the apartment, Ryan took me to the bathroom, and placed me in a warm shower, softly cleaning my arms and washing my hair and body. I would not speak. All I knew were the words that were shouted at me. They played over and over like a broken record in my head.

I only recall saying, "I want Ellie," but nothing more.

Ryan held me to his chest, as the water did nothing to wash away the dirt that I knew was permanently etched into me. Ryan gently dried me and wrapped my arms in bandages. I sat on the tub as he clipped my nails. He spoke, but nothing made sense to me now. Mrs. Logue's words were all I could hear.

"Hey!" Ryan said into my face. "So you hear me?"

I looked up at his beautiful, deep blue eyes.

"She was a woman grieving, looking for someone to blame, so snap out of it before Roger gets here," he said, smiling, as if Roger scared me.

I touched his face, and he pulled me up, kissing me.

While he stepped out of the bathroom to get my bag, I looked at myself naked in the mirrors that surrounded me. I touched the pink jagged scar where my baby was cut out of me. Even the baby couldn't stand to be with me and chose death instead of having me as a mother. I traced the many scars Jean-Paul had left me with through the years, but it was the roughly healed scars on the inside that hurt the most.

Jean-Paul would tell me I deserved everything I got, because I was born stupid and needed the shit kicked out of me every day of my life just to function. I could do nothing on my own, not without getting some sense slapped into me. It wore on me, but I never truly believed him until today. Mrs. Logue's words were absolutely true and were echoes of my own thoughts. I was touching the ugly scar on my shoulder blade when Ryan came back into the room. He saw what I was doing, and kissed the raw, red line.

"You should have that tattooed over if you don't like it," he said, smiling.

I played along, wanting to hurry now to see Ellie.

"Oh, Ryan!" I said, suddenly remembering, wanting to kick myself.

"What?" he said, looking me over as if he had hurt me somehow.

"You're meeting Ellie today."

Ryan picked up a towel and rubbed his hair. "Can you hurry it up, then? I'm running late as it is," he said, smiling.

For just a little while, the conclusion I had come to would take a backseat to what needed to be done. I had a few days to get ready for what was ahead, and I would spend them with my family.

CHAPTER THIRTY-ONE

The plan was I would go to Ellie alone and let her know she was about to meet her father, but that quickly changed as the door was thrown open and she came running to me, Bee not far behind.

"Oh, for goodness's sake, you can't go barging in like that! You have to knock! They might not be decent!" Beatrice smiled, as she saw me.

Scooping my child up in my arms, I kissed Bee on the cheek, promising to be downstairs to eat soon.

"Oh, my goodness, I missed you!" I told my daughter, sitting in one of the wingback chairs by the window.

"I missed you too, Mom," she said sweetly.

The bandages tugged at my skin as she sat up straighter on my lap to look at me. She was getting too big for my lap, but I had to keep squeezing her. Ryan stood in the bathroom doorway watching us patiently.

"If it were not for video chat, I would not have survived it!" I told her, meaning every word.

"Skype is one of the best inventions," she teased me.

I glanced at Ryan, and Ellie followed my eyes to him.

"Ellie? Remember I told you that you were—" but she surprised me by standing and walking over to Ryan.

"You're my daddy."

Ryan blinked nervously, something that would look stupid on any other face but his.

"I am," he told her simply.

Ellie had her head back, looking up at Ryan's face, mesmerized.

Ryan swallowed.

"It's nice to meet you, Ellie. May I hug you?" he said, unsure if she would accept him or not.

Ellie didn't hesitate and leaped into Ryan's outstretched arms. I hadn't realized I was holding my breath until I became dizzy. I wiped the tears from my eyes and took a much needed inhale.

Ellie was off and running, filling us in on the goings-on in the school and in the house. She showed us Christmas gifts, and artwork from school, not taking a breath.

We eventually joined the rest at the table for a late breakfast, and if Ryan took his eyes off of Ellie I never saw it. A housekeeper came to me later that morning to hand me the iPhone Roger had given me the night before.

"Miss? Mr. Roger called the house, and asked me to take you your phone," she explained as she handed it to me.

"Thank you," I said, leaving Ryan, Sheldon, and Ellie to their laughing and playing. Bee and the girls left for a birthday party. Nathan and Roger, I knew, were at the hospital, as Sheldon told me at the table while we ate. I began looking through the messages, afraid something was wrong.

Two from Nathan, the first saying, "Everything okay? No change with Josh." His next message read, "Best if you come after-hours to see him. Imogene way out of line, but understandably she's crazy at the moment. Don't believe what she said."

The next was from Roger. "Give Ellie my love and will be by later today." The next read, "Tabs know where Ryan is. Spotted last night. You all stay at the apartment today. I will send Titan to get you around ten to take you to see Josh. He will be alone then, and I know he would want to see you."

A third message said, "I will arrange a suite to be ready at the Plaza. It's all over Twitter that Ryan is there with you right now. Trying to keep everyone safe. It's not just the Cajun I'm worried about; it is also crazy fans of Ryan."

A part of me thought Roger sent that last one just so I wouldn't blame myself entirely, but I did anyway. I showed Ryan the messages, and he rolled his eyes at them.

Shrugging, he said, "The Plaza is nice and safe, and we will have Titan with us also." He kissed me softly on the lips and then returned to Ellie, who was now playing the piano as Sheldon strummed his guitar.

Watching the trio gave me an odd feeling. I was both comforted and uneasy, worried what cost would they have to pay. I was happy on the surface, but the wave of emotion kept me from being overjoyed at the moment.

I would fix this mess, all of it. Then Ryan and Ellie would be able to live a peaceful life. I knew, as I knew last night, that somehow I would need to lead Jean-Paul away from the ones I loved.

After dinner, Roger, Nathan, and Titan showed up. Just by the way Roger looked, his forehead creased and heaviness to his eyes, I knew what he had come to say was not going to be to my liking. He took enough time to show the kids he loved them, and then sat in the sitting room by the fire, waiting for Sheldon to shut the door.

I sat with Ryan. Sheldon sat on the floor in front of Nathan, who sat opposite Roger. My head hurt, and I was a mess inside, wanting to cry and willing myself to stay perfectly still, like I trained myself to do for the times Jean-Paul would lecture me for hours. I was a statue, still. Unmoving. Unfeeling.

My mind ran wild with planning, but I had to remain emotionless lest someone pick up on my plans. Roger sipped from a cup, then set it aside. Clearing his throat.

"Josh is still out right now. The doctors have him in a medically induced coma. I'm going to be honest. It doesn't look good."

I lost my composure for a moment. I physically hurt for Josh.

"The biggest thing now is him being septic, but we can hope and pray he will come out of this. One thing is for sure, had it not been him with Ellie, I don't think she would be with us now. Josh worships her and would gladly die in her place."

We all stayed quiet knowing the truth in Roger's words.

"He couldn't bear the thought of you hurting any more than you already have, Piper."

I nodded, spilling tears as I did. Josh's love was pure and unconditional.

"We must now agree on where you all will be safest. Jean-Paul will be free in four days, if not sooner. I will be alerted the moment he exits the prison gates. Sheldon?"

Roger turned his tired, dark eyes to the floor where Sheldon sat.

"Am I mistaken, or do you all have plans to return to London next week?"

Sheldon nodded.

"The girls have things to do, and I have a small venue tour. Bee has commitments, but in light of everything I think it would be best if I canceled appearing anywhere, and they went on ahead, and I meet up with them later. I would prefer to stay here," he told us.

Roger shook his head.

"No, I think it would be better if you all return together. Stay with your family, and separate yourself from Ryan and Piper."

I swallowed hard. I wanted my friend to be safe, but hearing they were better off nowhere near me reinforced my diseased state. Sheldon nodded. It would be better if they were far away.

"Ryan, you are due in Florida, in St. Petersburg in two days. Correct?"

Ryan shifted his legs uncomfortably.

"Yes. I spoke with Viola earlier, and there was no pushing that back, but before you say anything, I think Piper, Ellie, and I should stick together."

I opened my mouth to speak, but Roger cut me off, still talking to Ryan, convincing him.

"I think Piper and Ellie would be safer with you as well," Turning his attention to me now he said, "It's a safer place to be by far. We originally spoke of Denver, but honestly Piper, there will be plenty of security on hand, as you all would be with a film crew. The studios are extremely tight, and the house you will be staying at is a perfect location. It will also give Ellie the sense of being on vacation instead of hiding."

I caught myself biting my lower lip. The idea of contaminating Ryan and Ellie with the threat of Jean-Paul left me cold. I also began to see how this could work in my favor.

"Roger, we can't run forever. I want to go home soon. I will do this, but not forever," I told him.

Roger said nothing to that, but began to ask Nathan about his schedule.

"I have recordings here in the city for the next two weeks," he said. "Then I have nothing until next month in London with Sheldon."

Sheldon nodded.

"Okay. We need to all understand that Jean-Paul comes from a long line of bad guys with lots of family and tons of cash. Josh took out two, maybe three of his hired hands so far. The one thing I think is in our favor is Jean-Paul is not treated as the others are. He was a prostitute's son, and though he is a Duchete by name, the family does not treat him the same. I say this in the hope he is limited, even though the family itself has unlimited power and capacity for violence. Maurice took him to Tennessee, hoping his son would turn out to be decent and honest, but he is ruthless to the extreme. I stress to you all, go nowhere alone. He will use any of you to draw Piper out into the open. It is crucial we stay in contact with one another. Nathan, would you and Deedra stay at my apartment?"

Nathan nodded, scratching Dixie's ears.

"I will stay close for Josh and his parents, at least until he has improved. Do we all agree?" Roger asked looking to each of us.

They all nodded, but I chose to remain still.

"Piper?" Roger said, dragging me out of my trance.

I looked at him quickly before he saw the ideas on my face.

"I know Josh would want to see you. Perhaps when Ellie is asleep, Titan can take you down to see him? Frank has taken Imogene back to their hotel for the evening. He asked me to let you know how sorry he is about what happened, and hopes you will forgive her."

I nodded sadly, but still said nothing. I deserved what I got, because everything Mrs. Logue said was the truth.

We got settled at the Plaza later that evening. The suite was grand and majestic, with huge beds and a view of Central Park. Ellie did not want to sleep, and it was after ten when Ryan and I finally set out with Titan to the hospital.

I was nervous leaving Ellie, but she had a nanny—actually a well-trained female bodyguard called "Rhodes". There was also a massive bodyguard in the suite called Bryce, along with one at the door called Kent. All worked for Shields, a personal protection company Josh and Titan started a few years ago.

All of these things ran through my mind as Titan drove us to a back door into the hospital. At least two photographers were stationed at each door, so there was no helping this situation.

"Stay right with me, and don't look at them, okay?" Ryan said, as Titan opened the door.

Ryan held my hand, as we rushed through the automatic doors.

"The valet is getting the car, so I'll take you up instead of calling someone down," Titan told us in a deep booming voice.

Ryan kept hold of my hand as we made our way to the ICU. A breathless nurse rushed to us, only to meet the brick wall of Titan's chest.

"Oh," she said startled. "I just wanted to let you know we have been expecting you, Mr. Knox. You all may stay in the room while you visit to avoid any..." she searched for words, backing up a few feet from us as she did. "To avoid any unwanted attention," she said, in awe of Ryan.

"Thank you," he told her, and walked past Titan, who still stood between Ryan and the star struck nurse, as if she were going to jump us. I glanced into the waiting room, fearing Mrs. Logue was there. The only occupants were an elderly man, asleep on a small couch, and a couple quietly talking to each other in a corner, obviously crying. I said a silent prayer for each of them and their loved ones.

Josh was hooked to monitors and wires everywhere. Tubes ran from his nose and mouth, making no sense to me. His eyes were closed and unmoving. My knees went weak. Josh looked as if he were already dead. I let go of Ryan's hand and went to the bedside of my oldest and closest friend.

"Josh?" I said, not recognizing my own voice anymore. "It's Piper, Josh."

I raised my hand to stroke his now long brown hair. I cried for him for a long time, Ryan never interrupting me. I eventually lay down beside Josh after his nurse came to take notes and left without speaking to us. Ryan sat with his eyes closed, and his head against the wall. I began talking softly to Josh, trying to will him better.

"You saved my little girl. I'll never make that up to you," I said through quiet sobs. "I guess I owe you a lifetime supply of Nana's cornbread and apple pie, huh? Or have you changed your favorites again?" I asked him, smiling at the memories.

I talked more than I had the last forty-eight hours, allowing the clock to tick by unnoticed. Ryan lightly snored as I went on and on. I thought of Matthew and of Jean-Paul taking him from me.

"Josh, you can't leave me. Matthew didn't know, but you do. You're still here for a reason. You have people waiting for you to wake up. I need you to wake up, Josh."

My breath was now catching in my throat, and I tried to calm myself before I continued my pleading. I turned to see the sun peeking from between two buildings, rising slowly.

I unclasped a steel chain from my neck. On it was the black diamond ring Matthew had given me the night we first promised ourselves to each other, on my sweet sixteenth birthday. I held the ring now, running my fingers along the circle of dark stones.

"When Matthew gave me this, it was a promise of a life we would live, a promise of things not yet seen but hoped for, a promise to one another. Josh, he was taken from us and was unable to fulfill those promises."

I began wrapping the chain around Josh's wrist, the ring attached to it. I clasped it and took Josh's big hand in mine, placing his on my cheek.

"On days I was too injured to get out of bed, this ring, or rather what it represented, pushed me to go on even when I didn't want to. I had it on when I gave birth to my daughter, and when I finally fought back against Jean-Paul. I give it now to you, so that you may pull on its powers. Alone it is useless, but combine what it stands for with your faith that your spirit is as unbreakable as the circle, and Josh, you will get better. I promise you with all of my heart, I will make this right."

I lay my head down on his chest, and sobbed.

"Come back to me. Come back to your parents, and Ryan and Roger and Nathan and Sheldon. Come back to Ellie, and watch her grow and witness the life you saved. Josh, please don't leave me. Please don't go where I cannot follow you. Please stay and laugh with me."

My body shook hard, and I felt Ryan's hands on me. I stayed on Josh's chest listening to his strong and steady heartbeat. How could something sound so good if it were dying?

Finally, I rose from the bed, wiping my now swollen eyes. Startled by a movement from the door, I jumped seeing Mrs. Logue there. I was unsure how long she had been there. She watched me as I left the room, but said nothing. I could not read her face, as I walked past her. She did not look disgusted by my being there, nor did she seem pleased.

I did not talk as Titan escorted us out, nor on the drive back to the Plaza. Ryan said very little, but held me, and rubbed my arm as if trying to warm me. Ellie was still sleeping when we return to our suite. I lay fully dressed in the dark with Ryan. The scratches on my arms itched as they healed. I fought the desire to slice them open again. I didn't cry anymore, but softly told Ryan about the friendship Josh and I always had.

"In most ways, he was the only family I had for a long time. Nathan was so lost to us in drugs. We always stayed in touch, whether it was phone calls or him visiting. I was never able to visit him of course, being married as I was, but we always stayed close."

I finally dozed off and woke around noon. I found Ellie and Ryan watching *SpongeBob* together, happy and content. I kissed Ryan's hair, and sat with Ellie in between us. We wasted the rest of the day ordering in, and vegging out on the couch. It was blissful as the snow fell all that day.

CHAPTER THIRTY-TWO

Going from eight inches of snow, to seventy-five degrees and sunny in one afternoon was a shock, but a welcome one to say the least. We arrived in Tampa, Florida, to gorgeous blue skies. I couldn't look away from all the water we crossed. We drove over majestic bridges across the bay, and ended up in a beachfront mansion.

The small bridge we crossed to reach the house gave us breathtaking views of the surrounding properties. We stayed in the car, as Titan made sure the area met his approval. Ellie ran from the car as soon as the door opened.

The sun was blinding and heavenly. We could see speedboats racing not far off the coast. We had our own boat to use at will.

"We can take it out while we are here, if you would like?" Ryan said, noticing my interest in it.

"You can drive us?" I asked

Ryan chuckled.

"I can do some things on my own, believe it or not." I playfully jabbed a rib and he said, "Ouch. Watch it now. I can't show up on set with bruises. The boat is like driving a car by the way, except no brakes. Turn a key, and press the gas. Simple as that."

I noted the different things he said about the boat, thinking this might be a good idea for what I needed to do. I wiped the thoughts away. I had to save them for when I was alone. Right now, I had Ryan and Ellie. I wanted to enjoy them without the looming prospects of my future.

Ryan and I watched the sunset while Ellie chased seagulls. I made us grilled cheese sandwiches and chips for dinner, and then we played Uno until Ellie started nodding off. I followed Ryan upstairs to her room and watched as he tucked her into bed.

It was strange when Ryan sent for the female bodyguard they called Rhodes. I assumed that was her last name. We passed her in the hall, and said good night. Rhodes would stay in Ellie's room, reading, or watching TV, but she would shoot anyone who tried to enter, as would Titan or the other two guards, Bryson and Kent.

All in all, I felt pretty safe at the moment. Maybe it was my decision and the peace I got from it. Ryan and I showered together, not waiting for the bed to begin making love. When we were alone like this, it was as if we had always known each other, always loved each other. We collapsed in bed tangled in each other's limbs, sleepy and satisfied.

"I may be gone when you get up in the morning," he told me in the dark.

Off in the distance, the moon danced on the water.

"I'll miss you," I said.

"Piper?" he said, keeping me awake.

"Hmm?" is all I managed

"Let's get married."

My eyes snapped open.

"What?" I said, maybe a little too surprised.

"You don't want to?" He sounded defensive now.

I sighed, thinking how odd it was for his first thought to be *me* not wanting *him*.

"I've never thought about it. I never thought you would..." I stopped short of saying that he couldn't possibly want somebody like me. Instead I said, "...you would want to."

Ryan pulled me closer to him. His cool, naked body gave me cold chills and a rapid pulse.

"I do. I want you forever and ever. Would you want me? Even knowing I'm broken in many ways?"

His words shocked me.

"Broken?" I asked, confused.

"You know, the drugs? This twisted way of living with the paps, and the crazy fans? All that is not something I would wish on you, but I'm too selfish to not want you with me all of the time," he said simply.

I kissed him, amazed he considered these things issues.

"So, is that a yes? A no?" There was doubt in his voice.

"Ryan, we are currently in hiding from a man who wants me dead. If that were not a factor, I would say absolutely, yes. Without a doubt, yes, But my best friend is lying in ICU because I put him there. My childhood sweetheart is dead, cold in the grave because of me. I cannot, and will not bury you as well. Until Jean-Paul is dead, I'll never be free to live nor will you."

Ryan got out of bed, angry now.

"What are you saying, Piper? What do you mean Josh being in a coma is your fault? And what? You're going to allow this mother-fucker to control you? And no one is dead because of you. If anyone is dead because of you, then I am completely responsible for Molly blowing her brains out in front of me."

I watched as his chest heaved in the dim light from the bathroom. He was naked in more ways than one. I was not frightened but mad at myself for saying too much.

"Don't you love me, Piper? Am I so bad?"

I sat up and got on my knees still on the bed. I put my arms around his neck and nuzzled him.

"I love you, Ryan. Truth be known, I've loved you from the moment I saw you."

Ryan snorted remembering that first moment.

"Okay, the second moment. I never stopped thinking about you."

I felt his body relax into mine. He was awakening, and I felt his stiffness between us. He rubbed my back, shoulders to bottom, in long strokes like rubbing a cat's back. Running his fingers up and down, then moving to my sides, then breasts, bending and kissing my neck.

"I love you. I want nothing more than to be with you. Say yes." Now he had his mouth on my breasts, causing my breathing to speed up. "Say yes, if you want it too."

Giving in, my mouth on his now, I said, "Yes. Yes. Yes."

After drowning in each other, and long, light-hearted conversations, I asked Ryan to take me to a tattoo parlor.

"Now?" he said shocked. "But it's two in the morning." I pinched him lightly.

"It's your fault. You woke me up. Come on, please?"

Grudgingly Ryan had Titan locate an artist, and then take us to a local parlor called Guns and Needles. I was in awe of how easy things were to do when Ryan's name was used.

After listening to the artist carry on and on about Ryan's recent movie, and "how fucking wicked" it was, I sat with my back to him, as he gave me my first tattoo. Ryan watched, trying not to chew on his nails.

"Quit fussing over me," I said, amused at him.

"Does it hurt?" he asked, squinting.

"Not at all," I said, meaning it. I caused myself pain for many years with cutting, and had endured countless beatings. The tiny needing etchings didn't bother me in the least.

When the artist was finished, I stared in the mirror at the once ugly, scarred tissue given to me on my honeymoon. It now had delicate writing on top of it.

"To thine own self be true."

Through my horrible existence with my mother and Daniel, burying Matthew, Nana, Lana, Papaw, living years and years with a monster that used me as a punching bag, my daddy's teachings lived brightly in me.

That quote from *Hamlet* was one of my last memories of him. His handsome face and his voice I'd nearly forgotten, yet the words he loved so dearly stuck to my insides.

"To thine own self be true," he said in his best Shakespeare voice.

"But what does it mean, Daddy?" I asked from my bed.

I watch his mind click through his deep brown eyes, my own eyes looking back at me.

"Well, Piper, it means you can't ever be who you're meant to be, like God intended, unless you are truthful to yourself first. Always remember who you are—here." With a finger, he touched the spot where my heart was.

I placed my hand over my heart now, as it ached from the memory.

"Like it?" The artist asked me, unsure of his work.

Other than the eight-gauge earrings, the man looked like a Sunday school teacher.

"I love it. Thank you," I said, and hugged him.

Ryan and I posed for pictures with him, and made our way back to the house. I was happy, as I climbed into bed with my movie star.

Tomorrow, Ellie's name would be changed to Knox. Ryan would take us out on the boat for the day after an early morning meeting, and he would begin work on the film that evening. We would sometime file papers for a marriage license.

I said a prayer for my loved ones, saying an extra one for Josh, and slept, looking forward to a future with only the slightest doubt I wouldn't come out alive.

All I had to do was figure out my next move without anyone getting hurt, or knowing what I was about to do. Before I could move on with Ryan and our little family, I had to go back and do what I should have done before. Isn't that the way it goes?

You're walking along, then bam! You're in a spiderweb. But just because I walked face-first into the web, that didn't mean I had to stay there and wait to be devoured.

CHAPTER THIRTY-THREE

Ryan ~

It was the middle of March, and filming on *Treasure Island* would end the next day. I had been sober just shy of five months. I lay tired and happy in a chaise by the ocean. My daughter and her "friend" Rhodes were building sandcastles.

Rhodes had been an exceptional choice as Ellie's bodyguard, and I had faith in her ability to protect my child. Piper was returning from a sand bank where she had been fishing sand dollars out with her toes. I glanced twenty yards behind her, watching Titan keep his distance from her, but never quite out of sight. I knew Bryce was at the house, and two others were stationed somewhere I never knew, for Titan never told us.

"Just rest assured, your family is secure Mr. Knox," he would say at least once a week.

Josh had phoned earlier, and he sounded stronger every time I spoke with him. We thought we had lost him a time or two, but he surprised even his doctors when he woke and had no lasting effects from the infection. He refused to hear of any of us leaving to come see him.

"It doesn't make sense, bro. I'm on the mend. Piper and Ellie are safe with you. Let's keep it that way, okay?"

I couldn't disagree, primarily because I was selfish and wanted to keep Piper and Ellie all to myself as long as I could. Before I could argue he changed the subject.

"Roger spoke to some feds this morning. Looks like Jean-Paul lost a family member in a shooting off Highway 55, in the direction of Memphis. Just found his body. They think it had to do with what they were hauling." He said not hiding the disgust he felt at the thought.

"They, and the investigators Roger has working on him, believe Jean-Paul is sticking close to home in Louisiana. Ryan, you know how close you all are to him? Just stay safe, and listen to Titan. I'll see you soon. Tell Piper and Ellie hello for me."

We hung up, and since the phone call, I couldn't wait to get out of Florida. This place had been an escape, but the reality was, Piper was too quiet, and I worried constantly.

Photos of us ended up on a tabloid television show. I watched it, still shocked at how these parasites and their mega-zoom lenses could capture such clear images. This day they caught Piper and me on a boardwalk, then again later that day at Bubba Gump's, out at John's Pass. We thought we were being inconspicuous, but the photographer got us, holding hands, and feeding each other. At least it wasn't the million-dollar kiss.

We looked silly and in love, exactly what Piper and I were. The only thing that bothered me was while in the gift shop looking over the many different Bubba Gump shirts and hats, they took a photo of me reading a sign, and Piper was looking out of the window with that deadened look she sometimes got when she didn't know I was watching.

It was an empty look, as if she were waiting for something, and as quickly as I saw it, she turned it off and became the light in the room again. I had a bad feeling she was hiding something, something I was sure she knew I wouldn't like.

"Daddy!" Ellie squealed, running my way with a fistful of slimy seaweed.

She giggled as I acted like I was scared of it. I pulled her up on the chaise with me squeezing and hugging her, leaning back on the lounge.

"Ellie, honey, did you put sunblock on today?" I asked, sliding the strap of her shirt aside to reveal a bright white line.

"Yeah, but Momma says I'm as red as a pickled beet."

I chuckled.

"What in the world is a pickled beet? Is that some kind of Tennessee thing? Or is it another way of saying as red as a beetroot?"

Ellie shrugged.

"Tomorrow, I'll be as brown as a biscuit. Daddy you talk funny sometimes." She laughed.

"I talk funny? Ha! Just cause I'm not a country bumpkin doesn't mean I talk funny"

I tickled her ribs, and she squealed. She squeezed my neck and returned to the sand.

Piper started my way, and I watched her long legs as she walked. I loved every inch of her. I knew I had a stupid grin on my face, but I didn't care. Piper was gorgeous, inside and out. I noticed the thin layer of skin glue that covered her new tattoo on the inside of her left forearm.

Since the night of the first one, she began getting different scars covered with words, delicate, small letters, covering ugly reminders of her past. So far Piper had five tattoos. The first was *To thine own self be true.* Then there was the scar under her right breast that now bore the words, *Keep breathing.* That one had something to do with birth.

Then her right hip bore a nasty thick scar she had covered with, *Nana said there would be days like this.* Next on the inside of her left bicep, there was a tiny willow tree. This sat in the middle of several long pink scars. When I asked what they were from she shrugged.

"From my own hands this time," and I left it at that. I did not push her, knowing it would get me nowhere. Instead, I allowed Piper her space until she was ready to talk.

This last tattoo was my handwriting: *If music be the food of love, play on*, from Shakespeare's *Twelfth Night*. At first, it was just me goofing off with a Sharpie. I was pleasantly surprised when the following day I learned she had made my script permanent.

Kicking off her flip-flops, Piper sat her bag of shells on the sand beside me.

"What are you smiling at?"

She lay beside me, wrapping her arms around me. I kissed the top of her head.

"I was just thinking of your ink, love," I told her, squeezing her closer.

"I'm a bad girl," she teased.

I bent to kiss her full lips, something I couldn't stop doing when we were together. We lay in the sun, listening to the waves and Ellie's giggles. This was heaven. The sun. The sea and my girls. I would be sad to leave.

"Are we set to head across the pond tomorrow night?" Piper sat up and watched Ellie.

"Yes." I touched her shoulder. "You don't wish to leave?" I asked.

"No, it's not that. I'm excited to see London," she said, shrugging, the adult version of our daughter. I sat up with her, putting my chin on her shoulder.

"You're homesick? Missing your mountains and baby delivering?"

Piper giggled and pulled her shoulder away, making my head jerk.

"Your whiskers tickle, but yes, I'm homesick, among other things." She hesitated, talking in the direction of the waves so I couldn't read her face. "Ellie wants to go back to school. She brought it up again this morning."

I leaned back and closed my eyes. The day was setting into my bones.

"You told her she could be schooled with Libby?" I asked, exhausted with the topic.

Ellie seemed to bring up her big New York City school every chance she got. Turning toward me, Piper touched my exposed stomach with one finger.

"Hey, now," I warned her

"I can't hide out forever, Ryan. I won't. As much as I love you, I can't just sit and wait to be found."

She turned her face from me again. This had been our only disagreement. Piper felt it would be better if she somehow trapped Jean-Paul. To draw him out from whatever rock he had slithered under.

"I'm not accustomed to being 'handled,' Ryan."

I got up.

"Goddamn it, Piper, the man will stop at nothing to get to you. This time it might mean the death of you. Why must you bring this up again? The investigation..."

"...could take years, Ryan," she cut in before I could finish.

I stood looking down at her.

"I want you to be happy and healthy. I want you and Ellie to be safe. What could you possibly do to ensure that? How can you stop him hunting you both?" I asked.

I reached to touch her cheek. Turning her head to receive my touch she kissed the palm of my hand.

"What are thinking, Piper?"

She said nothing.

"I can't lose you. You know that, right?"

Piper looked up at me. Her expression was unreadable.

"Nor I you," she said simply, clearly not wanting to continue the conversation.

I would bring this up again and soon. Something was just not right. My phone vibrated in my pocket. I fished it out, recognizing the number.

"Shit," I said to the phone. "I forgot to tell you I have an interview in the morning with one of the more tasteful magazines. The photographer wants pictures of us together. It won't be printed for a while, if you would like to be photographed with me. Very tasteful stuff. There's interest in you, love." I pulled her up to me and began to dance with her. "I see no problem with it. What do you say? It'll be a nice album for the grandkids."

Piper allowed me to dip her and then I brought her back up gracefully.

"Can we negotiate my keeping the wardrobe?" she said in her scary business voice.

I shook my head, smiling.

"I'll ask."

The magazine people were willing to give Piper whatever she wanted to get the first official photos of us. We were packed and ready to head to England as soon as we finished up. The film wrapped, so it was all fun for a few days.

I had plans, one of which started before the dresses were chosen. Rhodes had taken Ellie to a studio room, and they were playing Mario Kart on a Wii.

Once she was settled, I went to Piper's dressing room. The door was open, and the make-up artist was having a field day with her.

"Oh, Lord, honey, your skin is fabulous. I dream of working with skin such as this." Catching sight of me in the doorway, the tall, thin, bi-racial man said, "Oh la la, Mr. Ryan Knox! You hit the jackpot with this one here."

I smiled, knowing this already.

"Yes I did, but Jar Jar? Can you give us a minute?"

Jar Jar, with whom I was very familiar, from dozens of shoots through the years, sighed again, placing brushes and powder on the counter in front of Piper.

"Don't you ruin my canvas," he warned me, leaving the room.

"Jar Jar?" Piper said incredulously.

"His nickname, because he talks like Jar Jar Binks. You know, from *Star Wars?*" Piper had no idea. "No, I guess you wouldn't know, considering you don't even watch movies in color," I teased.

Piper stared at old black and white movies like they were lifelines. I enjoyed them, but I was determined to bring her up to date on a few. I shut the door, noticing my palms were sweating. Rubbing them on my pants, I got down on my knees in front of Piper, reaching up to kiss her.

"Oh no no no! You will mess up Jar Jar's canvas," she said, smiling.

I chuckled nervously.

"Why did I agree to this?" she asked again.

"Because once the market is saturated with your flawless skin, the paparazzi hunt will die down, at least in comparison to what it is now. That, and you need some exposure before we legally change your name."

She smiled down at me.

"Speaking of which, you are a little naked you know," I said.

"I'm not wearing this, silly."

She gestured to the robe she was wearing.

I took her delicate hand in mine.

"I meant here. You are naked," and I kissed the top of her hand. "Piper, will you do me the absolute honor of being my bride?"

I placed a new ring with old diamonds on her finger. I swallowed my emotions, trying not to be so soft, trying instead to be the cool actor I was meant to be.

Piper's rich brown eyes filled with tears.

"The diamonds are your grandmother's. I had them reset for your ring. Nathan gives his blessing."

She said nothing as she looked at the ring, tears now sliding freely. I reached for a Kleenex, now unsure of my design.

"If you don't like it, I can have the diamonds placed back into the original."

Piper hugged me, and I sighed with relief.

"Oh, Ryan! It's gorgeous. How did you do this?" She was a little breathless. Pulling away from me she blotted her eyes. "You realize how old these diamonds are? They were my great-great-grandmother's. You have made me so happy," and she hugged me harder.

Jar Jar knocked on the door. Not waiting to be told to come in, he swung it open.

"Time's up," he started to say, then went into an angry Latin rant about Piper's makeup, or at least, that's what I guessed it was about.

He began nudging me out the door.

"Wait!" Piper said, before the door shut. I pushed it open against Jar Jar's force.

"Yes," Piper told me, her hand over her heart.

I was still laughing from nerves and excitement when Jar Jar shut the door in my face.

The photo shoot went beautifully. The photographer, Maximus Bryant, bargained with Piper on this and that, having her change dresses several times. I watched mostly, and loved doing so. Maximus was an artist, and I had confidence this shoot would show Piper in a much better light than over-exposed pap shots, or cell phone pictures taken while we took Ellie for ice cream.

This photo shoot would be a good thing, I hoped. The speculation about who Piper was to me would, for the most part, be made clear. Maximus was a gentleman of his trade, and one of the few photographers I trusted. He was taken with Piper instantly, commenting on the color of her deep brown eyes and ivory skin.

After Piper briefly explained one of her new tattoos, and that it was to cover an "injury," the photographer began to beg for nearly nude photos.

"No. No. They will be tasteful. I will not push you, darling, but think of it as a road map for other women from abusive relationships," he assured her, knowing all too well what the scars were.

Piper looked at me, nervous.

"What is it you want her to do?" I asked him, while watching her face.

"We will have her out of the dress like this," he demonstrated, "and again like this," again showing us. "No breasts, no buttocks, I promise, but the body with the scars and tattoos. It is genius. I want a photograph of you, fully dressed, in front of her, naked. The knight and his lady," he said in his heavy French accent. "You are a very beautiful woman, but have endured much. No? I see it in your eyes, darling. Same as my mother, God rest her."

Piper smiled sadly and asked what I thought. I shrugged, but Piper looked uncomfortable.

"It's just your tattoos, and it really is a good idea. You might actually help someone. You're gorgeous, Piper, but it's your call. Of course, I'm going to say go for it. So long as it's tasteful." I added, eyeing Maximus sternly.

He again assured us it would be "Art in its purest form."

I looked at Piper, watching her face but spoke to Maximus.

"You're aware of the bounty?"

Maximus made a distasteful sound with his lips.

"But of course," he said dryly.

I kept my eyes on Piper as I spoke.

"I want you to cash in on it. I want the money from it to be placed in a fund I will later name, but label it Matthew Logue." I looked away then, back to the photographer. "You do that, and we will do as you wish. Agreed?"

Maximus blinked, confused.

"Of course, Ryan, if this is your wish, I will do this for you."

I nodded.

"It is our wish."

Knowing Piper and the love she had for me, I was utterly unthreatened by a man dead and gone, even if he was so obviously still a big part of Piper. If Matthew Logue loved her half as much as I did now, then he was worth remembering.

In the end, the photographer outdid himself. I was very proud of my soon-to-be wife. The marks on her showed where she had been, and where she, by all accounts shouldn't be, but truly was.

"Soon people will know who your Piper is, Ryan. Congratulations to you both. I will send you proofs soon," Maximus promised as we said good-bye.

After we finished up, Piper and I, with Ellie and company in tow, boarded a studio jet and headed to London.

I laid Ellie down on a reclined chair. She had fallen asleep on my lap. I covered her with the suit coat I'd worn at the photo shoot. Titan, Bryce, and Rhodes were seated in the rear of the jet.

They were not speaking, but instead read a magazine, or typed on their phones. I readied myself to bring up the subject I knew Piper did not wish to discuss.

"You're so quiet. What troubles you, my love?" Reaching for her hand, I said, "Tell me."

Piper shrugged and glanced at our bodyguards.

"The same. I just want Jean-Paul located. I can't rest, thinking of him getting to Ellie or you, or anyone I love." She looked away and said, "Ellie wants to return to New York. You know that. My being her mother prevents her from having normal things, or the things she wants."

I squeezed her hand.

"Piper, you can't help the way things are right now."

She looked at me, and for the first time I saw anger in her eyes.

"Can't I?" she asked.

I took her other hand, forcing her to keep her face toward me.

"This is temporary. You'll see," I tried to reassure her, although I was not sure I believed it myself.

There was something, some thought, that was taking physical form right in front of me through Piper's dark eyes, whether fear or resentment of the situation, I didn't know, but I would do my best to keep her from drowning it. Her face turned soft again.

"I feel him, Ryan. I know he watched my house from the woods when I believed him away working. He watched me with Matthew when we were young. I feel him watching us now. Waiting. I can't just wait for him to harm one of us. Josh is lucky to be alive, and Ellie…"

She stopped, barely able to think of what Jean-Paul would do to her.

"Don't you think if I could somehow trap him? Ryan, he killed Maria, and I couldn't stop him. All I see at night is him doing that to Ellie. I won't let that happen. I will do something before that becomes a possibility."

I got on my knees in front of her, mad now. "You listen to me, damn it. There is nothing, NOTHING you can do. We will be safe together, and Ellie will go back to school when the investigation finally turns up something solid on him, something we can get him put away for. Piper?" I said, a little sternly, but pushed by the fear she would do something stupid and end up dead. "Do you hear me?"

She nodded, but I was unconvinced. We spoke very little the rest of the flight, choosing instead to be peaceful and loving. I believed we would be okay, or I was hoping we would be. I didn't want to think about the full extent of the dangerous situation we were in.

We were being hunted, something I was somewhat used to, although being hunted by cameras was obviously minor in comparison. Yet, I was so used to being "hunted," that it didn't seem strange to me. Roger and I agreed, along with Josh, that exposure might be a good thing for my family now. If tabs were being kept on us so closely, that just might make someone rethink harming us.

Only later did I remember the saying, "You will only find tomorrow on the calendars of fools."

CHAPTER THIRTY-FOUR

Piper made the cover of *Prestigious Profiles* magazine. The spreads were incredible. Soon after that, she was a regular in print. Sometimes she was captured with me, other times walking just behind Titan. The tabloids were crawling all over each other, trying to get shots of her.

One week, it was reported we had been secretly married for ten years, and the next week, they said that we were fighting all the time. Only one magazine made reference to Ellie, but it did not stick, thank God.

I was not ready to share my daughter with the world. We were extra careful with her. Rhodes and Bryce would accompany her wherever she went. By late April, Piper, Ellie, and I had adjusted to life in London. Even knowing it would be brief, it was nice.

Piper and I attended the premiere of *Douglas* while there. The crowds were crazy, and showed their love for Piper. At our makeshift home, we read scripts together, shopped, and I rented a cinema just for us, for an entire day, while we caught up on movies. Yet the heaviness was still in Piper's eyes no matter how happy the times.

I watched her become distant and vacant at some days. I knew she was waiting for something to happen. Whenever I saw her do this, I would touch her face and say, "Everything is all right."

This only put her at ease for a moment. Bee and Sheldon helped with Ellie. Their girls treated her like a sister. Roger flew out to stay with us, bringing Rebecca with him, and followed a couple of days later by Nathan, Dixie, Dee Dee, and Josh.

On a cloudless April day in England, church bells rang in the city. I was up early, having already planned the day. I was a nervous wreck trying to keep everything quiet. It would go one of two ways, and for my sanity's sake, I prayed it would go my way.

Ellie and the others were at Sheldon and Bee's house and would meet us later. I took Piper to breakfast and then down an alleyway I knew she would love.

"Look around," I told her. "There is something here you told me you wanted to see one day."

She gave me a sheepish grin.

"That could be a number of things."

Titan was a few yards back, giving us privacy. Most of the time, I didn't even know he was there. We walked slowly down the ancient stone alleyway. Piper looked curiously from the doors to the windows.

"I give up," she said, just before something caught her eye. "No way. Ryan is that…" She let go of my hand, and walked to the heavy, tarnished door knocker, touching it in amazement, as if it were pure gold. I walked to her side.

"The door knocker that inspired Dickens' greatest novel," I said in answer to her unfinished question.

Piper watched *A Christmas Carol* year round, any version.

"Wow," she breathed, as bright-eyed as Ellie would get.

"Wow. I thought its location was unknown?"

I chuckled.

"That's what they say, but it's because they don't want this thing ruined or worshipped. Lovely, isn't it?"

Piper nodded.

"Thank you. *A Christmas Carol* is my favorite."

I glanced at my watch and back at Titan. He walked ahead of us to make sure our path was clear. Once he returned, and nodded to me, I took Piper by the hand.

"We have somewhere to be, but it's a surprise."

She looked delighted.

"Another one?"

She gave the old knocker one last look, then began to look around for a new treasure.

"It's not Jack the Ripper stuff, is it?" She wrinkled her nose at the thought.

I shook my head.

"Not today, love," I teased.

"Tell me then."

I chuckled.

"Nope. Not until we are inside,"

I led her a few yards away, to an old wooden door. Opening it, I pulled her in with me. Titan remained outside for the moment.

"What is it?" Piper whispered.

"A church, my love," I told her.

I led her to a balcony where she could see. Once she caught sight of everyone her breath caught and she placed a hand over her mouth.

I took a deep breath.

"You did say yes?"

On the floor below was Roger seated with Rebecca, Viola, and Dee Dee. Nathan stood to the side with Josh. Bee fidgeted with Ellie's hair bows. Sheldon was talking quietly with the priest.

"Your dress is there," I said, pointing to a closed door.

Piper looked a little panicky, and for a second, I doubted my plan.

"Piper, we filed the papers months ago. We have the license here as well. Today, not far from here, the world is watching royalty say their vows, so I thought, why not do it while everyone is focused on them? We can do this, and it can be ours. Not intruded upon by strangers. Say the word, and we can do it another time."

Piper smiled at me.

"I'll meet you at the altar," she said in a conspiratorial whisper, and nearly ran to the room that housed a gown Maximus had handpicked for her, and which I was not allowed to see.

A designer did a huge favor for me and my bride, and in return I would give Maximus and the designer exclusive photos of the event. I had no problems with this, as I wanted pictures for Ellie and her children. I also wanted Piper to feel as pretty as the princess getting married down the street.

Twenty minutes, and a fussy Jar Jar "masterpiece," later, I watched in my tux, Sheldon by my side, as Nathan walked an angel down the aisle. The dress was understated, and allowed Piper's natural beauty to shine.

It hugged her curves in all of the right places, emphasizing her hourglass figure. The bottom flowed open, like flower petals. She wore no veil, but tiny white flowers at her left ear. All was the whitest white, and in her hand she carried six pale pink roses, matching the one in my lapel.

I had held my breath, and Sheldon actually punched me in the back to get my attention. I realized the priest had already asked me to repeat after him. With all of my heart, I did.

"I, Ryan Thomas Knox, take thee, Livia Piper Mitchell, to have and to hold, through sickness and in health, for richer or for poorer, for as long as we both shall live."

I heard Bee sniffing and had to choke back tears myself. I had already married Piper in my heart. We both had promised these things to one another many times, in many different ways, but standing in front of a priest, reciting vows that had been said millions of different ways, and swearing these things in front of my daughter and family, meant the world to me.

I heard a soft click, click, click. For the first time, it did not bother me in the least. Maximus and his assistant were hard at work, and I was thankful these moments were being captured. We were pronounced husband and wife. Kissing and sealing the deal, we were swept up in the emotions and laughter of our loved ones.

This day, there were no clouds, or thoughts of bad things in the world. People did not want to harm us. I briefly thought of Molly, and thought if she had only loved her father and me enough she could be here with us, celebrating, but like my own father, other things were just more important.

I would focus on my future, with the ones I was important to now. This day was the first day of the rest of my life. I greeted it with clarity and gladness. On the caravan ride to a feast fit for royalty, Piper leaned into me, whispering in my ear, "In spite of having every reason not to, I dare to have the audacity to love you with all of my heart."

I smiled at her.

"That's all I ask of you, love."

CHAPTER THIRTY-FIVE

We celebrated our union the remainder of the week. Putting off a honeymoon until something gave with Jean-Paul, we opted for great food and late night Monopoly tournaments. Roger owned the entire board by the third night.

We feasted and when that was exhausted we opted for pizza. We were all happy and whole—for the moment. When we were alone in our room, Piper and I talked about what we wanted to do next. For my next project, I wanted very much to produce.

"You're very gifted, Ryan. There's nothing you can't do," Piper told me many times.

"What about you, Piper? I know there are things you want to do. I can take time off, and concentrate on you, I want you to have things you want."

Piper reached for the papers she had been reading earlier.

"Now that you mention it, there is something. Years ago, when Matthew and I were young, we talked about spending time helping victims of rape."

371

She made a face.

"I hate that word, victim. Anyway, I feel my trials, the crosses I've borne, could maybe help others in some way. Young girls—and boys for that matter—are sold into sex slavery every day. I want to do something, shine a light on a very dark thing. That, and work at clinics in third world countries, delivering babies," she added, smiling at the thought.

I was a little amazed.

"That's some ambition, Piper. You've been thinking about this for a while?" I asked. Piper nodded. "Now that you're a star yourself, you could pick some of the most prestigious photojournalists to document such noble works. Piper, I've got to admit, I'm impressed. You can have what you want, shop all you want, live a very fluffy lifestyle, but this is most impressive. Then again, I'm not that shocked. Your giving heart and unbreakable spirit are but two of the reasons I love you so." I bent to kiss her. "And those gorgeous pink lips."

Scripts and movie ideas all over the bed didn't stop our lovemaking. As it was every time I was alone with Piper, I was home, and as long as I was with her, I was whole and complete. No matter what came our way we would face it together.

The little nagging at my heart, telling me that something was amiss with Piper, stayed quiet while we enjoyed our new status as husband and wife. It returned a couple of days after everyone had returned home.

Nathan was taking care of everything in Tennessee, the investigation of Jean-Paul and his family continued but had nothing to report. Ellie settled for schooling with Sheldon's girls for now, but brought up her New York school at least once a day. I got a call to let me know there would be some reshooting needed of the Tampa Bay scenes.

Leaving Rhodes and Bryce with Ellie, who would stay with Sheldon's family in London, Piper and I flew back to Florida for at least a week. Titan was joined by Josh at the airport, and they both accompanied us on our trip.

"I don't like you being this close to Louisiana, Piper," Josh was saying as we walked to our car.

"I don't either, but we agreed this is what we would do," I said.

"It's just a week, Josh, and then Ryan and I will go back to London," she assured him.

Josh glanced at me, wishing I would make her go back now. I shook my head at him.

"She won't listen to me, if that's what you're getting at," I told him.

On this trip, we decided to stay on a luxury boat, instead of the house we had occupied before. Being in the water, a couple of miles from shore, gave us privacy and the feeling of a small Honeymoon.

Titan and Josh would stay on shore, but we had to have walkie-talkies at hand at all times. When I was due on set, Titan and Josh would accompany Piper wherever—if anywhere—she wanted to go. It sounded simple enough.

None of us knew we were being followed. Not by the madman trying to hurt my family, but by various fans, simple everyday people who snapped cell phone photos, giving away our location.

Our arrival was captured by a luggage handler, who tweeted the photo, along with our location, instantly. Unknown to us all, Piper had been exposed as soon as we stepped off the plane in Florida.

A teenager at the dock videoed our boarding the boat, the name and location plainly included on her Facebook page. Josh and Titan could be seen, staying behind on their own vessel, waving us off.

Before we had anchored, our location was compromised. The tweet was retweeted to the public via fan sites and to tabloid newspapers, hundreds of times in just a few minutes.

Roger's calls to warn us went unanswered on our silent phones. The Facebook video went viral in less than an hour.

Jean-Paul and a beast of a man quietly came aboard our boat not long after. Monstrous hands were choking the life from me. The smell of gasoline burned my eyes and nose.

Jean-Paul had Piper by the hair, holding her head back, a knife to her throat. There was chewing tobacco wadded in his cheek. I fought the brute holding me, making no impression at all.

"Set him up. I want him to see this," Jean-Paul told the man.

Picking up the belt I had tossed on the floor when we arrived, the man held me down with his knee in my back, locking the belt around my arms. I fought and cursed, but it was useless. Standing me up like a child would a doll, Jean-Paul spat on the floor where I stood.

"So Mister Big Shot, you've enjoyed my wife for some time now. What do you think of the whore?"

"Fuck you," I spat at him. "You have to bring one of your goons to do your bidding. Can't fight me like a man. Oh, but I forgot. From what I understand, you only like beating on your women, you pussy."

Jean-Paul snarled back at me. I got the effect I was going for. He removed the knife from Piper's throat and handed her to my captor.

"Hold this," he ordered.

Piper's face was red, and blood leaked from her month. The sight of it made me insane. I head-butted Jean-Paul, his teeth cutting into my forehead. He was momentarily stunned and stumbled backward. Touching his teeth, he spat out the wad of tobacco, along with, to my pleasure, a tooth.

Smiling like the devil himself, he walked back to me, knife raised to my side.

"I will let you suffer. I was going to let you watch, but you have changed my mind. I'll let you live long enough for the sharks to eat you bit by bit,"

And before I could fight back, or take a breath, Jean-Paul plunged the steel hunting knife into my side, tearing me open like a deer being gutted. I crumpled, swearing, knowing I was screwed.

"Toss him overboard," Jean-Paul told his accomplice.

Lifting me by the belt, holding my arms behind me, blood poured from the open wound. I was dragged up the steps, and outside, fighting like a wild animal.

Piper was screaming, and I heard fists on flesh. The man tossed me over the side of the boat with little effort. The salt water burned me like acid. All was black as the night. Only a small beacon, to alert passing boats to our presence, lit the water's surface.

I squirmed and fought against the belt holding me. I managed to get out of it, and stealthily swam to the back of the boat. There was a platform at water level, used for diving, or to easily board the boat from the water.

Watching for the goon, I climbed up bleeding and willing myself not to pass out from the blood loss. I had to get to Piper. I silently prayed as I wrapped the belt as tight as I could around my middle, literally holding my body closed.

The pain was there, but I was so hell bent on getting to Piper, I didn't take time to notice it. A tool box sat, buckled to the deck. I blessed the man who stocked it.

I silently began sifting through the contents. A filet knife, used to part the delicate skin of fish, was all I came up with. Praying to God I was not too late, I made my way back down the stairs. I no longer heard Piper. This scared me worse than her screams had.

The huge man stood in the doorway, and from the side of his face, I could see he was mightily entertained at what he was watching. Just past him I could see Jean-Paul kicking Piper, who was obviously unconscious, and simultaneously unbuttoning his pants.

Before the man could register my presence, I plunged the knife as hard as I could down, into his neck. He screamed, and lunged at me. I felt my wound part further, as I hit at the man. It took several seconds, but he finally fell over, coughing and spitting blood.

His eyes still open, I heard the death rattle from his throat. I didn't stop. Instead, I turned to Jean-Paul in time to see him running toward me, knife held up, to do the same to me as I'd done his partner. I wrestled the knife from his hand, cutting mine in the process. I slammed him as hard as I could, breaking a dresser mirror.

He grabbed at the belt holding me together. I screamed, as he shoved fingers deep into my open side. He gained a footing, and began to punch my face. I heard the unmistakable crunch of my nose shattering.

I grabbed his balls, and squeezed. That got him off of me, at least. I staggered up to begin a new round of fighting when my knees gave way. Taking a moment to catch his breath, Jean-Paul started my way, cussing and spitting.

"I'll kill you. I'll kill you," he muttered, breathless now.

Blank spots were in my vision. I looked for the knife, but saw it nowhere. I turned to the dead man, reaching for the fillet knife still in his neck. From the corner of my eye, I saw Piper move like a snake.

Jean-Paul, his attention on me, did not see her. I had just enough time to think, "Thank you, God. She's not dead," before Piper tried stabbing at him, the knife landing in his upper arm.

He grabbed hold of his arm, looking around at her, wild-eyed. I tried to will my legs to move, but swayed like the boat itself. Jean-Paul fell on top of Piper, trying to strangle her.

Piper struggled to get free, clutching at his hands.

"You took everything from me!" He was nose to nose with her, screaming into her face. I grabbed hold of his shirt, but I was nearly gone now.

"Then this piece of shit!" He kicked at me. "I tried with you. I loved you. You never loved me back! And now they're saying Ellie isn't mine?" he screamed like a crazy person.

I pulled with all the strength I had left, but he shrugged me off with little effort. A deafening blast kept me in the here and now long enough to see Jean-Paul fly off of Piper from its force.

I watched as Josh pumped the shotgun, ready to fire again. Jean-Paul lay still, not breathing, a monstrous hole in his shoulder. Josh darted to Piper, yelling her name. Titan had me then, pushing on the wound at my side.

"Come on, Ryan, let's get you out of here. Stay with me now." He placed something under my nose, and my senses perked.

"Piper?" I knew I said it, but heard nothing come out of my mouth.

"Piper!" I screamed it this time.

I felt my ears, throat, and eyes burning from blood and seawater.

"Piper!" I screamed at her.

Josh was pushing on her chest, breathing into her mouth. Titan pulled me up, and I watched Josh carry Piper out of the room, taking two steps at a time.

Titan half carried me out behind them, dropping a lit flare as we took the steps. I could see Josh as we exited the stairs now, still working with Piper. I could feel the warmth was at my back. I did the best I could, stepping onto the boat Josh and Titan had used to reach us.

Titan sat me down on the floor next to them. I put my head down beside Piper's ear. She was not moving. She was not breathing.

"Damn it, Piper, breathe!" Josh was screaming.

I felt the boat jerk into gear, and we sped away, the night sky ablaze now.

Josh continued pumping her chest, tears streaming from his eyes now. He bent to her mouth, then back to pumping her chest. Blood spilled on the boat's surface.

I drifted in and out of consciousness. All was dark for a long moment, and I opened my eyes to see Josh climbing into the boat holding his now bleeding leg. There was a deep cut on his shoulder.

I tried to speak, but no sound came. I was numb and freezing. Josh crawled to me and pressed on my side. I screamed in agony, but I was seeing clearer. I sucked in the salty air.

"It hurts like hell, but it will keep you alive. Try to stay awake," Josh was saying.

"Is she alive?" I asked.

Josh didn't answer. He just kept messing with my wound. I felt the boat shift into gear, and Josh was yelling something, but I couldn't understand it. I closed my eyes again.

CHAPTER THIRTY-SIX

I was aware, at some point that I was going to pass out and not wake up again. My hands had already turned cold from blood loss. The reality of what had transpired in the past half hour left my brain numb.

I tried fighting off the dark haze that threatened to close over me, as doctors began to undress the poorly wrapped wound. Gloved hands loosened the belt that held the ripped tissue together, and lifted it slowly. I snapped my eyes shut at the sight of the gore.

It was bad, far worse than I had imagined. For the second time that night, I realized that this situation might actually end my life. If Piper didn't make it, I hoped I would die.

Blood dripped from the bed. The wound pulsed and gushed, like an open spout. I swayed and could feel cold hands pushing me down, forcing me to lie still on the bed. I could not think of the pain.

I began to do as I'd always done when I was scared or nervous. I sifted through the countless songs stored in my head and began to sing. The room was chaos, but I kept my eyes closed, and my mind on the song as warm blood spilled.

I fought the words that came. This was not the time for this song, but too late, I thought, as I realized which song my mind had reached for. Behind closed eyes, I began to sing, "Let me fly." All resistance gone now, I could no longer feel my fingers, and something that felt like acid burned through my ribs.

I thought, sardonically, "Damn, there goes months of sobriety."

I caught words from time to time like "deep tissue," "possible damage," "bowel and spleen," and "immediate surgery."

Someone, a nurse I presumed, placed a needle in my arm as I began to softly pray my deathbed prayer. Words from the sad song began to grow louder as the room became darker.

I sang and prayed, just above a whisper. No one noticed as I mouthed the haunting words that were now my lament, "And like an eagle, I took to the sky."

CHAPTER THIRTY-SEVEN

"Piper?" I asked the dark.

The smells told me I was in a hospital. I tried to clear my throat and started choking. Someone came from a fold-out bed beside me and placed a straw to my mouth.

I drank gratefully. I saw the pale light of a phone and Sheldon's face lit by the glow. He was texting someone.

"Piper?" I struggled against the drugs to speak. I heard movement around me.

"Hey, Ryan," Josh said to my right.

I must've slept some more, because the sun was bright outside when I looked again. Sheldon lay on his back on the fold-out bed with his mouth open, softly snoring. I looked around my hospital room, clearer now. Josh dozed in a chair to my right.

"Josh," I said, and he raised his head instantly.

"Ryan. Thank God," he breathed.

"Where is she?" I said without preamble.

I cared for nothing but my wife right now. Josh dropped his head, and to my horror, started crying. I pushed my head back into my pillows and shut my eyes.

"Tell me," I demanded.

Josh got a hold of himself, but it was Sheldon who responded.

"We don't know, Ryan."

I heard Josh suck in a deep breath. I looked from one to other.

"Tell me, damn it!" I nearly yelled now.

Josh put a big hand over his eyes as if to block out an image.

"They took her," he said. "They took her directly from my hands."

He looked at me, and I saw blood in his left eye where normally white would be.

"I got her breathing normally again. I sat her upright, and she was banged up but otherwise all right. I mean her throat was badly bruised, and all that." Josh paused, and took a swallow of water from my cup. "After a minute of making sure she was stable, I went to you. Ryan, you had lost a lot of blood, and I tried to pack your wound the best I could. I got your bleeding under control anyway." Josh shrugged.

Sheldon said, "Probably saved your life," in a low voice.

Josh glanced at Sheldon and then looked me in the eye. Here it comes. I braced for the impact.

"A boat rammed us in the side, throwing me and Piper overboard. Our boat did not capsize thankfully, but Titan hit his head and was pretty much useless. You were unconscious. I reached Piper in the water, and we began working our way to the boat, which had drifted. It was about fifty yards away by now, and then I heard the other boat approach again. I had Piper in my hands, when all of a sudden she let go and swam away from me."

Josh licked his lips and touched his temple like he had a headache. I started to tell him to go on, but he held up a finger for me to hold on.

"I grabbed wildly for Piper, but she got away from me fast. She held an arm in the air for the boat to see her. It was a gesture of surrender, like at a battle, but without the white flag. I begged her to stop. I screamed for her, and finally I got her, and tried to get away. Jean-Paul reached down and took her from me, and all I could do was watch as they drove away."

Josh hung his head defeated.

"Just before the boat reached us, she told me it was the only way we would ever be left alone. I grabbed at her and tried to hold onto the boat as it took off. They turned, and shook me loose. The propeller clipped me in the shoulder."

Josh looked back at me, tears pouring down his unshaven face. "I'm sorry."

I looked at my friend and understood that he would gladly die in Piper's place if given the chance. Josh had saved my daughter and had risked his life for both me and Piper, but right now I could not think about that.

"Where's Roger?"

I felt like he of all people could fix this. Sheldon left to get him. Josh leaned closer to me, and I smelled alcohol on him.

"I'm going to get that bastard." Josh said with Venom.

I looked him hard in the eyes.

"Not if I get there first."

~ The end